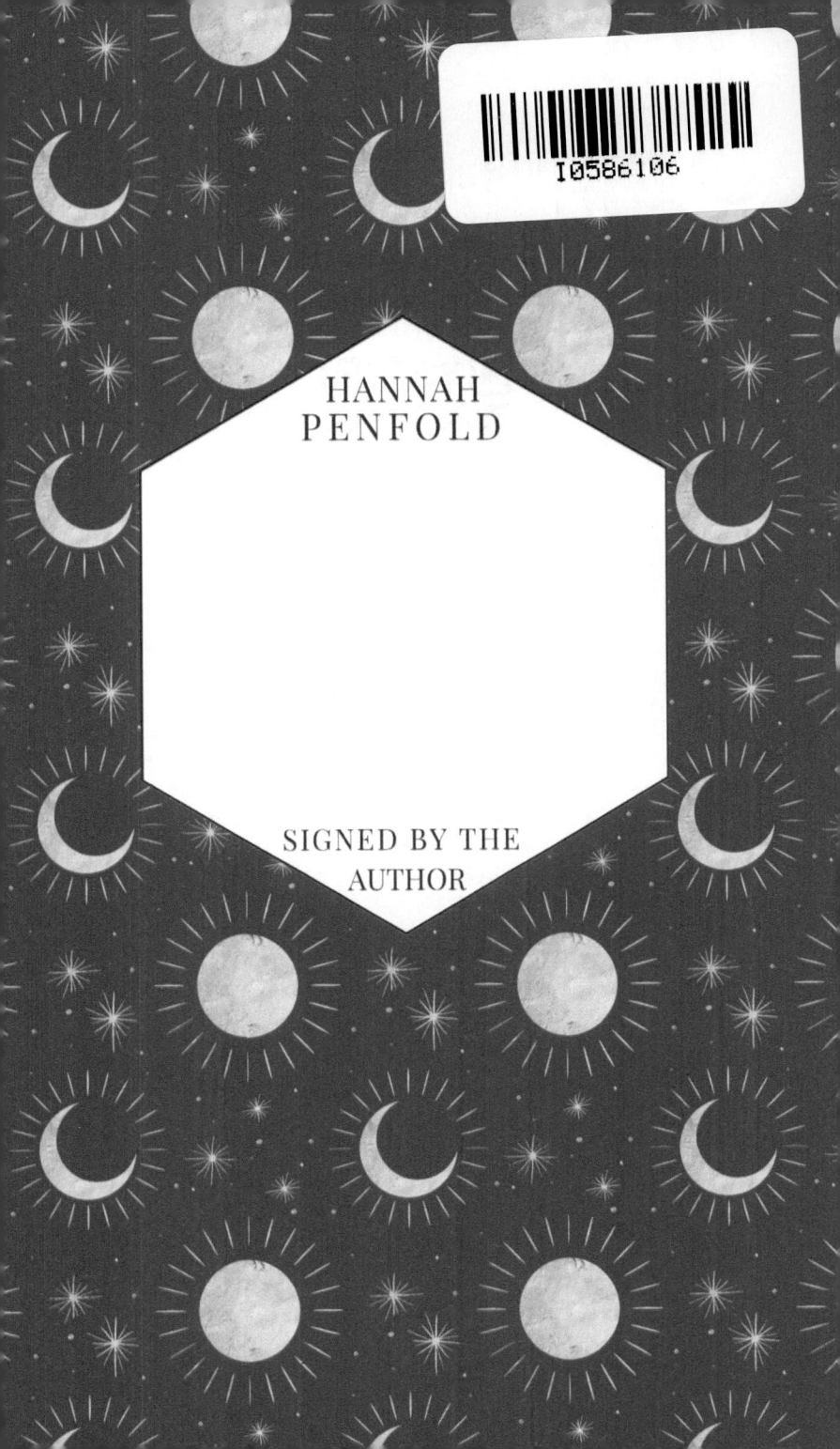

HANNAH
PENFOLD

SIGNED BY THE
AUTHOR

CONTENT WARNINGS

This book contains material that may be triggering for some readers. Reader discretion is advised. For a complete list of content warnings please scan the below:

PRINCE OF NIGHTMARES
Editing by Eden Northover
Cover Design by Get Covers
Character Art by Ekaterina Vasilevna
Map by Danielle Greaves
Ebook ISBN #978-0-6458468-2-9
Paperback ISBN #978-0-6458468-3-6
Hardback ISBN #978-0-6458468-4-3

PRINCE

OF

NIGHTMARES

BY HANNAH PENFOLD

This book is dedicated to my Nan.
For strength comes in many forms and she is one of the strongest
women I know.

I

THE PAST

Firm hands shake me awake.

'What–'

'Ellis! Quickly! Get dressed,' he says, tossing the bedding off my body. 'Come on. Quickly!'

My brain is fuzzy, my eyes blurred from the sleep he shook me out of.

Why is he in my bedroom?

'What's happening? Is the castle under attack?' I ask, my voice gravelly from drowsiness.

He doesn't answer. Instead, he throws me a shirt and helps me put on a pair of boots. I wrinkle my nose. What's happening? Where are we going?

Taking my hand, he rushes me to the window and flings the curtains wide open.

'Don't! The owl will come in again,' I protest, recalling the last time that pesky bird made a home in my bedroom. My aunt and uncle had to involve the guards, who were far too rough with their handling.

He ignores me and peers over the ledge to the grounds below.

Lifting me up like I weigh no more than a bag of feathers, he sits me on the windowsill.

'Do not fear, Ellis. Trust me. Everything will all make sense soon.' He smiles, a warm gesture that makes me slowly nod. He can calm me on my worst days – much like my brother can with his mere presence alone.

'I trust you,' I say, and he ruffles my hair.

'Good.'

Then, he pushes me out.

Before I can scream, strong arms catch me, cocooning me in their embrace.

'You didn't think I'd let you fall, did you?' he asks. His arrogant grin grows as he hovers midair, a pair of invisible wings keeping him afloat. Flying has its perks, but it doesn't mean he can treat me like this.

I huff, crossing my arms over my chest as he tightens his grip around my back. 'Where are we going?'

'To Gwenore Forest,' he answers as we launch high into the air. It's dark at this time of night, and I gape as a flock of birds soar above us.

It's not the first time we've done this – flying in the cool evening air, allowing the wind to ruffle our hair and whip our faces. He loves to soar over the kingdom and watch it at night while the people below live their lives.

'Are you taking me to a party?' I ask, peering down at my dangling feet. My bootlaces need tying. If we're heading to some sort of private celebration, I should have worn something more suitable.

He seems to think for a second, then angles his face towards me as the trees of Gwenore grow larger before us. Our bodies are weightless under his magic as we close the distance, I smile at the feeling despite having been disturbed from sleep.

'I suppose it's a gathering, but I'm not sure I'd class it as a party,' he admits with creased brows.

Darkness lingers below, where the trees cast long and intimidating shadows across the woodlands. The foliage rustles as he lowers us through the branches that graze our arms and legs. I sit up in his hold, searching for a clue to where we are. He sets me down by a large brown tent, which is so big, I crane my neck to see the top.

'I am lacking in theories,' I tell him. I crouch to finally tie my laces. The loops are big and sloppy, but I get the sense that wherever we are going, he wants us to be there soon. 'You aren't bringing us here to murder me, are you?' I grin.

Someone screams, and I bolt upright. My heart rate spikes. Maybe I spoke too soon.

'Easy, Ellis.' He grabs my hand and tugs me along inside the tent to where the discerning sound arose. 'Stay close to my side and you'll be fine.'

My eyes widen as I see groups of children in thick collars and chains, their wrists and ankles clamped with thick black metal. There are more than I can count with both hands. A girl with red hair seems to be the one who screamed, the large man behind her roughly stuffing a rag into her mouth.

'What's going on?' I try to sound demanding, but my voice betrays my emotions. It comes out timid. I shuffle closer to his frame and entwine my hands to keep from shaking.

'They're being experimented on,' he replies, dragging me past them.

One girl meets my eye, and her gaze makes me shiver. Her piercing purple-blue stare is void of all feeling, and dirt mats her long blonde locks. I don't recognise her, but she is the only one not reacting to everything around us. She keeps her mouth shut and emotions on lock.

'What type of experiments?' I ask feebly.

Smiling, he bends down to eye-level and his large hands cup my shoulders. 'We are going to make you all powerful, Ellis. We will give you the strength to move mountains and take over kingdoms, if you wish. Doesn't that sound fun?'

'You all?' I wrinkle my nose.

'Yes. You and them.' He dips his chin towards the girl still staring at us, and tightens his grip, locking my arms beside my body. 'You'll be even more powerful than me.'

A prickle rushes over my neck, and the hairs on my arms rise.

'Don't be scared,' he coos as I tense under his grasp. Unfamiliar hands hover over my head, bringing a large metal clamp before my face. I pull back. I don't understand what's happening until it's too late.

'What are you doing?' I cry, trying my best to wiggle from his vice-like hold. He is hard like stone. A collar crafted of the same black metal as the other children is secured around my neck, and the cold hardware stings as the metal digs into my skin.

'Keeping you in line. It won't be easy to begin with, Ellis, but I have faith you'll be the best.'

'I don't want to be the best!' I argue. I try to move my arms but fail, struggling to escape his unyielding grasp. It's no use, though. He is over twelve years my senior and much stronger.

His sharp eyes roam my new collar with a look of approval, and then he releases me. Smiling fondly down at me, he ruffles my hair again. 'My little slayer.'

2

ELLIS

'Are you paying attention, Ellis?'

I slowly lift my head while my aunt drones on, I can't seem to feign interest like my brother, Alex, who shoots me a pointed look. Yet a small tug of his lips gives away his amusement, though he won't reveal it in front of the queen of Tealwaters.

I exhale heavily. Aunt Melody watches me like a hawk, expecting an answer.

'No, I am not paying attention, Your Majesty. You keep repeating yourself, and it's tiring.' I run a hand through my dark blonde hair and sigh again for emphasis. 'Are we finished?'

Without waiting for a reply, I rise and brush down my trousers as if I've sat for so long I've begun to gather dust. My aunt, otherwise known as the queen, scowls.

'I am not repeating myself,' she snaps. I pause.

'I tuned you out on the *third* mention of Alex's birthday being beach-themed,' I state plainly. 'A theme that everyone expects, no? It's the same every year, and seeing that we reside in a city that lives and breathes the *ocean,* every guest presumes it.'

Aunt Melody turns to Alex for support, but he averts his gaze, covering his mouth to contain his laughter. She scoffs with indignation before she closes her eyes and massages her temples as if the sight of me irks her. 'I've had enough of you today.'

'I must be losing my touch,' I quip.

She shoots me a sharp glare. Not many people in the kingdom of Tealwaters can say they've been scolded, on countless occasions, by their sovereign, but as her youngest nephew, I have a special skill to push her limits.

'Excuse me?' She flicks a long strand of blonde hair over her shoulder, as if readying to fight. The queen reminds me of a wild alley cat dressed in a fine silk gown, sharpening her claws to strike someone foolish enough to go too far. *I* am that someone. Daily.

I stride to the window, my back turned. My next words are nonchalant. 'I usually infuriate you by mid-morning, which is when you often say you need space from me. But it is what ...' I peer at Alex and tap my wrist for the time. Without hesitation, he withdraws his pocket watch. 'It is late in the afternoon now. This is the longest we have spent together without you losing your temper. I'm losing my touch.'

If I knew a woman could look so outraged, I would have shut my mouth sooner, but when the queen of Tealwaters bares her teeth, I smile.

'Ellington Irvine!' She grasps her knees through her lavish dress, and her knuckles turn white as she tries to quell her anger. It takes her a moment until she finally breathes in, containing her rage.

'Are you done?' I goad. Her cheek twitches.

She is silent for a good minute before turning to Alex. The difference in her tone is laughable, her words are softer and significantly more encouraging as she asks, 'Can you please give your brother and I a moment alone?'

Alex glances at me with a *don't make things worse* look, but I offer my brother a casual wave. I will do no such thing.

'Of course, I'll leave you to it,' he says, with one lingering look before leaving.

When he is gone, the queen motions for me to sit with a jerk of her hand towards the pair of armchairs. I consider her for a moment before doing as I'm told.

As I make myself comfortable, she asks the guards to stand outside. They don't look too thrilled about leaving their monarch with me, but the queen's order is firm and clear, and finally, they leave us. When she deems it safe to talk, she leans forward, perched on the edge of her seat as if readying herself – though for what, I am not sure.

'You need to learn manners, Ellis,' she starts, and I lean back in my chair. I must get comfortable because it is a long and tiring affair when my aunt lectures me. 'You cannot talk to your sovereign in that tone. I am your queen, and it does not uphold appearances in the presence of our staff. They will think I am incapable of keeping you in line.'

Aunt Melody is far from pleased, jaw tight and hands clenched, she leans closer with quiet determination. I have never seen eye to eye with the queen – nor will I ever. We have our reasons for being distant, and she knows I will never confide in her like I would my mother or father when they were alive.

'I talk to you not as my queen but as my family,' I say. 'If we are speaking not of business, you are nothing more than my aunt with a fancy crown.' She's seething but does not answer, most likely, she's conjuring up an effective counterattack. 'When we talk of Alex's birthday, I do not present myself as a prince of our fine kingdom. I am simply Ellis, his younger brother, and if you do not respect that, then do not invite me to these tedious discussions.'

She exhales, her face no longer simmers with anger, but something else just as sharp-edged. She places her hands gently on the arms of her chair.

'Your uncle is worried about you.'

You're not, then?

But her confession surprises me. Those pale blue eyes roam my face for a hint of a reaction, but I offer none. I am a man who has learned to always don his mask. Perhaps she loathes the fact she cannot decipher the complex thoughts addling my brain.

'There is no need for him to worry about me, Your Majesty,' I say flippantly.

The queen tilts her head, pursing her lips. 'The king and I have talked about you and your ...' she trails off, as if weighing her words. '*Problematic* behaviour. We thought you would grow out of your adolescent phase, but you continue to talk down to peers and distance yourself. You even push away family when all we do is try to help.'

I almost scoff. *Help* is an interesting word choice.

'If this is about the ocean-themed birthday —'

'No,' she replies evenly, her temper having faded – but

only just. I get the sense I am walking into a trap. 'I am used to your inappropriate comments and moments of rebellion. I am used to you building a stone wall around yourself to keep people out.' She studies her well-manicured nails, pretending to find something the matter with one. It is a manoeuvre to make me sit and wait, wondering what she'll say next.

'One day, Alexander will be on the throne,' she continues, lifting her ocean gaze to mine. I hold her stare and patiently wait, playing the game we always play when we're together. 'He will take over everything your uncle and I have built over the years and make it his. He will need you by his side for support, to be his hand to hold in dark times.'

A flicker of emotion passes her smooth face, and though it is gone in a flash, I marvel having witnessed it at all – that I noticed her glint of sorrow.

She is not old but has worked extremely hard for many years to govern our kingdom. Being the eldest daughter of two, she was born to rule, and Uncle Hector by her side helped to bring further success to our kingdom. But her plans of handing over her title changed. Her son was killed, the only heir to the throne gone. With Alex next in line, she had to quickly pivot her plans and accept the hand fate dealt. It grieves her to talk of my brother in such a way, to have him be her successor and not her own beloved child.

'When that day comes, Ellis, you will be unable to act so self-indulgent.'

I refrain from rolling my eyes. Her perception of me has never been a secret, but to hear her describe me as *self-indulgent* is nearly laughable. 'Alexander will be left to fend for the kingdom alone. You may see yourself as unimportant – the spare, as people jest – but just because you won't be on the throne does not mean you can avoid your duties.' Her eyes narrow and bore deep into mine. She digs her claws into me one by one, knowing the single thing – or rather, the single *being* – who will make me reconsider. 'You are the person who will need to keep Alexander's head above the water, and believe me, it happens more often than you think.'

I absorb her words as I picture my brother as king, with a large crown balancing atop his golden head and a grand smile.

I knew from the moment I lost my cousin that Alex would be the future sovereign of Tealwaters, taking the role and making it his own. My brother is kind, funny, and thinks of others before himself. I know our people will be his priority, which is what they deserve after all the suffering we've endured.

'I am the last person Alex will need to worry about,' I murmur. 'I am loyal and devoted to the crown, and most of all, to *him*.'

Anguish glints through her pale blue eyes, they are the same colour as Alex's and identical to my mother's. The queen reflects on my words for a moment, while I silently question the queen's loyalty to her nephew, which wouldn't be the first time.

'I believe you are genuine in that regard,' she replies, pursing her lips. 'But I am not sure you won't run at the first sight of difficulty. I must know that I am leaving my legacy in safe hands, and that means I must trust you and Alexander wholeheartedly when the time comes for him to step up.'

My jaw tightens, but she continues. 'You do not bother attending royal events anymore, deeming them below you, you do not see our people, and thus, they do not trust you. You need to prove to me that you are worthy to stand by Alexander and that you will not falter when you are needed most.'

My mind spins, and her words confirm the suspicions I've had for years. I cannot deny it. My people do not like me, yet they adore Alex's sunshine personality and compare us all the time. Though as I am no longer around to weed out rumours, they spread and twist into lies that fester until I am deemed something I am not.

I don't correct the queen. Her opinions are set in stone when it comes to my reputation. 'Alex will be in safe hands with me,' I say firmly, though again, she's unconvinced. With the way she looks at me, I might as well have a second head. 'If you lack faith in my abilities then why bother having this conversation?' My tone is calm but edged with challenge. 'If you do not deem me fit to rule beside Alex, why bother with all of this? Why not send me away and be done with it?'

'The king insists we give you one last chance to change your ways.'

The words sting but I don't let it show. The queen is happy to get rid of me and dust her hands of a difficult nephew yet my uncle has hope, which isn't surprising, really. He has always had a kinder heart out of the two. He had married into the royal family, not born to wealth and power like the queen.

I bring my hands together, my fingers steepling. 'And what does Uncle Hector need from me to prove my worth?'

'You will shadow Alexander at events and make peace with those who do not favour you. You will swallow your pride and make our people trust you again. You have had enough time to wallow in your insubordination. Enough is enough. I will not coddle you any longer.'

'Just a few things then,' I say, suppressing my sigh.

'And lastly,' says the queen, and my brow lifts. 'You will find yourself a lady to accompany you to Alexander's birthday and all the other events that follow.'

I stiffen. 'Excuse me?'

'It will do you good to present yourself as something other than unapproachable and aloof. A female companion will soften the hearts of those we must impress. I have compiled a list of ladies in accordance to—'

'No,' I state. Clearly, this is something she and my uncle have thought deeply about. If they have compiled a list of women for me to choose from then it's a request I cannot refuse. Though if that's the case, I must do it on my own terms. I will not be prancing around with some insufferable woman the queen deems appropriate. I can imagine it now ... their overly polite mannerisms, their inability to speak their mind in fear of being scolded. 'I will choose the girl.'

'You will not choose a courtesan or someone of the like to spite me. They must be—'

I cut her off again. The act does not go unnoticed. 'She will be to your liking, Your Majesty. Do not fret.'

The queen's mouth presses into a thin line. 'Fine. You have three days until your brother's birthday. Do not disappoint me.'

3

ELLIS

Alex and I stand with the king and queen of Tealwaters, who don their usual garb of pale blues and silvers – the colours of our kingdom. Their crowns sit large and obnoxious upon their heads, glinting beneath the moon that hangs in the darkened sky. The sovereigns sparkle like stars.

My brother's crown is smaller, a circlet of pearls and crystals. He fiddles with it, exposing his nerves as he readjusts his clothing for the fifth time that evening. The queen casts him a sidelong glance, seeming to want to reprimand him but thinking better of it.

'Enough,' I tell him. I pull Alex's arm down as he reaches for his crown again. 'You have nothing to worry about.'

He gives me an amused look. '*You* are worried about *me*? I should be worrying about you. You haven't attended one of these tributes for years.'

I shrug, though, in reality I am quivering with nerves.

Tonight is the ten-year anniversary of my return home. The return of all lost children.

When I first attended the tributes, I was a hopeful young boy, I dreamed of overcoming my trauma and to live a normal life once more. But as my new – and much darker – magic grew stronger, I couldn't take the pressure of being in the presence of so many. I was a threat, and I wouldn't take that risk.

Before I can answer Alex, my uncle comes to my side and claps my shoulder. His pale blue eyes peer down at me, a slither of grief passes in his gaze, but mostly empathy lines his tanned face. 'You'll be fine, boy. Just take a deep breath if you feel overwhelmed.'

My gaze flickers to the queen. Though she is facing away, her stance is less poised than usual, her body tight with what I assume is uneasiness. Tonight, she remembers all the people she lost, too – not just the children who never made it home, but those who fought to save us, those who sacrificed their lives to liberate us. There were too many casualties that night, including my cousin, Athos. Her only son.

Anguish and anger burns through me but I keep my thoughts to myself. My uncle's hand rests on my shoulders, his expression expectant.

'I am fine,' I assure the king, averting my gaze. In previous years, I would have hid from the palace guards, who always failed to find me. My family would be forced to leave without me to attend some royal event or other. 'Ten years feels exactly like nine years.'

'Ten years already,' sighs the king, tightening his hand

around me. 'I can't believe it. How can time pass so quickly yet the grief feel so raw?' He moves away, and instead, reaches for his wife's hand. Her lips wobble and he pulls her in close. 'There, there, my love.'

She doesn't cry, but she allows him to hold her. Alex and I stand stoically, we make no move to break the bubble of emotions erected around us.

When we are escorted into our separate carriages – the king and queen in one, Alex and I in the other – I can breathe easier. My brother shuffles until he is comfortable before swiping at my waist coat, a strand of thread comes loose from the bottom. I scowl.

'So, I hear you must find a lady love by the time I turn thirty two,' says Alex. I hum in answer, staring out the window. 'That is in three days' time. Can you find a willing girl by then?'

Turning my head, I look at him, affronted. 'Have I ever fumbled one of the queen's challenges before?' I remark, though I do not wait for his answer. 'I will show her up as I usually do.'

'So, you have someone in mind?' He grins. He may not have a precarious relationship with the queen like I do but he still enjoys our drama. 'Is she wealthy? Or are you going to break the rules and find someone unbefitting for the role?'

'She will be exactly what the queen would want,' I say cryptically. 'I only hope she will agree to such a farce at such short notice.'

'I'm sure you can charm her to do your bidding,' Alex offers, his faith in me unwavering.

* ☆ ° ₀ * ☾ * ☆ ° ₀ *

The sky is no longer streaked with purples, blues or pinks as the sun disappears behind the horizon. Yet the night sky is a sight to behold, and all the stars shine brightly tonight.

Sapphire City is busier than I have seen it. The streets are full of carriages arriving to drop off civilians, small rowing boats in the water roads which are anchored and tied to keep from floating away, while the taverns bustle with activity. I peer out of the window at our own horse-drawn carriage.

The festivities appear to be in full swing by the time my family and I enter the fray, our arrival only ramps up the mood.

As we exit our carriage, a mass of guards surround us. The Tellian people scream and shout for my family, and I notice Alex is unusually quiet, his bright smile dimmer than usual. From his sombre gaze, I know he's deep in thought, simply putting on a show for the public. I long to touch him and ease his obvious unease, but when I step closer, my hands feel like lead when I try to lift them. It's as if the simple task of reassuring my brother is impossible, like the small movement will be viewed as a weakness that I can't afford for him – or anyone else – to witness.

Instead, I take a deep breath to calm my growing unease as the guards escort us to our royal box. The main square is like a stage before us and Alex continues to wave. I must show my brother that I am reliable, and, despite the unending darkness in my mind, I will be right beside him every step of the way.

'I am always here for you, Alex,' I say, watching from our safe space. Across the square are three stages, where performances have been scheduled throughout the night. Tonight is a way of showing respect to the fallen, to celebrate the return of all survivors, and to remember our kingdom's horrid past – to ensure it never happens again.

I sense my brother glancing in my direction but I refuse to look back at him. Instead, I observe the city as if my words are of little value. 'What you did for me ten years ago will never be forgotten,' I continue, watching from the corner of my eye as he sharply inhales. 'I will always be thankful for what you did. For me and the others you rescued.'

Nearby, girls scream Alex's name and erratically wave their hands. He does not notice them.

Finally, I allow myself to look at him, absorbing his mournful expression. I want him to understand and feel the depth of my words. Because our experiences of that time are not ones to take lightly. I was a child in need of a hero, and Alex was that and more. 'You saved us. I am forever in your debt.'

Alex shakes his head. 'You owe me nothing, Ellis.'

'But I do.' My smile is soft but unpractised. It feels forced, but I endure it. 'I thought I would die in that prison camp, Alex, and that I would never see your face again. By killing Fral, you gave me and many others their lives back. It's because of *you* we stand here today, reunited with our friends and family. Because of you, we have a future we never expected.'

My brother lowers his head, his gaze unblinking as he inspects his shoes. Our family never speaks the name of the man Alex killed, the topic being too hard to bear. But our people gave him a moniker that has stuck throughout the years. Fral, the angel of darkness.

Having been the closest to him, Fral's true name triggered me as a boy, whereas now, it only sets off a dull ache in my chest that I've grown used to. When I hear his name it is a reminder that even those closest to you can never be trusted, while Alex remembers the blood on his hands, no matter how many times he washes them.

'Today, we remember those we lost,' I remind him. I turn to find a servant in the corner of the royal box, a tray propped on her arm. I take two crystal flutes of blue bubbles and hand him one. 'But we also remember those who were given a second chance at life.'

He nods, promptly clearing his emotions. 'You're right.'

'I know I am,' I say, noting the glint of amusement on his face. 'I am rarely wrong.'

Alex smiles and the warmth returns. I nearly sag in relief to see it.

'The first speech is about to start,' announces the king, motioning for us to take our seats.

My brother takes his place beside the queen, my chair is at the end, showing our line of procession. Alex leans over, taking a small sip of his drink. 'Are you ready?'

This is the first time in eight years I have attended an anniversary as the mass of people makes my skin crawl. The darkness inside my head, though quiet, is present, and though I am in control of my powers now, it does little to settle me as I peer across the square to the stage, grabbing everyone's attention.

No, I am not ready, is the answer springing to mind, but, instead, I nod, remembering I must be there for Alex no matter what. I must show my family and my people that I am capable of holding their trust.

'Yes. I'm ready.'

4

ELLIS

We sit through hours and hours of entertainment. Music plays all night long, and a large bonfire is ignited for the people to dance around. By the end of the performances, I am somewhat calmer, that is, until the sovereigns are given free range to roam the city square.

'Go mingle with the people,' says the queen, eyeing me up. The warning is clear in her gaze. 'Remember your manners.'

If I weren't so transfixed on the fact I had to walk through crowds of civilians, I would have given the queen a sharp response, but instead, Alex drags me into the fray, with several guards surrounding us.

As we amble the streets, I try my best not to touch anyone, but it proves an impossible task. My stomach churns with apprehension but I feign a neutral expression. I cannot have Alex think I am incapable due to my childhood anxieties.

To my dismay, we are to visit each vendor attending tonight's homage and try their wares. All stall owners are delighted with my brother, who eats copious amounts of food that they insist he tries. But when they greet me, their expressions are the same – confused. The sight of my presence is no doubt strange to them.

When a large man with a long beard offers Alex and I some meat from his stall, I politely refuse. I am too tense to have an appetite. Instead, I let Alex take my sample, though my refusal seems to fortify the stall owner's opinion of me. I grit my teeth. This is why people hate me. They judge me on my surface-level actions, never daring to look deeper.

It's not your job to explain yourself. If they do not wish to know you better, don't waste your time making the effort, my mother's voice reminds me.

I have lived my whole life by that mantra, which has taught me that very few people care.

'Are you sure you don't want to try some of these?' Alex offers me the meat and I avert my gaze. The smell of it makes my stomach roll.

I shake my head. 'I'm not hungry,' I insist while the stall-keeper stares at me. 'But I'm sure it's delicious.'

When we head to the next vendor, my gaze wanders, keeping a watchful eye for the one person I hope to spot tonight.

'Is she here?' asks Alex, his own gaze roaming the mass.

'I can't be sure,' I mutter. I follow alongside him as we approach a bakery.

The woman smiles brightly at us. Her stare lands on Alex first, which is unsurprising, and then finally flickers to me. Unlike the other workers we've conversed with tonight, she does not falter. Her smile never wavers as she studies my face. I nod in greeting but feel a sense of appraisal from her like I have met a certain expectation of hers.

'Your Highnesses, welcome to Danes Bakery,' she greets. 'I hope you have enjoyed the festivities tonight.'

I peer down at her name tag. *Maura Danes*.

My heart rate spikes.

Danes.

Instantly, I know who I'm talking to. My memories overlap until one comes to the forefront of my mind.

Maura Danes, business owner of Danes bakery, alongside her husband, Calvin, and mother to two daughters.

When I peer down the long table, I spot a man, probably my age, and a young girl I somehow know is Maura's youngest daughter, despite never having met her. I squint at the boy's tag – Luca. Yet no matter how hard I try, I can't remember the name of the girl now offering samples from a large silver tray, she's waiting on customers, occupying them with happy chatter and food.

'It's been marvellous, as I'm sure the rest of the night will be, too,' says Alex, returning me to the conversation at hand. 'I have no doubt your products will further that theory.' I suppress the urge to roll my eyes at his charm. The woman appears to melt at his words, and I can see why he does it. My brother enjoys making people smile, their laughter like music to his ears. He gestures to me. 'I am an enthusiast for savoury pies, but my brother here has a serious sweet tooth. Do you have something for me to try now and something for Ellis to take home for later?'

Clever move. My lips twitch at his way of pleasing Maura but keeping her from scolding me. He winks at me when I meet his gaze.

Maura nods. 'Of course! Let me gather our best sellers for you both.'

'Why the face?' Alex mutters, leaning in close as the owner skirts around the table and workers with ease. 'You look like you've seen a ghost.'

'The girl I have in mind,' I say, and he nods in encouragement. 'I just realised this is her mother.'

Alex leans back, surprise etched across his features. 'Wait, you aren't thinking of *Violet* Danes?'

We are interrupted by Maura returning with a large plate. She points out and names the different slices for Alex, having given him a slice of nearly every pie in their parlour. My brother's smile widens. One talent of his is the ability to eat copious amounts of food and still feel hungry. While he begins to consume them, Maura hands me a bag.

Inside are cookies, two muffins and some donuts.

'Thank you, this is very generous,' I say, dipping my chin in thanks.

'Violet's back!' The young girl calls. Maura and Luca glance up with expectant smiles.

My heart hammers as Violet comes into view, hurrying behind the table with a large box of pastries. She begins to arrange them into groups, displaying some on the racks and readying others onto plates.

Violet Danes has always been a stunning sight to behold, with her long blonde hair and striking eyes of purple and blue. But it's her smile that has always captivated me most. Even though I saw it hundreds of times when we were children, I can't help my sudden intake of breath when I lay eyes on her now. It's like she's punched me right in the gut. The very sight of Violet brings back all the memories I've done so well to control and lock in a box somewhere deep within my mind.

My hands curl into a fist, my first instinct is to hide my tingling hands. My brother peers down at me, concerned, while the tips of my fingers turn a dark shade of grey. This is not the place to lose focus.

Breathe, Ellis. You are in control.

'So, it *is* Violet,' my brother muses, staring at her like she's a spectacle he can't look away from. 'Why am I not surprised? You always were infatuated by her.'

I don't answer because he's right. She always had a special place in my heart, and because of me, I ruined the friendship we once had as children.

Violet rests a hand on Luca, her expression softening. They talk amongst themselves, yet their demeanours betray their closeness. The taste of envy lingers on my tongue at the sight of Violet enjoying herself with another man, who, in return, looks delighted by her attention. Something he must have said pleases her as she throws back her head and laughs.

Breathe. Breathe. Breathe.

'Are you going to approach her, or should I?' asks Alex, a quarter of the way through his pies. My gaze lingers on him with quiet admiration before flicking back to Violet.

'You are not going anywhere near her,' I state. Before I second-guess myself, I round the crowd and approach the other side of the table.

Will she remember me?

When I reach the stall, it is Luca who serves me. The moment he registers my presence, he stiffens. I narrow my eyes.

'Your Highness,' he greets with an edge to his voice.

The greeting catches Violet's attention, who is helping her sister restock the sample trays. Her piercing gaze snaps to mine.

So, she does remember me, I think smugly.

I tuck my hands inside my trouser pockets as the darkness inside me opens an eye as if remembering her, too. I cannot make a fool of myself. I must stay in control.

As we share a look, I realise I have never felt so magnetised to another person as I do her, and I know she feels it too. A flicker of hope ignites inside my chest until she looks away, pretending I don't exist.

When I regard Luca, my annoyance evident, he seems entertained by the dismissal as a slither of a smile lines his lips.

'Three of those,' I say, pointing to some freshly baked goods displayed on the tiered cake stand. I certainly don't need to purchase more food, but if I don't, I will look like a fool.

Luca serves me, but slides in a fourth. 'To help with the *sting*,' he says before turning to another customer.

Humiliation floods through me and I grind my teeth together with the need to make him suffer for his outright disrespect. A firm hand drags me away.

'Do not do what you are clearly thinking,' warns Alex, taking the pastries off me.

'I am thinking of nothing,' I reply.

He gives me a pointed look before eating the bag I bought. 'Yes, and I am not the crown prince of Tealwaters,' he quips.

I take a deep breath as we head to the next vendor, sparing a quick glance over my shoulder. I will talk to Violet if it's the last thing I do.

5

THE PAST

One thing I know for certain is that I am not going home anytime soon. Children of all ages surround me, sleeping across the cold floor. Our wrists and ankles are chained to thick eyelets jutting from the floor. As much as I try to yank myself free, the metal restraining me is too strong. Even when I try to conjure up my magic, I fail, it no longer feels present, as if it's been snuffed the moment I was shackled.

The moon shines through the tent canvas, providing me with some vision. No matter how hard I try, I can't fall asleep. The unfamiliar space keeps me on edge.

'It's no use,' murmurs a girl. Her voice is quiet so as not to wake anyone. 'These chains render our powers useless. The guards call them obsidian metal – they are supposedly very hard to come by.'

Her unusual eyes have my full attention. They're a strange mix of blue and purple, and the combination makes her look startling, her gaze is sharp and penetrating, as if she can see what lies beneath the surface.

'And what powers do you possess?' I ask, wondering if she can read minds.

A soft smile lines her lips and a thoughtful look crosses her smooth features. 'I can shapeshift. My preference is a wolf, they are such lovely creatures.'

My aunt would reprimand me for my reaction as my mouth drops open in awe. 'That's incredible.'

'Not here,' she says, sagging. 'Here, it means nothing. I can't do a bloody thing to help anyone.'

'I can conjure up lightning,' I say when silence envelopes us. I want her to keep me company, as the prospect of closing my eyes to see what awaits me is too frightening to bear.

'That's impressive.' She nods. 'Does that mean you can control the weather?'

I shake my head. 'Not yet. My brother thinks I will one day, though, if I train hard enough.'

Again, silence falls and I shuffle with unease. If she decides to lay down, will I stay awake all night by myself in this horrible place? I sniff and recoil. The stench of dirty bodies and blood invades my senses.

'You get used to it eventually,' she whispers, tilting her head to the rows of small bodies before us. 'The smells, the lack of space, the screaming.' Her mouth twists with sudden regret as she notes my flash of fear. She reaches for me and shuffles closer until she's sitting beside me. 'I'm sorry, Your Highness, I don't mean to scare you but I'm afraid I can't hide the truth.'

'How long have you been here?' I want to alter the course of this conversation but the feel of her warm hand is comforting – something I've missed in the few days of being in this horrid camp.

She shrugs. 'Weeks? Months? I'm not too sure. All I do know

is that I was the second kid to be taken. Caleb over there was the first. You can imagine how much he misses his family.'

She points to a boy with dirty blonde hair resting fitfully across a blanket of hay that looks weeks old. Long wounds cross his arms and legs, the flesh looks fresh, as though it's still healing. To my dismay, they look similar to the girl's, whose tanned skin is marred with painful-looking cuts and scabs.

'You must miss your family, too,' I remark, dragging my gaze away from her in case she finds my staring rude.

She answers with a solemn nod. 'I do. My parents must be worried sick wondering where I am. We are super close – and my little sister – but I'm afraid they might think I've run away ...'

'I'll make sure you see them again,' I blurt. I'm not sure what makes me sound so adamant, but it makes the girl smile, her gleaming teeth a sight I thought I'd never see in a place like this.

'Good, I'll hold you to that.' She begins to move away, but my hand shoots out to grip her fingers. They are wonderfully warm. Her other hand coils around mine in surprise, the touch seeming to soothe us both.

'Please,' I utter, the rest of my words stuck in my throat.

Please don't leave me.

Understanding dawns across her features until she eventually nods.

'Get some rest. You'll need your strength in the morning.' She lies beside me in a small area of ground that isn't taken by another body. She pats beside her, and I do as I'm told, making myself as comfortable as someone can be on the hard ground of a forest. Facing one another, I watch her sigh.

'Goodnight, Your Highness.' She closes her eyes, and suddenly, darkness creeps in, the lack of colour making my nerves fray once more.

'Ellis.'

She opens her pretty eyes before lifting a brow. 'Excuse me?'

'Call me Ellis,' I amend, enjoying her quizzical stare.

'Ellis,' she echoes, as if tasting my name for the first time. She smiles, and I swear I feel my heart shiver in delight. 'I'm Violet.'

6

VIOLET

I attend the anniversary every year but, for some reason, I always expect it to be easier the next time round, like the horrors of those memories will finally have faded away. Instead, they return with full force – the taste of salt on my tongue, screaming ringing in my ears – all of it comes rushing back.

Working through the performances and speeches helped. It allowed me to avoid the retelling of our tale, and the statistics of how many died and those who survived. I don't need to be reminded, the figures are burned into my brain for eternity.

A large fire blazes in the middle of the main square. I am thoroughly drunk at this point, my family's stall now closed. My mother, tired and eager to get to bed, wanted to take my little sister home. Hazel's eyes drooped as we packed our stuff away. However, Luca and I wanted to make the most of the night – Luca because he never wanted to work tonight but was duped into it because my mother needed extra hands, and myself because I desperately wanted to forget seeing *him*.

'One more?' asks Luca, lifting his empty glass of beer.

I swear we refilled it a few minutes ago. I peer down at my own empty goblet.

'Huh,' I mutter, flipping the cup upside down to make sure there are no drops left. To my dismay, there isn't. 'Yes please, kind sir.'

Luca winks before sauntering away, a few girls catch his eye as he approaches the tavern. I shake my head. Luca and I have been friends for years due to him working in my mother's bakery, and though we had a moment where something *more* happened, I knew it wouldn't work. He enjoys the chase while I prefer stability – though that doesn't mean we can't appreciate each other from time to time.

At this late hour, only one tavern remains open, the barmaids still serving the drunkards slurring their way through conversations. I sit along the street curb, watching the world go by as I wait for my topped-up beverage. The bonfire still crackles, the flames so high I must crane my neck to see it all.

'Are you enjoying your night?'

I smile, thinking some intoxicated fool is trying to find a lady to bed tonight. When I turn towards the voice, my mouth drops open. Something dark and dangerous ripples through my ribcage, my traitorous heart dropping at the sight of the beautiful man.

Prince Ellis crouches beside me, tilting his head to accommodate our height difference. My gaze trails towards his hands hanging off his knees. The prince's strong fingers are adorned in several silver scars that glint beneath the bonfire's blaze.

'Are you enjoying your night, Violet?' His voice is wolfishly low, sending a shiver running through my spine.

This can't be happening. I'd not seen the prince in ten years and now he appears *twice* in one night. What are the odds?

And where is my drink?

A piece of dark blonde hair falls over his forehead, beneath, his dark blue eyes pin me down, challenging me to turn away like I did earlier. I debate my next move. Do I keep the royal hanging, pretending I want nothing to do with him, or do I have a civil conversation?

How about the latter with a splash of pettiness?

I nod to myself. *Deal.*

'I was having a *splendid* night until now,' I say, forcing myself to look anywhere else but him. Perhaps if I keep my answers short, he'll leave me alone, or Luca will eventually find us and shoo him away – he's always been the jealous type.

'Is it better now I'm here?' Ellis drawls, readjusting himself so he sits on the curb beside me, resting his elbows on his knees.

'What? No,' I scoff, unable to help myself. I spin with indignation, though amusement glides across his hand-some features.

Is he taunting me?

'You are not doing a good job of ignoring me now, are you?' he remarks. His confidence makes me uncertain. How can he act so casually with me when we've not seen each other in a decade? 'I've always liked how stubborn you were.'

Memories flood back – images of chains, open wounds, and sleepless nights. After ten years of not seeing one another, our paths have never crossed. Until now. When I was young and foolish, I thought it was cruel to be separated from the young prince, but now I wonder if it was for the best.

He's here for a reason, and it's most likely not because he misses you.

'You know nothing about me,' I state. My jaw hurts from tensing it. I need to get away from him, and quick. I can't fathom being near him for much longer in case old feelings bubble to the surface. 'Please, excuse me, Your Highness.'

I stand and don't bother to curtsy as custom dictates. Turning my back to the prince, I plan to find Luca and go home, but before I take another step, Ellis encases my wrist with a firm hold. His gentle fingers curl around my skin, and I turn, glancing at the contact between us. My body vibrates with nerves. How does he still have an effect on me after all this time?

'Now, now.' He tuts, and his jaw twitches. 'I don't mean to rile you up, as entertaining as it is. I am merely here for a friendly visit.'

Slowly, he releases me, as if the act is hard for him to do. I unconsciously touch the place where his warmth still lingers.

'What do you want?'

'To talk,' he says simply. 'To see how you are.'

I'm speechless. *Now* he wants to know how I am? Yeah right. He wants something.

'I'm trying to figure out if you're *acting* a fool or *are* a fool,' I say, narrowing my eyes. 'Because I don't believe a word you say.'

'Can I not visit an old friend?' He shrugs, a crease appearing between his brows.

'Friend?' I snap, letting the silence ensue.

He seems uncomfortable with me staring at him. 'What happened to your hair, Violet?'

I blink, lifting a hand to my head self-consciously. 'Why? Do I have something in it?' I fret, searching for my reflection somewhere, but Ellis grasps my wrist once more.

'No, that's not what I mean. It's streaked in black.'

Confusion hits me hard until my drunk mind realises what's happening. 'It's been like this for years,' I huff, frustration welling inside me. 'If you had bothered to *visit* me before, you'd know it's been slowly darkening for a long time.'

My tolerance for the prince is at its limit and I turn to search for Luca. I needed a drink five minutes ago. Yet Ellis follows close behind, pushing drunk men away from me as I dart through the tavern. The lady at the bar singles me out from the crowd of males and asks for my order, and I do something unlike me, ordering the most potent and disgusting potion they have.

She places two down and I wonder if she thinks Ellis is with me. When he reaches for the small glass nearest to him, I grab it first and swallow it in one gulp. I shudder when the disgusting taste trickles down my throat.

'That was rude,' mutters Ellis before reaching for the

second. Before he can get near it, I pour it into my mouth, a dribble escaping. The prince watches intently, unimpressed.

'Whoops,' I laugh humourlessly. I go to wipe it away with my thumb, but he stops me, seizing my hand.

'Don't,' he warns, and leaning forward, he licks it off my skin. The whole time, his dark cobalt eyes watch to see if I'll move away. He closes the distance between us and for some reason I stay very still.

He just licked me, my mind fumbles. The cogs turn inside my head. *The prince of Tealwaters licked my face.*

'Mother of pearl,' I curse, unable to comprehend his actions.

'My thoughts exactly after you drank my liquor,' Ellis answers, licking his lips. His eyes rest on my mouth as if waiting for more alcohol to lap up.

'It wasn't yours,' I retort. 'She brought me an extra one.'

'Did she?' he asks, tilting his head. His dark blonde hair shines beneath the lanterns.

From where we stand at the bar, I see the bonfire in the street, raging and burning enough to light the whole main square. In this moment, it's like I can feel its heat emanating from here. I pinch the front of my shirt and waft it to let some air in. Ellis scowls.

'Are you alright?' he asks.

It's not him, I assure myself. *It's the bonfire making you hot and flustered.*

'That's right,' I agree, earning a small frown from the royal.

'What is right?'

'It's the bonfire that's making me feel hot and flustered,

not you.' I poke his chest for good measure. It's broad and feels like stone when I prod him, hurting enough that I cradle my finger.

His brow quirks but I don't understand why, yet the tone of his voice makes me narrow my eyes. 'I make you feel ... hot?' He ponders. It would be funny if he wasn't on my list of people to avoid at all costs.

'Excuse me?' I lean forward, hands on my hips defiantly. This man is infuriating. 'Why would I think that?'

'You just said, "It's the bonfire that's making me feel hot and flustered, not you." So, I merely answered.' I watch those lips of his move, lifting slightly at the edges as amusement flickers in his cobalt eyes. 'Are you *drunk*, Violet?'

'No,' I protest with a vigorous nod of my head. 'No, wait!' I backtrack, shaking my head instead.

The prince searches for the exit of the establishment and grabs my arm. 'I'm taking you home.'

'No, you certainly are not,' I hiss, pushing his hand away. 'I am old enough to look after myself.'

His expression doesn't hold much faith in me but I spin and head for the restroom, travelling around couples who are entangled in each other's space, kissing and fondling throughout the passageway. I sigh at the queue for the restroom.

'Why,' I moan, throwing my hands in the air.

Ellis motions for me to follow him into the male restroom, instead, but I shake my head.

'Definitely not. I know how men work and I am not giving you *anything*.' I cross my arms and glance away, closing my eyes briefly to avoid looking at his face.

Strong hands press against my back, urging me forward. I stumble and my eyes fly open. Ellis catches me before I crash into the door frame.

'I am a gentleman, Violet. I won't take advantage of you,' he promises as another man heads for the door.

'Says the man who licked me,' I mumble.

Ellis doesn't bother to answer and instead focuses on the approaching male. 'Come back later.'

The man, who is just as large as Ellis, frowns, he's about to protest until lightning sizzles across the prince's body. The smell of magic sears my senses and his power crackles as the men stare each other down. The only part the prince doesn't light up are his hands that still grasp onto me. The man grumbles something under his breath and walks away.

'After you,' offers Ellis, opening the door to an empty washroom.

It smells unexpectedly pleasant thanks to a dish of scented flower petals. I bend over and breathe them in.

'Lavender,' I sigh, smiling. My eyes lift to the looking glass before me, where I find the prince observing my every move. 'What are you looking at?'

'You.'

It's so intense the way he studies me that my stomach tightens, and my hand rises to my chest. I need him to leave and to let me move on with my life. I was fine until he showed up, and now it's as if all the emotions I harboured as a child have rushed back in.

'Stand outside,' I order, pointing to the door. He quirks a brow and I motion for him to move. 'Please.'

Reluctantly, he obeys, closing the door behind him as I

relieve myself in peace. When I've washed my hands, I peer up at the only window in the room. It's long and thin, but thankfully, it doesn't take long for me to stand on the sink counter and shimmy myself through.

Enjoy being my guard for the rest of the night, I think proudly, running far from those alluring cobalt eyes.

7

VIOLET

I feel extremely vulnerable the next morning. Having eventually found Luca after my bathroom escape, we finished the drinks he had bought on our way home, and I didn't see the prince again. I began to wonder if I had conjured him up from my memories, the ten-year anniversary making him spring to mind.

When I finally stumble out of bed and wander downstairs to where our small bakery resides, I find my mother in the kitchen with Hazel, teaching a lesson about the importance of measuring ingredients.

My mother always loved to bake, so much so that my father found her this bakery to live and work in so she could do what she was passionate about. Unfortunately, with him leaving years ago, we have progressively lost our clientele. We're barely getting by with the small number of customers we get each week. We're unable to afford workers—except for Luca, that is.

So, when Hazel was old enough to not need supervision around an oven, Mum hired her in the hopes of helping the business. And it has. My sister seems to be following in my mother's footsteps, eager to create new recipes and always mixing wonderful new flavours together. They are twin flames, similar in ways I'll never be. But it's not enough. The three of us – occasionally four – cannot produce enough pastries, bread and pies while serving customers out front, too. We are stretched too thin, and the business suffers the consequences.

'Good afternoon,' greets my mother, her tone amused. 'I assume you had a good night with Luca?'

I smile sheepishly, winking at my sister when I'm certain mother is not looking.

'I had fun,' I say, sliding in between them. I wrap my arms around their shoulders and give them each a peck on the cheek. Hazel giggles when I blow a loud obnoxious raspberry against her skin. 'Another midday open today?'

My mother nods grimly. 'I may have to keep it open all day, but only on the weekends from now on.'

There is more to the statement, but she doesn't continue. I nod. I understand what her words truly mean. *I cannot afford to keep it open all week. I need to find another job to make ends meet.*

I nibble my bottom lip, knowing Hazel is too young to have a job elsewhere, and besides, she enjoys spending time alongside our mother. It's out of the question.

'Well, I can ask for more shifts at the saddlery? I'm sure Otto wouldn't mind the extra hands. He is always complaining about the lack of hard workers around here.' My mother attempts a smile, pride lingering in her gaze as she peeks up at me. 'I'll go visit him now.'

I head for the arch leading through to the hallway, the smell of bread in the oven is potent before Hazel pipes up.

'Can you get some things from the market on the way back?' she asks. Both mother and I glance at her questioningly. 'We're running low on some ingredients.'

'Sure, kid. Write them down and I'll get whatever you need,' I shout, heading upstairs to change. I catch my sister's smile before she returns to mother's lesson.

* ☆ ° ₒ * ☾ * ☆ ° ₒ *

An hour later, I'm trailing along the market stalls. My feet hurt and multiple bags weigh down my arms. I have one more stop before I must leave the markets. Searching for the colourful flower stall, I peruse the options – lilies, daisies, peonies, sunflowers. The choice is too difficult, and the mass of beautiful blooms has me debating which ones Maple would like the most.

It doesn't take long for my body to sense someone watching my contemplation. Their presence makes the hairs on my arms stand on end.

So, he wasn't a figment of my imagination, I think, wondering how he found me so easily.

'What's the occasion?' asks Ellis, towering over me with his hands in his pockets.

The urge to study him is immense, but I take a long deep breath and avert my attention. 'Wasn't last night not an obvious enough sign for you, Your Highness?'

He doesn't answer. We stew in silence, and I give into my temptations to find he's already watching me. The prince seems unimpressed by my lack of answer.

I purse my lips. 'It is my best friend's birthday today, and I wanted to drop off some flowers to let her know I'm thinking of her,' I answer, returning my focus to the plants. Taking a step away from the royal, I lean over a set of daisies before a bucket of bright orange blooms catch my attention.

Perhaps Maple will like tulips?

'What is her favourite colour?' he asks.

My eyes narrow. All I want is for him to leave me alone. 'Pink.'

He leans forward and plucks a few flowers from their holders, arranging them into a bundle of pink and white before adding a few stems of yellow and purple.

'Snapdragon, meadowsweet, and hyacinth,' he says, gesturing to the pink blooms. 'Marigold and violet for your namesake.' His fingers caress the petals of yellow and purple flowers before pointing to the white ones. 'And lastly, lupine and a classic rose to finish it off.'

To my dismay, it's a very beautiful yet strange combination. Never would I ask for such a bouquet, nor do I think a florist would think to group them all together but somehow, they work. They're the perfect gift for Maple and her unique personality.

'How do you know the names of them all?' I ask, frowning.

Ellis shrugs before requesting for the flowers to be wrapped in brown paper. 'My mother enjoyed her garden, so I made sure to pay attention.'

My heart constricts at its own accord. Ellis' mother died when he was young – too young – and she'd been the topic of many conversations when we were children, the grief from losing her was still fresh back then.

'I'm sure she would have enjoyed seeing you use that knowledge now,' I offer as the florist hands over my purchase. Her eyes linger warily on Ellis. It seems she's aware of the young prince's reputation, like everyone else in the city.

Manoeuvring my groceries so I can free a hand, I attempt to retrieve some coins from my skirt pocket, but a bag of flour purchased earlier nearly falls from my grasp. The prince catches it, hands quick like an adder. I sag in relief. If I had to go and get another one, I would cry – too achy and tired for another trip around the markets.

'Let me,' offers Ellis, putting his own hand into my pocket. A wave of heat rushes over my cheeks, surprised by his warmth as his body nears mine. Bending his head, his breath brushes my neck as he takes out the currency I need. When he lingers a little too long to count the coins, I know he's doing it on purpose, hoping for a reaction. He finally hands over the money and takes my flowers before roaming his gaze upon me. 'I'll walk you home.'

'Absolutely not,' I reply, like I said last night.

'You cannot possibly hold these, too,' he says, lifting the bag of flour and bouquet of blossoms. He stares at my full arms, where the weight of the shopping already makes my shoulders throb from holding them up so long. 'If you do, you'll collapse, and I don't want you hurting yourself.'

Without replying, he grabs some bags off me and carries them away to my chagrin. He seems to know where I live as he heads in the right direction. It doesn't surprise me. He probably followed me home last night like he threatened to do before I escaped.

'Maple lives this way!' I shout. He turns on his heel and heads in the opposite direction. I wait for a moment or two after he passes me before shouting, 'My mistake, you were right the first time!'

Glee flits through my chest as I get a head start in the direction he originally headed.

The prince flashes me a cold glare when I peer over my shoulder. I grin, striding so quick in the hopes he struggles to keep up. It's a fool's hope, though, his long legs gaining distance in seconds.

'That was cruel,' he murmurs, watching our surroundings with those deep cobalt eyes.

Were they always that dark?

'No,' I utter thoughtfully. 'It was funny.'

I mirror him, wondering if he's searching for something or if he's just usually this cautious. Groups of people mill around, collecting their own produce and wares. It's not as busy today, probably because of the amount of alcohol consumed last night.

'I try to help you and that's the treatment I'm given.' He huffs and the sight is comical.

'I didn't need help, Your Highness. You made it your mission to save the day when I am *not* a damsel in need of saving.' Our eyes clash and his jaw suddenly tenses, as if biting back a response.

He appears to debate his next choice of words. Is he thinking of the prison camp? Is he thinking of all the times he's seen me weak and vulnerable? Chained up like an animal, screaming and shouting for help?

'I do not think of you as a damsel, Violet.'

I swallow. My name on his lips is something I never thought could sound so ... *intimate*.

'No?' I ask, waving my hand towards him. 'Then, give me my bags back.'

He shakes his head. 'Absolutely not,' he says, echoing my prior sentiments. 'Just because I won't allow you to break your back doesn't mean I think you are weak.'

I have no answers, only questions.

'Why?'

He peers down, frowning. 'You'll have to be more specific. Why what?'

'Why are you here, helping *me* of all people? What are you doing in the markets? What were you doing last night?'

You never attend anniversaries, I want to add, but I don't want him to think I go out of my way to search for him. Because I don't.

When the prince finds something distasteful, he wrinkles his nose, and while he does so less prominently now, I still see it. The gesture sends a rush of memories flooding back.

You need to be less observant of his every move, I chide.

Ellis abruptly stops and I stumble, confused. I scowl. All I want is to get these bags back home before I literally break my back – not that'd admit that to him now.

'What are you doing?' I huff, lugging a bag higher on the crook of my elbow to keep it from slipping.

His free hand reaches out and delicately moves a strand of golden hair from my face. The look he gives me is achingly soft, the steel is gone from his eyes as he gazes deep into mine. Instinctively, I lean forward, wanting to be closer to him.

'Why wouldn't I help you?' The prince murmurs, concern and genuine confusion lining his words. I shake my head, words escaping me. 'We are *friends*, Violet. Why wouldn't I come and help you with your groceries?'

The hurt in his features makes my chest tighten with guilt.

Because you've not been my friend for years, I want to bite back.

But his expression is open and vulnerable, immediately, I know I can't answer truthfully even if I want to. Even after all this time, I want to hurt him – want to hurt him like he hurt me. But I can't. No matter how hard I try, I can't do that to him. Not now, not ever.

'Friends,' I begin carefully, testing my words to sense his reaction, 'are people who see each other often. I've not seen you in a *decade*. I don't know who you are anymore.'

'I am the same person,' he murmurs, briefly averting his gaze. 'I am still me.'

The bubble breaks and I press my lips together, berating myself for being so close to him. He left me once, he can do it again. His words sound sweet and alluring but what happens when he leaves me behind once more? Will he hide for another ten years while I'm left stitching myself back together?

Leave. Leave now before you start to remember your feelings for him.

My hand reaches out for the bag of flour, and he reluctantly lets me take it. Then, I gingerly grasp the bouquet and hook them inside a bag around my torso. I'm like a pack horse, but he doesn't protest when I cast him a long lingering look.

It's for the best, I remind myself.

'I'm not interested in having a friendship with you. Goodbye, Ellis.'

I walk off, and though I feel his eyes on me, I don't turn around, my emotions erratic and my heart unsteady.

8

VIOLET

Otto was kind enough to give me more shifts, accepting my request without a moment to mull it over. So, when I enter Swyndle's Saddle Shop early the next morning, I'm sprightlier than the day before. He is ready and waiting with a cup of tea, which he hands over as I approach the front desk. I breathe in its lemony scent. He is the only person who makes it with both sugar and honey.

'Just how I like it,' I say approvingly. 'Thank you, Otto. This is why you are my favourite human.'

He chuckles. Our relationship is more similar to a grandfather and granddaughter than an employer and employee. It is relaxed, easy and comfortable. I first met Otto when I stumbled across a poster in the street advertising extra help in his tack shop. At the time, my mother was still getting over my father's departure, as was my sister, and I couldn't handle another betrayal so soon after losing my best friend. So, I asked for the job knowing full well I had no experience or qualifications, but somehow, I hoped it would work in my favour.

Otto had laughed, asking why a twelve-year-old would want a job.

'Do you have bills to pay?' he had asked.

At the time, Danes Bakery was doing well for business – so money wasn't an issue.

I had been honest. I admitted that I didn't need any money but time away from a household that was drowning with sadness and grief – two emotions I'd already had enough of in my lifetime.

Otto sympathised with me, finally agreeing to take me on. Now, nine years later, he is one of my closest confidantes. His granddaughter was also a sufferer of Fral's prison camp, however, unlike me, she did not make it out.

'You are the only person I know who enjoys that ghastly drink,' says Otto, giving my cup a frigid look. 'You should broaden your horizons. Try peach tea or something more mature.'

'More mature?' I echo.

He nods. 'Yes, like green tea. It has its benefits unlike that sickly stuff you consume.'

'I'll consider it,' I reply. Both of us know I'll do no such thing. I head out back and sit in the weathered chair by one of the old wooden counters. Sprawled on top, open for the day, is the leather book filled with Otto's neat handwriting.

He is a meticulously organised man, something his late wife taught him. So, when I peer down, I give a small nod at today's schedule. Today, we have Rosen Dunne coming to pick up her order of a saddle and a matching bridle. She is not a regular by any means, but her commission was a nice change to my usual requests – her products designed with ivory coloured thread and engravings. I cannot wait to see her reaction.

'I want you to start the Arthur Goad order today,' Otto shouts, while I look further down the page. Right there is his name: Arthur Goad, who apparently needs a new saddle rug for his son's birthday later this week.

I nod to myself and check the sewing machine is out – it is. I take a sip of my warm tea before I get to work. I take the horse rug Otto has already made from the shelf. Its quilted texture is a fine quality not many other shops in Sapphire City can live up to. Sitting before the sewing machine, I lose myself in the task, pumping my foot in a steady rhythm to keep the flywheel turning to control the sewing needle.

A bell chimes alerting me to a customer, but I continue my work, knowing Otto will deal with whoever has entered.

Most likely Rosen, I think mindlessly. I peer to the corner of the room, where the saddle she has ordered sits on a stand ready for her arrival. I go back to my sewing.

'I am looking for Violet Danes,' says the customer.

The hairs on my arms rise at the voice. A very *familiar* voice.

I pause and my shoulders tighten. My foot pauses mid-air as I listen carefully to the conversation in the other room. My breathing falters as I try to hear every word shared between the two men.

'Is she helping you with an order, Your Highness?' asks Otto, his tone polite but curious. I know without a doubt he would never let the prince behind the desk to see me, not without consulting me first. 'If so, I can help you. Violet is busy right now.'

There is a pause. 'No. It is not related to saddlery. I am merely here to visit.'

'Oh, well. If that's the case, you can come back at –'

'I will not take up much of her time.' The prince is firm in his demand, authority carving his every word. 'I only wish to ask Violet a question.'

By Otto's lack of response, I know he's taking a moment to compose himself. The sound of his footsteps shuffling alert me to his presence as he pokes his head through the door frame. I am already looking his way, and as our eyes meet, he shoots me a questioning look.

Do you want to speak to him?

I huff and make my way to the shop front. Otto allows us space and takes over the sewing machine. I can hear its whirring by the time I come face to face with Ellis, whose midnight blue eyes assess me carefully. His demeanour is more rigid than yesterday. I almost smirk. Perhaps he is uneasy seeing me. After what I said to him, I would be the same, which makes me wonder what he's doing at my place of work.

'How did you know where to find me?' I ask.

Ellis steps forward, resting a hand on the desk between us. His fingers flex against the hardwood, and his scarred skin makes me swallow. I can't help comparing them to mine, covered in the same thin white lines.

He shrugs, glancing around at the space. To my left are tall shelves filling two sides of the room with organised riding attire in all colours and sizes. To my right are finely crafted leather helmets with leather boots to match.

'What are you purchasing today?' I ask, pretending to have not overheard his conversation with Otto. Reaching across the counter, I take the box of gloves used to entice the customers and reorder them into neat lines.

'Nothing,' he replies, and I raise an eyebrow.

'I am very busy and do not appreciate you wasting my time. If you are not here to buy something, I suggest you leave.'

It's the prince's turn to raise an eyebrow, amusement glimmering in his dark eyes. 'Is that so? And if I refuse?'

'I'll *make* you leave,' I answer, lowering my voice in warning.

I'm confident I could escort him out without shapeshifting into something threatening, but if I must, I will. It wouldn't be the first time Otto has had trouble in this shop, I chased the last fool out having morphed into bear form.

'I have no doubt you would,' Ellis agrees, and I give him a tired look. This seems to change his mind about playing coy. He moves closer, bending over the desk and lowering his voice. 'I came to see you. To say you were right yesterday.'

Something cold shoots through my spine and I stiffen at his confession. My hands stop mid-movement, unable to look away from the prince.

Ellis goes on, oblivious to my shock. 'My appearance at the markets was not a mere coincidence, and I have an ulterior motive for being here today, too.'

My brows lift in surprise and my mouth opens before I remember myself. 'I thought as much.' When he doesn't elaborate but silently stands there, gazing into my eyes, I wave an inpatient hand. 'Go on then, what is it?'

'I need you to be my ...' The last word catches on his lips and his throat bobs. He looks pained. His knuckles turn white as he presses his hands into the hardwood between us. I sense that if he pushes any harder, the counter will start to creak beneath his weight, little cracks spider webbing beneath his touch. The royal sighs before spitting out the last and most definitely unexpected part of the sentence. 'Companion. Partner. Fake lover. Whatever you wish to call it – for a brief period of time.'

The gloves fall from my grasp, the box tumbling to the floor along with them. I jerk away. Ellis observes my every move as the products surround my feet, his expression grim.

I am unable to move, unable to speak even. I am dumb-founded as I look away, wondering if I had imagined his words or if the prince of Tealwaters did in fact say what I thought he said.

'*What did you say?*' I almost shriek. My emotions rise the longer he stands there without a hint of emotion. My tone is accusing yet quiet, as if at any moment, something inside me will snap, and I'll experience a sudden meltdown where I wreak havoc upon the shop and everything in it – including Ellis.

'Don't make me repeat myself, Violet. You heard me just fine,' he grumbles, snapping me out of my trance.

Anger fills me, swift and burning. 'You come here to my place of work with no intention of buying something, hassle me with a preposterous request and then have the audacity to give *me* cheek when I merely want you to confirm that you *did* in fact ask me to be your companion, partner, and *fake lover*,' I rattle off, repeating his words back to him.

He winces but does not back down. 'I suppose when you say it like that ...'

I huff and rest my hands on my hips, trying to appear larger and more intimidating. 'You, Prince Ellis, are a *menace*. You have no boundaries, do you? Why would I want to parade as your fake lover? I haven't seen you in years!'

The prince gazes at me as I fume. His lips twitch, and it's only then that I realise this is all a game to him. Right now, he finds me entertaining and is beguiled by my temper. He tilts his dark blonde head, as if getting a better angle of me.

I carry on, having found my rhythm. 'The gall you have to step in here and —'

'Violet, *enough*.'

Ellis presses his finger to my mouth and my words fade instantly. His demeanour softens as he slowly drags his fingers over my bottom lip, as if caressing it. A flash of hunger lights his cobalt eyes, and my thoughts catch up with the reality of what's happening. I smack his hand away, but his eyes linger on my mouth. I'm breathless, my chest rising and falling, as if I've run up and down the street multiple times.

'I refuse your absurd offer,' I murmur. I intend to sound harsh but it comes out the opposite. To save face, I growl, and a wolf's warning leaves my lips. My mouth stings as the long canines I've conjured pierce my lower lip.

'Why don't you listen, so I can explain how this

arrangement could benefit you?' asks Ellis calmly, stepping back to give me space. I will the air deeper into my lungs but I don't answer. He takes this as a sign to continue. 'I need someone to parade around with. I need a dependable woman to smile alongside me, make conversation, and create positive relationships with the wealthy families of Tealwaters.'

'Why?'

'Politics.'

This is not a good enough answer for me, and I tell him so.

'It should not matter what I need, Violet,' says Ellis, with a dismissive wave, as though his requirements are small and insignificant. 'You should consider what I can give *you*.'

'And what is that?'

He shrugs. 'Whatever your heart desires. Jewellery? Clothes? Whatever Sapphire City has to offer. I can get it *all* for you.'

I narrow my eyes and cross my arms. 'You think I'd agree to be your arm piece because I want a new *dress*?'

'Perhaps you have come to like those things now you are ...' he struggles to find the right words before finally choosing, '*grown*.'

I shake my head. 'I refuse your offer,' I say firmly. 'Now, if you excuse me, I have work to do. Some of us must endure daily labour to afford the basics in life.'

Ignoring the floor covered in horse riding gloves, I circle the hardwood desk and wave for Ellis to follow. He does, albeit reluctantly. When I open the shop door, and the bell chimes, I motion for him to leave. The prince steps halfway before meeting my eyes, his expression serious.

'You may not like the sound of being mine, even for a while, but think what you can gain from it. I'll offer you anything. *Anything* you desire. That is my promise.'

I shake my head, ignoring the feeling inside my chest when he says *mine*.

Ellis steps outside, and as I close the door, I hear him declare, 'Consider it, Violet. Asking anything of a *prince* could be a life changing opportunity you may regret passing up.'

I watch as he strides away with his hands in his pockets before sidling up to a woman in a royal uniform – most likely his personal guard. I release a shaky breath and don't take my eyes off him until he's out of sight. I spin on my heel to return to work, but I pause. Otto is standing in the doorway, his face wary. 'You alright, Blossom?'

His nickname makes me sigh. I rub my forehead, feeling a headache coming. 'How much of that did you hear?'

He chuckles. 'I'm old but I'm not *that* old,' he says, admitting to overhearing every bloody word.

'I thought as much.'

I follow him to the back room, where another fresh steaming hot tea awaits on the desk, its lemon scent filling the air. As Otto returns to the sewing machine, I perch on the armchair by the order book.

'The young prince is right y'know,' mutters Otto. He doesn't wait for a response before firing up the machine and pumping the pedal once more. 'He has a much further reach to many more resources than you and I. If you play your cards right, you could have him do many things to ease your life.' He peers at me with a pointed look.

'What are you saying, Otto?'

'I'm saying, consider his offer. Sleep on it, but don't make a final decision right now.'

I wait a beat before nodding. 'Fine, but only because you asked it of me.'

Otto grins, the skin around his mouth stretching with delight. I smile back, even with a ball of uncertainty growing in my stomach.

9

ELLIS

I have no doubt that if I keep pushing, Violet will eventually bend to my will. I could see it in her eyes when she denied my offer – the curiosity and inquisitiveness as to why I kept pestering *her* and no one else.

I smile as I recall seeing her yesterday, fired up and defensive. While it's not the first time I've been cursed at, it's the first time I've wanted more harsh words slung my way. Violet's insults sound more like a challenge than abuse.

'I've found her,' Hera announces, pointing at the fountain where Violet sits with another girl.

I made a bet with my guard that whoever found Violet first would win a favour. Hera is one of the best trackers I know, but with my ability to sense souls, I thought I had her beat. It seems I was wrong.

Tilting my head, I find I vaguely recognise the girl Violet is with, but I'm not sure where from.

'Go buy yourself a treat.' I hand Hera some silver coins

while she passes me a long thick cloak made from sapphire velvet. 'And think about what favour I can give you.'

'Oh, I will, Your Highness,' she says before heading to a nearby shop that smells strongly of coffee. Hera will stay at a safe distance until I am ready to return to the castle.

Violet and her friend leave the fountain, and I follow as they exit the city square. They are about the same height, but where Violet's hair is gold streaked in onyx, the other girl's locks are light brown with a hint of red when it catches the light. They talk animatedly between them-selves, their hands waving all over the place, they occasion-ally bend at their knees, reaching for one another as they laugh obnoxiously loud. People glance at them but they don't notice, the pair in their own bubble.

I feel a twist of envy, but a carriage load of satisfaction at hearing them cackle and witnessing Violet so relaxed. It's nice to see. Those piercing eyes of hers glow with mirth, and her perfect smile is wide and full of joy.

The friends hug, wrapping their arms tightly around each other before the other girl leaves. Violet stills, watching her friend go like she's saddened by their farewell.

This is my chance, I think.

I have one more day to convince Violet that being my other half won't be so terrible, ensuring she attends my brother's birthday that is being prepared as we speak.

Violet heads down a quiet street away from the city's busy centre and toward her home, which I recognise after following her back home when she was drunk. She and Luca had been foolish and intoxicated enough not to notice being shadowed, they hadn't even detected me when I was only a stone's throw away as Luca waved her back into the bakery.

I bend my knees and shoot into the sky. I'm flying without wings and relish the wind in my hair. I land on a roof she has yet to reach, so I sit on the edge and let my legs dangle, whistling a fine tune to mimic a Tellian bird.

As expected, Violet's head shoots up. Clearly, her adoration for animals and nature has not changed. I smile and whistle again. She pauses, spinning in a full circle before her brilliant eyes land on me. Those pretty pink lips purse with distaste and the sight makes my trousers feel suddenly tight.

Mother of pearl.

I lean back on my arms and watch her, saying and doing nothing. Violet continues walking, pretending not to have noticed me, so I whistle again – this time louder and more urgent.

She passes beneath me and finally stops, looking over her shoulder with a questioning glare. I finally move and pat the edge of the rooftop, silently asking for her to join. For any normal person, this would be impossible, but with Violet's shapeshifting abilities, she can fly whenever she wishes to.

She appears to debate her next move, the cogs working so furiously inside her head that I can practically hear them screech to a halt. She narrows her eyes.

'I can't,' she shouts, resting her hands on her hips.

'Why not?'

'Because I don't have another set of clothes on me.' She motions to her attire.

Shapeshifters are notorious for constantly shredding

their outfits, especially if changing into a body much larger than their human form. I lean back and grab the cloak Hera gave me, holding it up for her to see.

'I have you covered,' I say. Her eyes sharpen with questions. 'Now, make haste. I don't have all day.'

'If that's the case, I won't bother.' She huffs.

I roll my eyes, though I secretly enjoy how difficult she is. 'Are you denying the order of your crown prince?'

She glances up at the sky, murmuring something under her breath. 'An order? Really?'

I nod and pat the spot beside me again, tilting my head in challenge.

Violet sighs but heads into a nearby alleyway, no doubt taking her time to find a place to stash her clothes. I don't move, allowing her the privacy to strip and change into whatever form she chooses. Yet my mind wanders to how she must look – that long, pullable hair, those plump angry lips, that soft body of curves and —

Breathe, Ellis, breathe.

I peer at my fingers, darkening at the tips, and curl them into fists. I try to control my hammering heart and relax my very obvious and straining crotch area.

An eagle, sleek and dangerous, shoots upwards from between the two townhouses. I spot Violet's sharp talons and beak first as she nears me, aiming straight for my eyes. I do my best not to shuffle or tense, acting as though Violet in animal form isn't highly impressive and slightly terrifying.

Violet trills at me. She flutters her long powerful wings, sending gusts of wind at my face. Her dark onyx eyes are bold before she settles and gets comfortable on the roof's edge. I gather the sapphire-coloured cloak and drape it over her head, and she warbles in a tone that sounds like annoyance.

In a flash, a set of long bare legs slide out from beneath the velvet. Violet's messy head of hair sticks out, too, frustration lining her features.

'Why couldn't you come to me? It would have been a whole lot easier,' she complains.

'What man would pass up the perfect opportunity of sitting with a nearly naked woman?' I counter. She scowls.

'You are a scoundrel, Your Highness,' she hisses and rearranges herself so she can sit comfortably without revealing any more skin. 'Now, what is so urgent that I had to unwillingly come and sit on a roof with you?'

She knows the answer, I can see it glimmering in her eyes —- eyes that have returned to their normal shade of purple-blue. I play along, allowing the illusion that my next question isn't expected.

'I presume you have thought about my proposal. Slept on it. Mulled it over. So, I came to tell you the offer still stands. In exchange for helping me, I will offer you something you need in return. *Anything* you want.'

Violet nibbles her bottom lip, averting her gaze to the street below us. A stray dog sniffs around a flowerpot before disappearing down an alleyway – thankfully not the one Violet left her clothes in.

Her features furrow with consideration, yet Violet's thoughts are so loud I can practically hear her debating my words. She is worried, but about what, I'm not sure. However, that unease doesn't seem to warrant another refusal.

'When you say anything, do you really mean *anything*?' she asks, intrigued.

'Anything.' I nod. 'But I will draw the line at murder.'

'What about staging an accidental death?' she ponders, her curt tone having softened, but only slightly.

'Let me guess, you are thinking of getting rid of me?'

Violet lifts her gaze to meet mine and smirks. 'Am I that easy to read?'

Silence lingers between us, which feels strange. A long time ago, when we were stuck together with chains and rope, we talked all the time, chatting about anything and everything. The limit was non-existent. Now, I can feel her uneasiness and how her body stiffens anytime I'm near. I want that rigidness to ease, I want her to feel as relaxed with me as she was with her friend from earlier.

'So, have you thought about what to ask for?' I press, needing her consent before I can execute my dismally last-minute plan.

'I have been thinking about what you could give me,' she admits, and I nod slowly. 'But I feel improper to ask for such extravagant things.'

'Nothing is too extravagant for me,' I assure her, my voice low and soothing. 'My family and I rule over this whole kingdom – over you and your neighbours. What could possibly be too unseemly to ask of me?' Violet sharply exhales and rolls her eyes at my answer, likely the arrogance of it.

'Fine. I have two requests,' she says, surrendering to her mixed emotions. 'My mother owns a bakery.' I nod.

'I remember.'

Violet casts me a lingering look before averting her

gaze. 'I saw in the newspaper that our sovereigns have arranged for many businesses to attend your brother's birthday celebrations tomorrow. I want her there as a vendor. It will be good exposure for her.'

'Consider it done,' I reply, making a mental reminder to ask Alex if such a thing will be allowed. If not, I'll make it happen regardless.

Violet pulls the cloak tighter around her and presses her lips into a thin line. 'I need my mother's business to thrive, Ellis. I want to help her in any way I can. That means more staff, more advertisements, more *everything*. We need all the help we can get, otherwise, we may lose the shop altogether, and I can't let that happen. I cannot fathom such a thing occurring – she adores that place.'

Violet seems outraged by the simple thought of her mother's bakery being taken away, and that slither of doubt and worry makes me nod without careful consideration for what I am promising her.

'Of course, I will do everything in my power to help your mother's business. What is the second appeal?'

I expect this to be something for herself or maybe something personal.

'My sister, Hazel,' says Violet, tilting her head this way and that. 'She loves the bakery as much as my mother. She's always spoken about attending some classes to hone her skills and better her creations in the kitchen.'

'You want to send her to baking classes?' I muse. Violets nods faintly. I shrug. It's a simple enough request. 'As you wish.' I wait for more, but she is quiet. 'Is that really it? Two things? None of which benefit yourself.'

'They do benefit me. Those two things will make my

family happy. What else is there to ask for?' She wonders. A line forms between her brows, and something warm unfolds within my chest, coursing through my arms and legs. The need to touch her is suddenly all-consuming.

She goes to say something before smiling, a slow animalistic smile. I swallow at the sight of it.

'Uh oh,' I mutter.

'Now you mention it, there is something you can do for me specifically. Something you can give me today – just to make sure you're not fooling with me.' Violet's sudden excitement makes me suspicious.

'Do share.'

'If you want me to be your faithful companion throughout the *politics*,' she muses, quoting my reason for being in this fiasco. 'I want you to ask me *nicely*.'

My body stiffens, but when I meet her purple-blue gaze, I know she's deadly serious.

'I did,' I state neutrally.

'Saying "I need you to be my companion, partner, and fake lover" is not how you would ask a lady to be yours in any way, shape, or form. Now, ask me nicely, Ellis. Ask me as if this is *real*. I want it to be believable as I assume you want me to act like this,'– she motions between us –'is real in front of whoever has made you wish to carry out this absurd plan.'

She's testing me, and a part of me knows I deserve it. When Violet swivels round to gain a better look at me, I roam my eyes over her bare shoulders. I do not mind her assessing my limits – seeing the lengths I will go to for her to agree to my proposition.

She stares expectantly at me, keeping nothing hidden

as she assesses every part of my face. The sensation of her taking me in is thrilling and my head throbs, deciphering what it might mean. She rouses the darkness inside me, which watches her as intently as I am. I take a moment to push the monster away, refusing to let it take over my control.

Just ask her and be done with it. Allow her this slice of power and then make sure she knows who's really in charge.

The fact that she wants me to ask isn't the problem, it's knowing that she wants me to be vulnerable – to expose my neck as a show of trust. Violet knows that I must be desperate if I keep reappearing.

'Violet Danes,' I say softly, reaching for her hand. She is relaxed under my touch, letting me do as I wish in the hopes of executing her request. 'Will you do me the honour of being mine now and until we state otherwise?'

Violet is silent, letting me swim in my own self-doubt for a moment before the corner of her lip lifts. 'You're laying it on thick but fine. Yes. I will be yours until stated otherwise.'

Yours.

My heart falters with equal parts relief and exhilaration.

10

THE PAST

I become attached to Violet – her clever words, mind, and the steadiness of her presence. So, when they take her nearly daily for tests, the loneliness looms over me. Violet is the only one brave enough to talk to me, all the other children are either in states of recovery from their own experiments or are too daunted by the sight of me.

I suppose their hope dwindles upon seeing their youngest prince as helpless and desperate for escape as them. If a royal can't leave this nightmare, then how will they?

I twiddle my thumbs, trying to occupy my thoughts. I am not used to nothingness or being chained up like an animal, left to my own devices. I am constantly doing something back home, but here, it's a never-ending pit of nothingness.

I peer towards the entrance. Violet has been gone for hours – longer than ever before. I only know this because her rare smile and gleaming eyes keep me going – they reignite my hopes in this place of pain and torment.

I'm alerted by movement. The tent's canvas flutters open when the very person I've been hoping for is thrown inside, *where she collapses into a heap by the entrance. My heart stutters at the sight of her – the lack of movement. I'm by her side in seconds, my chains rattling, pulled taut against the eyelet as I lift her head off the ground.*

'Violet,' *I fret.* 'Violet, talk to me.'

She groans when I lay her across my lap. Her head nestles in the crook of my arm as I swipe away a dirty strand of blonde hair. She closes her eyes but the purple shadows beneath them are dark, the surrounding skin webbed with black veins.

'What happened?' *I whisper. Others watch us cautiously.*

'Pain.' *The word is near silent, so I crane my neck closer to listen.* 'So much pain, Ellis.'

'What can I do?'

Another moan escapes Violet as she tries to readjust herself, her eyes reluctantly opening. 'Hold me. Talk to me.'

My hands tremble as I pull her closer to my chest, cradling her body to mine. She closes her eyes once more, as if content. 'Talk of what?' *I ask.*

'Anything. Tell me something happy.'

I nod, though I suddenly find it hard to think of such things. 'I have a brother called Alex.'

'I know,' *she replies, a faint tinge of amusement in her voice.* 'He is our prince.'

'Oh right. Of course.' *I clear my throat, trying to think of something else.* 'I like to bake but I'm not very good at it.'

Purple-blue eyes meet mine. 'You *bake?'*

I smile, enjoying her surprise. 'I particularly like sweet treats.'

'My family owns a bakery,' *she confesses, and I lean forward.* 'But they specialise in mostly bread.'

'Perhaps when we go home, you'll convince them to make pastries? Mermaid cakes are my favourite.'

'I wouldn't have guessed,' she muses, a slither of a smile across her lips. My heart gallops. 'I pegged you as too regal to make your own food.'

'I am.' I nod playfully, and Violet chuckles until a horrible cough shakes her body. My only response is to rub her back until she stops. Blood covers her palm as she moves it from her mouth, yet with her eyes still shut, she doesn't see it. But when she closes her hand to hide the evidence, I know she feels it and has probably experienced it before.

I press on, not wishing to focus on the meaning of that crimson substance. 'I like to sneak into the kitchens and bake brownies or cookies if we have the ingredients. Alex used to love my late-night visits.'

'Past tense,' she murmurs.

'Excuse me?' I wrinkle my nose.

'You used past tense, Ellis. "Alex used to love my late-night visits." Don't use past tense with me. We are going to go home.'

I nod, scolding myself for the slip up. 'You're right. I'm sorry.'

'Don't be. I enjoy correcting your faults.'

I chuckle and she lifts her hand slowly to press against my chest. 'What are you doing?' I ask.

'Listening to your heart. Reminding myself.'

'Reminding yourself of what?' I ask, enjoying the feel of her touch.

'It's pounding, like you've been running.'

My nerves fray and words fail me as I try to conjure an excuse for why that might be.

'It's okay. My heart races for you, too,' she says, opening an eye to make sure I've heard her.

'Does it?' I ask, my lips twitching into a grin.

Violet removes her hand from my chest and places my palm over hers instead. To my delight, her heart reacts the same as mine, and the hammering beneath her tatty shirt prompts me to press my palm harder against her, like if I press hard enough, I can hold her racing heart in my grip.

'Three questions,' she says suddenly.

'Go on.'

'Would you take care of it?' she wonders, resting her cold hand atop mine. 'This little thing inside of me?'

I smile down at her without restraint. With her eyes closed, I can watch her as closely as I wish. 'I would guard it like a dragon would its baby.'

'Dragons kill to protect their babies.'

'They do,' I confirm, and her cheeks flush a light pink.

'Second question,' she murmurs, resting her cheek against my arm as if to hide away. 'When you and I get out of here, can we bake mermaid cakes together someday?'

'Of course. We can do it in our castle kitchen. We have all the fancy equipment needed.'

She hums in approval. 'Last question.'

'Yes?' I press. My face is so close to hers, eager to know what she'll ask next. Violet's voice is so soft, and her whisper tickles my cheeks.

'Will you, Ellis Irvine, be my best friend until the end?' My heart stops for what feels like an eternity. Violet sighs, her lungs rattling. 'Did I go too far?' she asks, regret lining her features as she reluctantly opens her eyes. 'Did I make a fool out of myself for asking that?'

I bring her closer, twisting my hand so my fingers interlace with hers. 'No. You merely took me off guard. I would proudly be *your best friend.'*

'Until the grim or happy end?' she asks lightly.

I nod. 'Until the happy *end. Don't forget, we're getting out of here.'*

'Of course,' she muses.

It doesn't take long for Violet to drift off, her body relaxing against me. Caressing her cheek, I absorb every detail upon her face, remembering every freckle, every line, and every spot of colour until it's scorched into my memory, hoping more with each day that we are rescued from this nightmare.

'I have a question for you, Violet Danes,' I whisper, and my breath tickles her face as I hug her closer. 'Did you intend to steal my heart?'

II

ELLIS

The next morning, I direct the servants while they move the decorations, tables, and ice sculptures to the rear garden. Tonight's ocean theme consists of blue, blue and more blue. The queen's voice echoes through the castle foyer, her commands becoming more ridiculous each time.

'You wouldn't think this celebration was for me,' muses Alex, watching the queen wave her hands at a sculpture that needs moving slightly to the left. 'The way she has chosen every ornamentation, every dish, every score of music ...'

'Perhaps if you stood up for yourself, you could have chosen something other than the date of the event,' I say, earning an unimpressed look from my brother.

'And be ordered to "find a woman," whom I must pretend to be liaising with?' Alex snorts at my expense. 'I am no fool, Ellis. Our aunt enjoys finding people's limits, and I do not intend for her to find or test mine.'

'Why? Do you have something to hide?' I narrow my eyes in jest.

He laughs, bright and loud, the sound capturing the attention of a few servants in the gardens. 'Me? Why yes! I am the prince of secrets,' he mocks. I shake my head, a slither of a smile forming on my lips.

We both know Alex is an open book. He wouldn't be able to hide his feelings if his life depended on it, exposed for everyone to see.

'Talking of secrets,' says my brother, shuffling closer. 'How is the hunt for a certain lady faring? Did Miss Danes agree to your ludicrous offer, or did she give you the expected response?' He appears highly amused, lacking all faith that I could swindle Violet into agreeing with the queen's request. I flash him an unimpressed glare, but I play along with his game. 'She refused?' he presses, acting appalled. In reality, he knew it was coming.

'Yes. Several times,' I say. He chuckles. 'But she yielded in the end.'

Alex blinks, shocked, then claps my shoulder with a wide grin. 'You lucky bastard,' he mutters as the queen now heads our way. Servants scatter at the sight of her frustration. 'Let's hope she is to Aunt Melody's taste. She is in a foul mood today, which is strange considering how much she loves hosting parties.'

I don't have the chance to answer before the queen interrupts us with her stern tone and penetrating stare. 'Are you both going to stand there like statues or help?' The queen demands, lips pressed with disapproval before turning to my brother. 'You have tastings that require your attention.'

My brother is not a fool and hurries off, but not before tossing me a smirk over his shoulder. The queen peers at me then and pauses, as if lost for ideas on what I should do. 'And you ...'

'I was just leaving. I must make sure my date tonight receives her gown, as I am sure you will not approve if she wears anything less than regal,' I drawl with a pointed look.

'Indeed.' She waves a dismissive hand, and then heads to the fruit trees lining the perimeter of the gardens. 'Who was in charge of trimming these? They are not circular like I asked – they are *oval*.'

I make haste and find the exit, finding Hera at the castle's entrance.

'Did you find a good enough excuse to evacuate the premises, Your Highness?' she jests, and I nod.

'Indeed. We are going to visit Violet and hand deliver her outfit for tonight. Arrange a carriage immediately.'

She bows her head. 'Of course. Right away.'

As we travel through the city, my mind drifts to yesterday. I had struggled to sleep last night, too focused on Alex's birthday preparations. My arrangement with Violet has been built on uneven ground – my need for her is far more desperate than her need for me – but I can't seem to shake the feeling of something big looming in the future.

What I thought would be a simple arrangement between two people who once knew each other has turned into something much more difficult than I anticipated. Two nights ago, I licked her face, and the taste of her skin ignited something in me that I haven't felt in a decade. What scares me most is I knew full well what I was doing. But, at that moment, I wasn't thinking. I didn't care, all I cared about was how she would react to it – and her reaction was perfection. Yesterday, I had insisted she sit with me, knowing full well she would need to strip her clothes and expose her skin. Again, I did not care, if anything I enjoyed it – enjoyed the frustration she lashed out onto me.

She will be my ruination.

The thought of a person having so much control and sway over my life would normally feel suffocating, but with Violet, all I feel is *familiarity* – a sense of returning home after a long time away. It frightens me. Over the years, I've done so well to leash my power and retain a solid wall of control, but now she's back ... I can feel it slipping. But why?

It's because you missed her, a voice pipes up. *She is like a drug you never recovered from.*

I push the thought away before it blooms into something heavier – something hopeful. I must focus on the plan and execute it well, or else the queen will send me away, no doubt somewhere I'll be forgotten.

You must remember your duty to Alex and the kingdom.

If I am not careful, I'll fall into the rabbit hole that is Violet. If we do not enforce boundaries, I may hurt her like I did a decade ago, and that is the last thing I want. I will act as her fake beloved until the queen is satisfied, and then Violet and I will part ways amicably.

I nod, satisfied with my plan.

Do not get too close. Do not form romantic feelings.

* ☆ ° ₒ * ☾ * ☆ ° ₒ *

Violet's mother, Maura, runs a bakery, yet the other bakeries in the city tend to do far better. What they lack is reliable help and a reputation to keep the city dwellers talking. What Danes Bakery needs is more income for workers to help grow their business, which must be why Violet wants her family to be at the birthday celebrations tonight. The more people tasting their products, the better.

Hera and I arrive at Violet's family home. It's located on a somewhat busy street where businesses make up the bottom levels of the townhouses lining the road, with the family homes on the top floor. For the Danes family, their baking business is downstairs, and the entrance to their home is also the entrance to the bakery.

Before I step foot into the establishment, I close my eyes and focus. One of the powers I gained in the prison camp was sensing souls, therefore, when I concentrate, I see unique glowing orbs of the living within my mind. Soul sensing, like my ability to fly, was one of the few gifts Fral bestowed upon me, but with its good side comes its bad.

I count a total of four people inside the establishment: two upstairs and two downstairs. When I peer inside the bakery window, there are no customers present. I swallow.

You can do this.

I step inside, and the door opens, where the owner herself, Maura Danes, greets me. She has golden blonde hair beginning to grey around the temples and wide brown eyes that behold me behind the counter. She is quick to bow, seeing the heavy crystal and pearl crown atop my head, an expression of surprise upon her features.

'Your Highness, what a surprise. What can I do for you?' I get the sense she doesn't know of the arrangement between Violet and I, so I turn on the subtle charm.

'I came to see your daughter, Violet. Is she here?'

Maura's brows lift and nearly disappear into her hair-line. I refrain from rolling my eyes. No doubt Violet is hiding this arrangement from her family.

'Oh, of course. Come in. I will go get her,' she says, ushering me to the other side of the counter.

Maura leads me into their back kitchen, where the tables are covered in various baking concoctions. The smell of fresh bread makes my stomach tighten. Luca is there, putting a tray into a large oven. I suppose they are all readying for tonight's festivities – the vendors are expected to arrive earlier than the guests.

When Luca spots me, his nostrils flare. I suppress my smile.

Luca does not greet me. He observes me with such intent I think he's trying to find something wrong with my attire – or, more specifically, me.

'I did not realise you were fond of men's waistcoats,' I say casually.

He frowns. 'Pardon?'

'By the way you're studying me, I would say you like my outfit.'

He scoffs and returns to his work. 'That would be a negative.'

The sound of footsteps on the stairs makes me turn towards the kitchen entrance, where Violet leans against the doorframe, studying the scene of Luca and I. She doesn't seem bothered by Luca, her eyes glaze over him before landing on me.

It's as if she has stolen all the oxygen from my lungs. Those piercing eyes linger from the crown upon my head all the way to my polished shoes. She's impressed, maybe even a little captivated by the sight of me. I can't help but smirk.

Keep looking at me like that and we will both be in trouble.

'Ellis,' greets Violet, her voice nonchalant – a serious contrast to her intrigued surveyance of me. She scowls at Maura, who squeezes past her daughter into the kitchen and picks up the rolling pin on the counter.

'Violet,' her mother warns, pointing the tool at her. 'Be respectful to our prince.'

Violet clears her throat, appearing suddenly uncertain as her eyes flicker between me and Maura. She most likely doesn't want to treat me with respect, and I lift a brow in amusement, my lips twitching upwards. She narrows her beautiful purple-blue eyes.

Go on, I challenge.

Taking a deep breath, she lowers into a bow. I can see her cleavage, and I know she knows this by the subtle way her eyes lift to mine with a smirk. 'Your Highness,' she amends with a mischievous smile. 'How can we help you? We are your humble servants.' Maura rolls her eyes.

'I apologise for Violet, Your Highness, I –'

I raise a hand and offer Maura an attempt of a warm smile. 'No need. Violet and I are well acquainted. There is no need for formalities.'

The woman leans back, an unspoken question in her eyes. She looks to Violet for confirmation, while Luca comes to stand by the baker's side, dusting his hands on his apron. He turns to Violet for confirmation, too, his features lined with distaste.

'Is this true?' he asks, briefly glancing my way before focusing back on Violet.

She nods reluctantly but comes to stand by my side. 'Yes. Well, now you are here, I suppose I should formally introduce you.' Violet waves a hand between us, an air of awkwardness in her stance. 'Mother, Lucas. This is Ellis, my ... partner. He is the one who invited me to tonight's celebrations.'

Maura opens her mouth, and her chocolate eyes flit between the two of us. For show, I rest my hand on Violet's hip, and though she tilts her head in my direction, she makes no move to touch me. Regardless, her warmth is pleasant, the smell of her hair reminds me of berries.

'So, you weren't invited by a lord,' says Maura, her voice small and far away. 'You will be attending with Prince Ellington?'

Luca looks stunned, though likely not because I asked Violet to tonight's celebration, but because Violet actually admitted *out loud* that I was her partner. A small flame ignites inside of me at her confession. I lean my body closer, enjoying her proximity.

Violet nods with an expression that shows that she, too, is as surprised as her mother. 'That's right. I have *very* high standards. A lord just wouldn't do.' She chuckles, and her mother smiles with a look of reservation before studying me.

'If you are happy, so be it.'

Violet nods, her act fool proof. 'We are.'

'You can't be serious?' protests Luca. 'He is *dangerous*.'

I refrain from spitting a response at him, not wishing to prove his opinions.

Violet shrugs. 'And where did you hear that? In the newspaper or from the source itself?'

Luca appears unimpressed by her lack of wariness. My jaw tenses as he continues to speak to her like she is a child and not a full-grown woman. 'The newspaper requires a certain amount of truth to be able to publish the stories in the first place, Violet.'

She purses her lips before peering at me. 'Do you intend to harm me, Your Highness?'

I shake my head. 'Of course not.'

'That's settled then.' She claps her hands together, ignoring Luca. Something unfamiliar coils inside me. Violet is quick to defend me and dispute Luca's taunts. I find myself glad she is by my side.

Turning to me, she frowns. 'Should we go for a walk? Is that why you are here?'

'That's right.' I face Maura, while turning my back to Luca. 'I'll bring her back soon.'

12

VIOLET

Prince Ellis has met my mother and Luca. I thought I could keep this arrangement secret and do what he needed of me while helping my mother's business. But he came to my *home*.

The bastard. Why would he do that? And how did he know where I live?

Ellis keeps quiet while his guard, who he introduced as Hera, trails some distance behind us. It takes a moment to find my breath when he grasps my hand like we're a normal couple taking a stroll in the afternoon sun. I frown, not entirely certain *who* we are supposed to be fooling with our ruse, but when his hold tightens, I slowly allow myself to play along, his hand warm around mine.

'You didn't tell your mother about us,' Ellis starts, his voice devoid of emotion. I'm not sure what he thinks of it – perhaps that he's my little secret.

'I was going to keep it to myself so I wouldn't have to lie to my family and Luca,' I explain, glancing back at Hera who scans the roofs alongside us. 'Why did you visit? What is so urgent you had to barge your way into the bakery?'

Ellis squeezes my hand and leans down, peering into my eyes. 'Keep your voice down. We are in love, remember?' I give him a hard look. 'I needed to drop off an appropriate outfit for tonight's celebrations. Besides that, I came because I thought we should establish some ground rules.'

'Ground rules?'

'Yes. We need to be on the same page for this to work, and to clarify our expectations of one another.'

Uncertainty bubbles in my stomach, but I nod. 'Fine. What are your expectations?'

'We are to act like a real couple – hand-holding and touching as and when it's needed. This must be convincing, or else it won't work.'

'But no kissing,' I say. His brows rise.

'And why is that?'

My cheeks heat up. 'Because I do not want you to kiss me.'

'Do you think I will be terrible at it?' he ponders. Amusement lights his features. I stare, not completely understanding why he is fighting me on this one small detail.

'I think it will make things more complicated than they need to be. Besides, I would rather kiss others than the likes of you.' I add the last part to annoy him, and to my delight, it does. His smile falters.

Ellis stops abruptly, and my arm is craned backwards as he still grips my hand. I turn with a scowl, but he is there, close to my face, his breath tickling my cheek as he wraps his arms around me. From afar, it appears as if he is whispering sweet notions into my ear, but his hold is firm and possessive.

'I expect you to be faithful to me until this arrangement is over, Violet,' he murmurs, his voice heavy and haunting. I can't help the shiver that runs through me as the sudden and unexpected thrill consumes my senses. The prince clings to me tighter, no doubt having felt it, too. His large hands are sprawled along my lower back and shoulders, and he tilts me slightly back, as if he is about to dip me. 'I cannot have you spotted with random fellows for the news to be brought back to my family. Do I make myself clear?'

The prince shifts away, enough to give me a stern look. 'You are *my* girl, and everyone will be reminded of that every time we are together.' Ellis untangles himself from me and straightens, assessing me with his cobalt gaze.

My girl. Why does that sound awfully appealing?

I shake my head and huff. 'If you say so, Your Highness, but that rule must apply to you, too.'

He snaps back to look at me, as if I said something blasphemous. 'Violet, the moment you step into that party tonight, you will have no doubts or qualms about other women.'

'Good.' I can't think of what else to say to that. All I know is I must leave soon because my legs feel traitorously wobbly from his promises.

'We must also keep as close to the truth as possible,' says Ellis, taking my hand again and pulling me along. We pass the florist, and the smell of blossoms surrounds me. I think back to the day he chose my bouquet.

My mother enjoyed her garden, so I made sure to pay attention.

I peer sidelong at the royal and his immaculate attire and his neatly groomed hair. He is a man of sharp lines and edged words with an unwavering stare, and immovable feelings. But is the boy I knew from a decade ago hidden beneath the surface?

'The truth,' I echo. 'I can do that.'

Nerves seize me as I imagine stepping into an event that no usual civilian of Sapphire City attends. I will be walking into a gathering full of wealthy men and abashedly glamorous women. Will they know I don't belong the moment I arrive? Will they know I'm a fraud?

'I can hear the wheels turning inside your head,' muses Ellis. 'Care to share your thoughts?'

'I would rather not, Your Highness,' I answer, hoping he does not order me to tell him, like he did yesterday when he ordered me to sit on the roof with him, fully naked.

'No,' he says, tugging my hand closer to his side. 'You will not call me "Your Highness" unless the moment calls for it. Until then, you must be personal with me. Ellis is my name, and you will use it.'

I don't argue because it seems reasonable enough. If we are to fool everyone that we're a couple, using his title will not aid in that illusion. 'Is that all, *Ellis*?' I ask.

Ellis raises a brow. 'We will have pet names for one another.'

I recoil, but he pulls me back in with a scowl.

'Pet names? Whatever for?'

'They're terms of endearment. They will solidify this ploy to help win over those who do not enjoy my company.'

'I am starting to see why that may be so,' I mutter.

He hums in what I think is amusement. 'I've missed your fire, Violet.'

I look up, wondering if I heard him correctly, but he stares on ahead as if oblivious to my churning thoughts and emotions. Ellis remains quiet, absorbing the scenery like he always seems to do while keeping my hand tucked inside his to keep me by his side.

'So, to clarify,' I say, needing to fill the silence and gloss over his confession. 'I must hold your hand, pretend you are the love of my life, not be seen with other men in provocative positions, stick as close to the truth as possible, think of a nickname for you that isn't offensive but intimate and romantic, and last – but certainly not least – refrain from using your title because heaven forbid someone thinks we are anything *but* a real couple.' I sigh dramatically, finally taking a breath. 'Is that all? Or should I write it all down?

'Your sharp tongue may land us in trouble someday, but I cannot help but find it amusing,' he says, briefly glancing at me. A crackle of lightning sounds and I glance up at the sky before realising it was Ellis.

'What was that?' I ask, struggling to contain my smile.

'Be more specific, Violet.'

'That crackle of magic. Why did that happen?'

He shrugs. 'Because I wield lightning.'

It's not an answer, and we both know it, but I let it slide this time. I realise we are back in my street, having walked a complete loop. When we approach the bakery, I peer through the glass to find it empty. My face falls.

No surprise there.

'Just you wait,' says Ellis, gently pushing me towards the door. 'Customers will be flooding this place in no time.'

I tilt my head, a shadow of a smile at my lips. He is trying to cheer me up, having sensed my dismay. My mind spins as I try to think of a response, but he steps away.

And though he doesn't hand them out often – if ever – Ellis gives me the smallest, most devastating smile.

'See you later, *sweetheart.*'

13

ELDIS

The castle bustles with activity, the outside grounds are now finished, thanks to the hard work of our staff, who seem grateful it's over. Tonight is one of the largest events of the year, where all the richest men and women congregate to celebrate my brother's thirty-second birthday.

'How do I look?' asks Alex, pulling at his collar. He wears a white dress shirt, which appears particularly tight around his neck, and a waistcoat of pale blue to match his eyes. The pattern reminds me of the ocean waves crashing to shore. It's perfect for him.

'Like the heir of a mighty kingdom,' I murmur, he flashes me a grateful smile.

'You don't look too bad yourself. I enjoy seeing you out of your usual dark attire.'

I refrain from rolling my eyes as I peer down at my usual dark attire. 'Funny.'

'The birthday boy wants to request something from his

younger brother,' remarks Alex, shaking his arms as if to try to loosen the shirt's fit.

'Yes?'

'No doing that face tonight.' My brother points at my expression, brows furrowed.

'This is my normal face,' I argue.

Alex dips his chin and narrows his eyes. 'No, it isn't. You switch it on and play with it like a cat taunting a mouse. It repels anyone from talking to you.'

'And that's a bad thing?' I drawl, glancing over his shoulder at the first throng of arriving guests. The itch to escape is overwhelming but I make the effort to give Alex my full attention. 'The younger brother wants to request something from the birthday boy.'

Alex's pale eyes follow mine to where the guests enter. He briefly waves at a man having his wine flute filled by a servant, then faces me with an exasperated sigh.

'Yes, Ellis. You may go. I'll see you later.' Alex claps my shoulder, knowing for the first few hours I'll be keeping my distance. After all, the last thing I want is to make conversation with everyone or hear the jolly, forced birthday wishes relayed on repeat. 'I will come and find you later. And I look forward to meeting your girl.' He winks, waving me off in time to greet a family of three.

The daughter flutters her kohl-lined eyes up at my brother, no doubt wishing to capture his heart. It's unsurprising, really. Alex is handsome, the richest bachelor in the kingdom, and soon to wear the crown. All he needs is a wife and he'll be set for the pearl throne, according to the king and queen.

Music plays, soft and mesmerising, as guests begin to

assemble on the well-kept lawn. Every now and then, their laughter drowns out the melodies, and I must travel carefully to evade them. However, no one approaches me, and I feel better for it, appreciating some time alone before I must put on an act before my family.

'Make sure the pastries are fully stocked at all times!' a familiar voice from across the lawn yells. I turn towards Maura, who helps to load shelves of products onto tiered cake stands.

My eyes narrow at the sight of Luca, he's arranging plates and forks for the guests while Violet's sister, Hazel, prepares a large silver tray of pastries. They are a team in every sense of the word, each of them clear on their roles as the guests begin to approach.

'Thank you for allowing them to come,' hums a low voice beside me. I don't need to look to know it's Violet. Her voice has me wishing to shuffle closer. My heart skips, and my mouth runs dry, when I peer down to peruse her outfit. She wears a lavender-coloured gown that softly embraces her curves, it's made of silk, matching the texture of her long, wavy hair, where strands of blonde and onyx fall over her exposed shoulders. If I were to place my hand on the small of her back, I would touch bare skin, her physique on display for all the men to see. I grind my teeth at the mere thought of it.

You look stunning, the compliment is on my tongue, but Violet continues talking and the moment's gone.

'My mother was thrilled that she got an invite,' she says, her face alight.

I am quick to recover, averting my eyes to the stall once

more. 'It's the least I can do. Shall we try some of your mother's creations?'

Violet nods, pleased.

The table is halved – one side savoury and the other sweet. The left side brims with sourdough, cottage loaves, and other bread concoctions, served with various dips. The right side is full of neatly arranged cake stands that smell delicious, but what captures my attention is a tray of mermaid cakes, their blue and purple scales glinting beneath the lanterns.

'What can I get for you, Your Highness?' Hazel asks as her bright blue eyes flicker between me and her sister. She smiles coyly, and it's the same expression Violet used to do once upon a time. Something hard twists in my chest, I try to ignore it and point out my choice.

'A mermaid cake please, Hazel.'

'I heard they are your favourite.' She serves them onto a plate.

'Did she now?' I murmur to Violet, who for once keeps quiet, her cheeks flushing pink.

'And I would like a pomegranate tart,' says Violet, pretending not to hear me.

'Coming right up.'

Seeming to be eavesdropping, Luca peers at me with an unimpressed stare. I give him a steady look back.

'Hazel, do you mind making those *two* mermaid cakes instead?' I ask.

We watch as the young girl rounds up our orders. Violet leans towards me, voice low so her sister doesn't hear. 'Hazel made the tarts herself – they're one of her favourite desserts. She has been experimenting with new flavours all day to offer the guests.'

'I'll make sure to rave about them then,' I offer. When Hazel comes back, I point at her tarts. 'I want to add one tart with each flavour on a tray.'

Hazel's eyes brighten, wide and hopeful. 'Truly?'

'Yes. I will have them handed out to all our guests.' I motion to a servant, who kindly takes the tray and begins walking the perimeter of the party. She's under strict instructions to keep making the rounds and refill the platter whenever it becomes empty.

With a mermaid cake and tart in tow, Violet and I head into the fray, but not before I hand Luca a bag containing one of my two mermaid cakes. He takes it, frowning at what's inside.

'To help with the sting.' I motion toward Violet, who doesn't realise I've broken off from her. Luca's face contorts into one of annoyance. 'I recommend you mind your step from now on, Mr Moye. Violet is not yours to touch or toy with. If I hear you have been causing her any grief, you will have me to deal with. And I am not a forgiving man.' Luca pales, but I don't bother waiting for his response. I turn my back to him before Violet realises where I've gone.

The crowds seem less intimidating with Violet by my side. When I bite into the pastry, warmth floods me, and I cannot contain my groan of pleasure. Violet laughs, watching closely. A flicker of delight crosses her features.

'So, the feared prince of Tealwaters can be bested by something as simple as a mermaid cake ... who would have thought?'

'I rarely have them, but when I do, they are as good as I

remember,' I say, gobbling it in minutes – and in a fashion the queen would no doubt scold me for. 'I should make the cooks whip them up more often.'

'They are good,' Violet agrees, eating her own tart. I can't help but wonder about the bakery. Violet spoke of it when we were children, and how her father encouraged Maura to build the business, so she could work in a job that she loves while he supported her every step of the way.

'Can I ask you a personal question?'

She hums, mouth full of food. 'If you must.'

'What happened to your father?' I keep my voice low as we stride the garden borders. Violet pauses and frowns deeply before peering up at me. 'You used to speak of him often, but I have yet to see him.'

She swallows thickly, pondering her response.

'If it's a difficult topic—'

'No,' she interrupts. 'I was not expecting you to ask about him, that's all.' Violet bites her lower lip, averting her gaze to the partygoers. A large crowd has formed in the centre of the gardens, their laughter echoing into the night. 'A few months after I returned home, he left us for another woman.'

Home. After being taken and tortured, after being kidnapped from her bedroom window, like me, and chained up like an animal.

From her stories, her father had seemed like the last person to do such a thing, she always portrayed him as a kind, caring man who would do anything for his wife and daughters. From the look on Violet's face, she thought the same.

'I used to blame myself for his leaving,' she admits, and

I listen closely, keeping silent as she spills her heart to me. 'He said when I had been missing for so long, he found comfort with another lady. She had offered him hope, and he could not imagine a life without her. So, naturally, as a child, I thought I had pushed him away and that my kidnapping was the reason he left us.'

I grit my teeth.

She notes my expression, and her eyes soften. 'I soon realised it was an excuse, of course. He had taken my trauma and spun it to make himself look better. My mother was devastated, obviously, and Hazel was too. But all I felt was *anger*. While I had been caged and abused, he had been gallivanting with another woman to escape the anguish of our household. If he were a true man, he would have been home to soothe my mother and sister.' Violet sighs while I struggle to think of a good-enough response. 'What was your family like when you returned?' The sudden change of direction catches me off guard, though I presume she wishes to move on from her father, her tone is lighter now – more casual.

The question is innocent enough, but I'm suddenly uncomfortable. Violet had shared something personal with me, and I don't wish for her to think I asked for some ulterior motive. I swallow my discomfort and answer honestly.

'One thing my family took a long time to realise was that I came out of camp as a completely different person,' I say carefully, thinking back to the day I returned to the castle again, and finally saw the open sky after months stuck inside tents.

Violet nods with understanding, she's probably one of the few people here tonight who truly would. We pause by a table where servants hand out flutes of shimmering drinks. She takes two and hands one over.

'I was very open about my experience – what happened to me, what I had done, what I had seen,' I say, remembering our first family dinner where I relayed every gory detail. They could not hide their horrified expressions, and the devastated sounds escaping their lips will forever be ingrained into my memory. 'But the king and queen were upset whenever I mentioned it. They see the camp as being their fault, with it being their kingdom, their children …' The rest of my words stick to my tongue as the thought of Fral makes me stiffen. 'I learnt that if I were to keep them happy, I had to keep that part of my life to myself.'

'That isn't healthy,' Violet declares, a scowl forming.

I shrug. 'That's how we coped.'

'And your brother, was he the same?'

'No.' I shake my head and take a sip of my drink. 'Alex was different. He would listen and allowed me to vent and cry on his shoulder. But anytime I mentioned Fral, I knew it fractured him a little inside. Every time I mentioned him, he would remember the blood on his hands after killing him, and I couldn't do that – I couldn't handle the dimness in his eyes when he relived it.'

'Even after all this time?'

'Even now,' I confirm. I search the crowd until finding my older brother. 'He has a heart of pure gold but that night I think he hated how far he went. I don't think he regrets taking that extra step but I think he wonders how else he could have stopped Fral. If he could have saved us without shouldering that burden.'

'Did he see someone? Receive any help?'

'Our family all had doctors throughout the years. Alex sees his the most. The king and queen attend less often than before.'

'And you?'

'I stopped seeing mine years ago.'

'Why is that?'

I frown. 'Is this an interrogation?'

She frowns back, the lines in her expression deepening with distaste. 'No. I simply want to know if you need someone to talk to – if you need me to step in.'

'I am fine without your interference,' I state, hoping to escape this topic. With the way Violet watches me, I feel like I'm walking a tightrope, unable to decide if stepping closer to her is my salvation or the opposite path.

Violet ignores me then and devotes her attention to her pomegranate tart. The inside oozes red, and a bit of fruit sits on the side of her mouth. I'm tempted to touch her and wipe it away. Her expression when I licked the alcohol off her face comes to mind – the bewilderment and shock – sends bolts of lightning through me. It's not appropriate here, not with all the important people around, but it doesn't stop me from swiping my thumb across her mouth.

'What are you—' Her protests come to a halt upon spotting the fruit on my thumb. I go to lick it off, but she beats me to it and sucks gently before swirling her tongue.

Fuck fuck fuck.

My cock twitches at the sight of it, and I feel the urge to step closer, to put my thumb back in her mouth and tell her exactly what I want. I stiffen. Violet appears unbothered that my thumb is now tipped in black, as if the sight of it is normal. I, however, am riddled with panic that she has touched me, the darkness having leached all colour from my skin.

Breathe, Ellis, breathe.

When Violet is finished with her tart, my heart is hammering from watching her mouth the whole time.

'Ellington!'

My head snaps up and I instinctually move closer to Violet. The queen raises a hand to capture my attention. I tense my jaw, and my hand slithers around Violet's waist. She stiffens but doesn't comment.

'It seems we are being summoned.' I prepare myself, quickly eyeing Violet's dress once more. I am certain she will make a positive impression with my family, but what I am uncertain of is how she may react to the questions they will no doubt fling her way.

Violet hums in acknowledgement and takes my offered arm, gripping the inside of my elbow. Her hair smells of berries again, and I can't help but inhale deeply. She pats my arm affectionately.

'No need to worry. I am a brilliant actress.'

And somehow, the words do little to soothe me.

14

THE PAST

O nly now do I understand how pain truly feels.

I had not been tested since arriving, so I wondered why I was taken if I served no use to them. Violet and Caleb are still their favourites, the pair always being whisked away every other day and returning looking worse than the last time.

Fear stirs in my gut. I am the lucky one, I tell myself. If they don't want me, do not fret, as it is for the best.

But when a guard enters the tent and points to me, I gape. My brain is unable to function as fear slashes through my chest. Violet is standing in the guards' way before I can muster a coherent thought.

'You won't touch him!' she demands, outstretching her chained hand as if to keep him away.

The guard, who I learned was called John, laughs. He finds Violet's fire amusing and treats her like an exotic animal performing tricks. Yet the way he looks at her makes me sick, and if she wasn't Fral's most prized test subject, I know he would take advantage.

'The prince has been here long enough. It's time for him to pay his rent,' says John, chuckling.

'I'll pay his rent,' Violet retorts, she moves to the right when John moves left. 'Just leave him alone. You don't know if he'll make it. It's not worth the risk.'

John doesn't step closer, though, not because he's scared of Violet, but because today he's impatient and isn't in the mood to play games.

'Prince Ellington can either come with me now or —' John flashes me a pointed look, guessing that if Violet is defending me, we must share a bond of sorts. '—I will kill your little girlfriend right here on the spot.'

He has me in a chokehold there. If it was a toss-up between her safety or mine, I'd choose Violet in an instant. I step forward as the thought of Violet being wiped from this world is unbearable.

'Don't do it! They won't kill me. I'm too valuable,' she warns, grasping my wrist with firm fingers. 'Please, Ellis. Don't go with him. Fral won't risk you, you know it, too.'

'I'm not taking that chance,' I mutter, allowing John to lead me out of the tent.

I look back as I exit, where Violet stands, betrayed and evidently horrified at the sight of me leaving. I know then that what I imagine to be terrifying is nothing compared to what she has endured.

Moments later, John is escorting me through the camp, showing me sights I could never imagine – guards whipping children for their disobedience, food being used as rewards, and limp bodies scattered in large piles, different coloured eyes of children stare back at me, no longer seeing. I retch there on the spot.

'Hurry up!' John shoves me between my shoulder blades. I stumble and he is quick to catch me, the chains connecting my ankles are too short to have done it myself.

When I am directed into another tent – this one much larger – I meet the dreaded metal table I've heard so much about. It's the place where kids are experimented on and is the reason why those children outside are dead. It is where Violet and Caleb lay day after day to fulfil whatever Fral requires of them.

To my horror, a girl is already strapped onto one of the tables, her dirty red hair streaming over the counter. She is gagged, and tears stain her cheeks.

'Ellis,' greets Fral, his warm smile seems fake to me now. After all I've seen, I realise he is good at that, enticing people with kindness to rip them apart for his own gain. 'Welcome to where the magic happens.'

He and the several guards surrounding the tent chuckle.

'Do you know what we are going to do?' Fral asks, motioning me towards the empty table. I don't move, my feet fixed on the floor. 'I suppose you don't. Well, here we make you stronger. We take magic from one person —' He points to the red-headed girl. '– and transfer it to another.' He motions towards me, and my throat bobs.

'Why?' I stammer as the girl sobs into her gag. It's as if we both know what's going to happen and the pain we are soon to endure.

'To make you stronger,' Fral says simply. 'You are already so powerful at such a young age, and I wish you to conquer lands. So, I will give you even more power. The lovely Rigby here is an air elemental, isn't that fun?' The girl cries at the mention of her abilities, no doubt mourning its loss already.

Fral's smile no longer fills me with excitement or joy. It does the opposite. Dread swirls in my gut and I fear I'm going to be sick.

'Get him strapped in. I want this over and done with,' Fral commands, his tone sharpens when he realises I won't be playing along.

Firm arms clasp my arms and legs and lower me onto the cold table. I squirm, but under their hands, it's useless. Metal clamps into place, keeping my neck, wrists, ankles, and torso fixed to the counter. My eyes flicker toward Rigby. She blinks three times. Three deliberate flutters that make me frown.

What does that mean?

I blink three times back, hoping it's the right thing to do. She turns away and stares at the ceiling.

Fral looms over me. 'This will hurt a little, but I'll be right here the whole time. Scream into the gag as much as you need, no one will fault you for it.'

The gag tastes like salt water as if it's been washed in a bucket from the ocean. I bite down on the fabric, attempting but failing to steady my breathing. Fral grabs the hand nearest to him and squeezes.

'You are so brave,' he says with a look of adoration, a gesture contradicting everything happening around me – the strange man behind him putting on gloves, the other with magic sparking from his hands ...

It's only when John places a hand over Rigby's stomach and another over mine that I know it's about to begin.

'Look at me,' says Fral and I can't help but obey. 'You are going to be alright.'

Pure agony rips through me and I choke on the taste of salt as I scream into the gag. Nothing has ever hurt like this. No one has ever inflicted this much torment onto me.

'You are doing so well. Stay strong,' repeats Fral, hoping to comfort me.

I hate you, *I think*. I hate you. I hate you. I hate you.

15

VIOLET

Ellis' arm feels solid beneath my grip. As we draw closer to the king and queen of Tealwaters, my heart hammers, their expressions expectant.

When I peer up at my royal companion, his gaze is solely on his family, appearing far more tense than I've seen him all evening. I wonder for a moment if he is as nervous as I am.

'Your Majesties,' Ellis greets, before tilting his head towards me. 'Please meet my lovely date, Violet Danes.'

Queen Melody reminds me of a predator with the way her pale blue eyes roam over me. It's as if she's trying to find a weakness or fault, but if she finds any in my appearance, she doesn't let it show. Her husband, however, is beaming, like he's been waiting hopelessly for my arrival.

'Violet, my dear, what a pleasure to meet you. I would say Ellington has spoken much about you, but it seems he has kept you his secret.' The king chortles. His golden hair is neat beneath his seashell-decorated crown, the design is similar to the queen's but is more masculine. Together, they look regal in their complimenting outfits of white and midnight blue. I feel a new wave of intimidation. 'And now I can see why!' He motions to my attire, and I bow my head in thanks. The king claps his nephew on the back and draws him closer, the motion pulling Ellis' arm away from me. My hands are now free to hover, yet I have no idea how to occupy them.

'Yes, she is a vision,' mutters Ellis, though his cobalt eyes give nothing away. He seems to tolerate his uncle's hold, his own body making no move to lean in or touch the king.

'What a wonderful dress,' the queen muses, her gaze pauses on my hair, no doubt wondering about its onyx streaks before meeting my gaze. 'And what extraordinary eyes you have. My, aren't they unique?'

Comments about my eye colour have always been something I've enjoyed. They're different, the purples and blues blending into something I've never seen before in another person. But when the queen watches me, I sense rather than hear her curiosity. Immediately, I know she is someone I must be careful around.

'I am a walking oddity, it seems.' I flash Ellis a brief look, and he nods encouragingly. 'Perhaps that is part of my charm.'

'So, how did you both meet?' The king asks, genuine interest lines his handsome features. The crown upon his head shines, the crystal weaved throughout it catches my eye as he moves his head.

My heart tightens, and my palms sweat. Ellis does not look my way to help me formulate an appropriate response, instead, he watches his family's reactions, his narrowed eyes observant.

'I met Ellis in Fral's prison camp when we were children. We found friendship in a very dark place,' I explain, remembering that I must play as close to the truth as possible. The mention of that vile place makes both the sovereigns' recoil.

I sense Ellis' gaze on me, and the hairs on my arm rise, but this time, I'm the one unable to return his look. I'm afraid if I do, my face will show much more than I'm willing to give away. Not only did we find friendship in the camp, but we also left it there the day we were rescued.

'Oh.' All the brightness drains from the king. Queen Melody looks equally shocked but is quick to recover.

'What do you do for a living, Violet?' she asks, evidently an expert at redirecting conversations. For some reason, it irks me that she won't acknowledge my answer, instead wishing to gloss over it as though it means nothing.

I feel him then, that warm hand of his pressing against the bare skin of my back. He strokes up and down the column of my spine, sending a shiver through me. I feel the scars on his fingers brush the raised skin against mine. Scars upon scars.

'I work at my mother's bakery. She's actually here tonight.' I point to the stall. The queen gives nothing away while watching my sister serve her tarts upon a tray. Her expression is pinched, utterly unimpressed.

'That's my sister, Hazel,' I clarify.

'Quite young to still be here at this late hour,' Queen Melody claims before giving King Hector a pointed look.

'She is fourteen, so it's not that la—'

'Do you know where Alex is?' Ellis asks suddenly. He makes a show of looking around in search of his brother, but the heir is nowhere in sight. Instead, Ellis waves over the servant from earlier, instructed to serve Hazel's tarts, and motions to the tray. 'Also, taste these. I wish for your opinions. They are too good for you to miss out on.'

I note he doesn't mention they are made by my family, and a ripple of something runs through me. Is he embarrassed of me? Does he notice the unconvinced expression on the queen's face, too?

'What are they?' King Hector ponders, leaning closer to look at the various colours on offer.

'Have one,' Ellis presses.

'They are different flavoured tarts,' I say carefully, keeping my sister's name to myself. But if Hazel was here right now, witnessing our rulers tasting her creations, she'd likely faint with joy. 'I just had a pomegranate one, and it was amazing.'

The sovereigns of Tealwaters choose one each, biting into them with moans of surprise.

'I have dragon fruit.' The queen smiles, delighted. It's the first genuine emotion she's shown all evening.

'I think I chose lime and apple.' King Hector remarks, turning to face me. 'You're right! They are delicious.'

'Well, we must get going.' Ellis tugs at my hand, calling over his shoulder to his aunt and uncle as we walk away. 'Enjoy your night.'

We don't stop moving until we are on the other side of the garden, Ellis' grip never wavers until the music of the band fills the space between us. I peer back at his family, watching as they finish their treats. They talk quietly amongst themselves, watching us watch them, and when they briefly look away, I smack Ellis in the stomach.

'What was that for?' I hiss.

'You fail to be specific with your questions, Violet. What was *what* for?' Ellis retorts, taking another drink from a servant and handing me a fresh glass. Standing so close to the other guests, I feel their eyes on us, studying *me* in particular for my association with their youngest prince.

I assume Ellis notices too as his hand finds my arm, tugging me closer into him, my head nearly resting against his chest. From the outside, we look intimate as his hold lowers to my waist, drawing me closer. But I know it's a vantage point, so we can talk without seeming suspicious.

'What was with that sudden exit?' I clarify with a huff. 'I don't think it was going *too* terribly.'

Ellis is silent, watching the crowd of dancing guests – many couples are twirling and smiling and laughing like tonight is the best party they've ever experienced.

'I do not trust the queen, and thus, I wanted us to leave before she said something to offend you,' he mutters, tenderly running his fingers through my locks. It makes my scalp tingle, and the feel of his strong hands tugging at my hair makes my mouth drop open in surprise. He catches my restraint faltering, and I shut my mouth immediately, my cheeks suddenly hot. I do my best to look natural, but he only smirks, making me regret my second of weakness.

'Does that feel good, Violet?' asks the prince, leaning to speak into my ear. I can't hear his words, but I can certainly feel them sliding over my earlobe and down my neck. I tilt my head away, giving him room to dip his lips to my throat, dropping one single kiss upon my flaming hot skin.

'No kissing,' I hiss, despite a small part of me enjoying his proximity, the other part wanting to shove him away. 'You know the rules.'

'We have an audience,' is his response as he finally draws back.

I stare into the star laden sky, where the moon glows brightly upon me. It's calming to know she's right there looking over me. Protecting me.

'Why would you care what the queen says to me? Or even thinks of me for that matter?' I ask, wanting to distract my body and intrusive thoughts about how his lips would feel on mine.

'I suspected that the conversation would move on to family, and that if she spoke harshly of your mother or Hazel, I'd have trouble on my hands.'

'The queen would make a scene?' I wonder, frowning.

'No,' he says, amusement in his words. 'But I know *you* would.'

I go to protest, but his pointed look silences me. I suppose he may be right to assume such a thing. I'm a she-wolf when it comes to protecting the ones I love, and no royal would change that natural instinct.

'I've seen you guard what you call yours, and it's terrifying,' Ellis murmurs with sudden seriousness.

Our eyes clash at the memory of me shielding the prince in the camp, a heavy feeling settles in my chest. There were many occasions where we stood up for each other, risking our safety to ensure the other would come away unharmed. It was always a temporary triumph in the camp – the fight to keep ourselves in one piece, a continuous and exhausting battle.

My hands tremble and I take a shaky breath. Ellis grabs onto my hand, tracing soothing circles across my knuckles.

'Am I wrong in assuming such a thing?' he whispers, shielding me from the onlookers.

I shake my head, keeping my stare lowered. I do my best to suppress the tears. 'No. You're not wrong.'

His large hand lifts my chin until I'm gazing into his deep, cobalt eyes. We are silent as we absorb each other. 'Say that again.'

I snatch my chin from his grasp, his quip making the edge of my lips tug up. 'Not a chance, Your Highness.'

A flash of challenge shows in his eyes at my use of his title, but he chuckles, the rumble of it sending heat through me. He should laugh more often, it's glorious to listen to.

'A shame,' he drawls. 'I had hoped to have an audience when the day came that Violet Danes said I was right.'

I glower half-heartedly at him. 'I didn't say you were right. I simply said you weren't *wrong*.'

Mirth lines his features and his eyes twinkle. He was one of the few people who enjoyed my cheek – even as children, he had always smiled at my jibes and retorts to his annoyingly charming cleverness.

'Would you like to dance?' asks the prince, taking me by surprise. I watch the guests who dance slowly, their arms wrapped around each other. He seems to sense my unease and takes a step forward. 'No need to worry, I won't let you stumble.'

'What if I tread on your toes?'

'You won't hurt me, if that's what you're worried about.'

'I'm not,' I blurt, crossing my arms.

'Then take my hand, sweetheart,' he murmurs, defiance in his eyes. He wants me to refuse him, to maintain my facade of annoyance. But he knows I won't – or rather, can't – in front of so many attentive guests.

'Fine,' I slide my fingers through his, presuming he will guide me through the midst of swaying bodies. But no, we stay in the same spot, his body enveloping mine. Ellis brings a hand around the back of my head, and slowly and tenderly, he coaxes me to lean closer so my head lays comfortably below his shoulder.

'Okay?' he asks.

'Okay,' I mumble.

We sway like an old couple would, we cling to each other as if the very thought of letting go would end us, and a small part of me revels in the feeling. Why does this feel so warm? So safe?

I allow the feeling to wrap around me like a blanket, willing my mind to go blank to keep from thinking. I let myself *feel* this moment and make the most of it.

Finally, Ellis speaks so softly I wonder if I conjured his voice myself.

'Three questions.'

16

VIOLET

I blink.

Three questions.

I step back and peer up at the prince. Ellis' cobalt eyes stare back, watching and waiting for my answer. My throat feels suddenly dry, it's hard to swallow the realisation that he remembers much more than he lets on.

Three questions was a game we played when one of us felt overwhelmed or scared after a considerably shitty day at the camp, and there were many. Any question was allowed, and only honest answers were given. Back then, we didn't keep anything from each other, we were happy to spill every detail about our lives, wanting to know *everything* about one another. After all, we were best friends, and best friends weren't people you kept secrets from.

But now ...

'Three questions,' he repeats, perhaps second-guessing if I heard him.

I sharply inhale before narrowing my eyes. What does he want to know?

'Go on,' I murmur.

'First question,' he starts, peering over my head. His watchful gaze scans the crowd as if ensuring no one will overhear us. 'Why is your hair streaked in black?'

This takes me aback. It is such a strange question.

'I already told you why it's darker.'

He shakes his head and exhales. 'No. You told me it's been slowly changing over the years. You never said *why*.'

My mouth twists. Do I want to tell him my theories? Or should I spin some lie for him to back off?

As if reading my thoughts, the prince whispers in my ear, 'I can tell when you lie, Violet. So, don't bother giving me anything but the truth. You know the rules.'

I glare before averting my gaze to a couple dancing nearby. Their love is evident by the way they can't keep their eyes off one another. A twist of envy coils in my stomach.

'I have a theory that the dark magic they used in camp has been slowly seeping from me. It has its outlets, and this is one of them.' I pick up a strand of hair, the curled lock a mix of gold and onyx. When my hair first began to transform, I had often cried to my mother, worried that it was a sign I was becoming evil and would eventually hurt those I loved, like Fral. Yet, with years of unwavering support and love from my family, I no longer believed it. The dark magic I possess is mine to command and use how I see fit. No manner of persuasion would make me agree with Fral's ideals. He was a monster, and I am not. That was the difference that counted and one I grasped onto in my moments of self-doubt.

Like my eyes, my hair is an oddity – something people

don't mind staring at. Realisation hits me, this is probably why Ellis' appearance is slightly different to how I remember too. 'I assume you can relate. Your hair was much brighter gold when we were kids. And your eyes, they are a much darker shade of blue now then I remember them to have been.'

The prince stiffens. I caught him off guard. I allow him a moment to compose himself and think of an answer, glancing away to allow him space from my revelation.

'Second question,' he utters, apparently not wishing to talk about the dark magic we possess. I've clearly hit a nerve. 'Why is it that your mother sells not only bread but sweet treats, too? You told me she never baked desserts. What changed?'

I gulp. Ellis is too observant for his own good. This is one answer I can't fathom to say out loud, unless I risk looking like a fool.

'Remember, I can tell when you lie to me,' he remarks with a glint of amusement. I do my best to pretend he never asked me such a question, but he meets my eyes with his pleading gaze, like the answer would mean the world to him.

I inhale deeply, tamping down my embarrassment. I pretend it doesn't matter. After all, I was a child and now I am an adult. I have moved on, I have lived without him long enough to not care what he thinks anymore.

'I asked my mother to stock them because you once told me sweet treats were your favourite.' I smile as naturally as I can, feigning playfulness, but it doesn't fool him. If anything, he doesn't appear surprised, though his features mask any emotions he may be feeling. I feel on edge by his lack of response or retort. I glare at him, daring him to make fun of me, or to comment on how pathetic that sounds. But he doesn't. He simply tilts his head and nods.

'That is very thoughtful of you, Violet.'

My mind spins, though his own expression is carefully blank, as if the thought of exposing his mind to me is inconceivable. Does he think differently of me? Does he think I'm silly and childish for having changed my mother's business to cater to him over something he told me when we were kids?

Looking back, I never regretted asking her. While she saw it as a business opportunity, I saw it as something that might bring my best friend back. If we baked his favourite cakes, he might wander in one day, having heard of their deliciousness, and thus find me.

I frown. Yes, I was pathetic. But I was a young girl with very big feelings and terrible loneliness, shoved back into a reality I was slow to acclimatise to. A girl who no longer had the one person who knew them better than anyone else around.

'Last question,' says Ellis finally, bringing me out of my pool of self-pity. 'Have you slept with Luca?'

It takes me a moment to absorb his question. My eyes glaze over as my mind works extra hard to discern if he voiced that question out loud or if I made it up in my head.

Did he just ask about my sex life with Luca Moye? I think.

When I see a glint of malice in his expression, I know he asked me this on purpose. We are surrounded by curious onlookers, and this is his way of making sure I don't burst into fury. That my reaction is leashed, so his question can be answered without consequences.

Bastard.

The urge to push Ellis away is so strong I feel my fingers tighten. Affronted that he'd ask something so personal, my magic bubbles to life, and small shadows curl around my hands.

I may be his date but that doesn't mean I will spill every detail of my life to him.

'How dare you?' I quietly seethe. Ellis seems unbothered by my anger. If anything, it seems entertaining to him. 'My business with Luca is private. No matter how many games you want to play, I will never give you the answers you seek.'

'We shall see about that,' he utters, glancing away as if losing interest in me.

I laugh humourlessly, shaking my head. 'Are you threatened by him?'

His attention snaps back, and this time, I look away, pretending to be engrossed in a servant pouring more alcohol into clean flutes. The prince's grip tightens around me and I refrain from smirking.

'Threatened?' he scoffs. 'Don't be absurd.'

I smile coldly, keeping my attention elsewhere. 'You sound defensive, Your Highness. If you knew your ego was so fragile, perhaps you shouldn't ask such daring questions that might affect your self-esteem.'

'If the day ever comes where I feel any emotion towards Luca – except distaste – I will let you murder me after all,' he mutters. He dips me and a gasp escapes my lips. I'm hovering, suspended solely in his arms. The prince can drop me and he seems to revel in this small piece of power.

'I like the way you lie,' I whisper with a long, searing

look. He frowns, his cobalt gaze immersed in mine. 'It tastes like wine and sugar. Sweet and *intoxicating*.'

'Better to taste like wine and sugar than disappointment and dissatisfaction,' he drawls, nipping my chin. He is no doubt describing what he believes Luca to be like in the bedroom. Closing my eyes, I let my head fall back as I loosely hold his neck.

'Who said anything about being dissatisfied? I wouldn't have gone back for more if that were the case,' I muse. Emotion flares across his features, and he roughly brings me to standing, releasing me as if I've burnt him. I offer a coy smile. 'Let's go find your brother, shall we?'

17

VIOLET

I spin on my heel before Ellis can answer, searching the crowd for a blond head with a crystal crown. It doesn't take long to find him. His laugh is loud and boisterous, and at this late hour, a little tipsy, too. Ellis is not far behind, so when he reluctantly offers his arm, I clutch onto it.

'Are you mad at me?' I whisper as we approach. Prince Alexander notices our arrival.

'No.'

'I don't believe you,' I say, but he ignores me.

When we stand before the heir of Tealwaters, Ellis' arm slowly slithers around my waist, staking his claim before anyone in his brother's group can make an assumption. They all stare but none make a move to greet us.

'Ellis! I wasn't expecting to see you so late in the evening,' Prince Alexander calls out with glee. He claps his brother's shoulder affectionately, instantly forgetting the crowd he is with. He faces me then, giving me his full attention. A prickle of nerves slithers over my skull. 'And you are the infamous Violet. So many whispers about you tonight and no wonder. Look at you! You are way better-looking than Ellis. No wonder he looks so serious, he's not used to being shown up.' He grins, waiting for Ellis' reaction, but when he doesn't show any, the heir moves on without a beat, probably used to his sibling's behaviour. 'Yes, he's heartbroken. I can just tell.'

Prince Alexander turns to me, taking both of my hands in his. He bends, kissing one in welcome. 'It's so nice to see you, Violet. Unfortunately, I've heard very little about you.' He peers up and flutters his dark lashes. Those eyes of his are so soft and beautiful I can see why the whole kingdom fawns over him. He is handsome, charming and a ray of sunshine – the complete opposite of his younger brother.

'I'm not surprised, Your Highness,' I say, watching intently as he returns to his full height. Him and Ellis loom over me. 'Are you having a nice evening celebrating your birthday?'

'Oh, please. Call me Alex. And yes, thank you. I'm having a splendid time.' He gestures to a servant who passes us with a plate of desserts. To my delight, Hazel's tarts have been continuously restocked, with there being more on the tray than last time. 'I heard your mother is here with her baked goods? I've been scoffing down those flavoured tarts, which everyone seems to be raving about.'

I grin, thrilled that Ellis' orders to share the sweet treats have been fulfilled. 'Yes. My mother and sister made them special for tonight. The latter is your number one fan.'

'Is she? If that's the case, I must meet her. She may be my future sister-in-law one day, so we must get acquainted.'

Ellis' display of alarm makes me burst out laughing, his horror evident. 'I'm not sure that's something we should worry about,' I offer with a tentative smile. Ellis' grip on me loosens somewhat. 'But yes, she'd love that.'

'Then it's a deal.' He nods, resting his hands on his hips as he peers between the two of us before offering his hand to me. 'As Ellis seems to be tiring of the crowds, would you care for a stroll, Violet?'

I glance sidelong at my date to see that he indeed looks weary and more on edge than before. It isn't *that* late in the evening, but I don't comment on it. There is likely much to Ellis I still don't know.

'I'd love to,' I answer before turning to Ellis. I lay it on thick to test his reaction. 'If that's alright with you, *my love*?'

Ellis blinks with a questioning gaze until he nods, motioning for me to go ahead, and though I search his eyes, nothing in them reflects his true feelings. I nod curtly before his brother pulls me away.

'You know he's lasted much longer tonight then he usually would,' offers the heir.

I scowl. 'What do you mean?'

We approach the drinks table. Alexander is quick to hand me a beverage, his behaviour expected of a prince – gentlemanly and respectable. Even his stance is regal, his posture straight as an arrow, his golden hair is neatly styled to fit the crown. I can tell he has been training since his childhood to do just this – to one day be king.

'He hates crowds,' Prince Alexander answers, unaware of my scrutiny. 'Or anywhere particularly busy. I assume it's something he picked up as a child. Anyway, with celebrations like this, he usually would have escaped hours ago.

So I am pleasantly surprised he's still here mingling.' I peer over his shoulder to where Ellis stands alone. He takes a flute from a servant's tray and swallows it whole before taking a second and sipping it instead. The servant doesn't bother talking to him, he scurries away, as if eager to escape the prince's presence.

'He's claustrophobic?' I wonder.

Alexander shakes his head. 'No. He doesn't mind tight spaces, he just hates lots of bodies in one space.'

My heart stutters at the admission. As a child, Ellis used to always mention the overcrowded tents and how he hated being stuck in the middle of so many bodies, all he wanted was room to breathe.

'I know about your little arrangement, Violet,' Prince Alexander confesses, his voice so delicate I fear it might break. My heart pounds, wondering what he will do with such knowledge. 'And I know you are here because you gain something from this agreement.'

My mouth drops open, hoping to say something intelligible, but nothing comes out.

'I do not say this to alarm you. I merely want to state that Ellis bringing you here tonight must mean you are someone extremely special to him. He would never agree to this pairing unless you were worth sharing. He is a man of limited words, but bringing you here says a lot. He clearly trusts you enough to allow our aunt and uncle to meet you. That is no small feat.'

My head lifts to observe the future king, who watches me intently as if trying to find what it is that Ellis sees in me. I try to smile but it doesn't meet my eyes.

'He was—' I pause, wondering if my use of past tense is

a smart decision. 'He *is* someone special to me, too,' I murmur as something unfurls inside my chest. 'Someone also worthy of sharing.'

The heir finally smiles – a little tug of his lips to show he's pleased with my confession. 'I can see by how you look at him that's true.'

I avert my gaze, not wishing to think of how I appear when Ellis' attention is elsewhere – the moments I take to ogle him, to familiarise myself with the features I once dreamed about, the memories that flood my thoughts when he does something I remember or the way my body reacts to his touch ...

'Love is a precious thing, Violet. Hold on to it tightly, never take it for granted, and do not let it go,' whispers the prince before happily slipping into more comfortable conversation topics.

18

ELLIS

The next morning, I eat an elaborate breakfast out on Alex's balcony, who is slumped in his chair, covering his eyes from the dazzling morning sun. His food is left untouched before him, and I begin to steal pieces to keep it from going to go to waste. He's in a fragile state.

'Why did I drink so much?' groans my brother.

'Because it was your birthday,' I say, and he huffs in reply. 'Because the servants can't simply say no to the future king when he asks for another drink in fear of having their heads chopped off.'

Alex glares at me through the gaps in his fingers. 'I would never do such a thing.'

'No? Just me then?'

He rolls his eyes but pauses upon noticing the missing food on his plate. Narrowing his gaze, he shifts the plate closer – a silent go-ahead before he returns to his moaning.

As I consume his breakfast, I admire the ocean, the air filled with the sounds of crashing waves against the shore.

It's calming to some degree, but the salty smell is the only thing I hate about it. Bad memories of it linger on my tongue.

'So, I think I remember Violet being nice,' murmurs Alex, his tone light and casual.

I know instantly where this conversion is going, but I'd rather be having it with Alex than anyone else.

'Nice enough to drink with her,' I remark, and he straightens. The moment he does, his face creases in pain, as if he's going to double over and be sick at any moment.

'I do vaguely remember indulging in fine wines with a highly attractive woman.' He winks. When I don't answer, he tilts his head at me and slumps in his chair. 'I want to see her again. She probably thinks I'm a fool with all my drunken blabbering. I remember thinking that I must keep her entertained in fear of boring her with my conversational skills.'

'She told me you were very charming. You even made her blush once or twice, apparently.'

He grins at the sky. 'Now *that* sounds more like me.'

My mind wanders to last night with Violet in her lavender dress, her hair curled and streaming down her back, and the annoyance that flashed across her stunning features when I asked about that bastard Luca and if she had slept with him. The moment she pushed me away, I knew it was something she didn't want me to know, but to have her admit it, to allude to having been pleasured by him ... the thought makes my jaw ache.

No wonder he looked so smug the first night I saw him.

'Tell me about her,' says Alex, keeping me from thinking

of all the ways I can make Luca's life a misery. 'I want to know everything.'

I glance over at Alex. Though he's covered his eyes with his hand, something in his tone alerts me to his curiosity. He must be wondering why I never spoke about Violet until recently and why I had chosen her out of every woman in the city.

I swallow. 'Violet is ...' Stubborn. Feisty. Kind. Witty. The list goes on. There are so many qualities to her that I remember from ten years ago, and even now, those attributes shine through in the little things she does. Her kind smile to ease the discomfort of others, her jokes to lighten the mood when times become tense – her fire when she stands up for what she believes in and what she thinks is right.

'I've never seen you speechless before,' Alex jests.

My brow creases with confusion.

Alex's face softens. 'I saw the words flood into your brain instantly. You knew *exactly* how to describe her. All men in love do.'

My eyes meet his. My brother was in love before with a beautiful and intelligent woman who chose a future without him to travel the six kingdoms. It had devastated him and crushed his heart into little pieces. He's been a sap about love ever since, determined to find the same love our parents shared – forever a hopeless romantic.

You knew exactly how to describe her. All men in love do.

'It's funny how hard you go to war with yourself over the smallest things. Like your word choice, for example.' Alex points at me. 'I understand you can't deny being in love. Otherwise, your little act with Aunt Melody and Uncle

Hector might be revealed, and that is why you're performing, isn't it? But I'm coming to realise you don't want to say out loud that you're in love because, deep down, you know it's true but cannot fathom it being *real*.'

I don't move a muscle, not wishing to expose my churning feelings. Somehow, my brother has laid every one of my thoughts on the table within seconds. My mind is a mess, stumbling over how I will fix this predicament.

Alex smiles kindly. 'I know that if you really *did* have a lover, you would have told me.' He seems proud of himself, as if figuring out my secret has inflated his ego. He rests a satisfied hand on his chest.

'Is that so?'

He nods. 'Yes, because the very girl you decide to bring to my birthday is the same girl who used to ask to see you when you returned home. No matter the answer, she returned to the castle day after day in hopes of seeing you. If that was not love and adoration, I don't know what is.'

My throat feels like it's closing up with the reminder.

'You recognise her?' I question, perplexed.

'Straight away.' Alex nods. 'She looks different with the darker streaks in her hair, but I remember her face – those eyes.'

I wrinkle my nose. If he remembered her eyes, he must have been close to her before. 'You met her?'

'The guards were getting agitated, she had told them all she was your best friend and demanded to see how you were. One time, I offered to diffuse the situation,' he says, as if the memory was one he found humorous. 'A prince doesn't forget a civilian who orders them around, let me tell you that.'

'She has a fire in her.'

'So, why her? Why not a lady that would happily accompany you? Someone with wealth and status?' he wonders. I shrug.

'Violet's the only woman I can wholeheartedly trust,' I finally admit. Alex nods, his expression devoid of judgement as I explain. 'We were best friends once, and I thought if anyone would help me, it would be her.'

'And now? You have rekindled the friendship?'

I shake my head, averting my gaze to the ocean waves. I'm unable to look my brother in the eye as I confess everything. 'No. I offered her anything she desired, and in exchange, she would be my date until the queen was satisfied with my … *performance*, as you call it. That is the only reason she is with me.'

Alex purses his lips. 'Are you sure about that?'

'Yes.' I nod firmly. 'She wants nothing to do with me otherwise. I hurt her once by staying away from her, and I'm sure she isn't foolish enough to let me in again, nor would I blame her.'

Is that why she was intimate with Luca? If I had been her friend this whole time, would she have even given him the time of day?

'You were a child, Ellis. Surely she can see past that?'

'Would you forgive your past love for leaving you?'

Alex's lover had left him willingly, as I had with Violet – albeit for very different reasons. She had wanted freedom, not a crown to cage or trap her into a certain lifestyle.

Leaning forward in his seat, my brother places his elbows on the table and cups his hands together. 'I would have forgiven her over and over again. I loved her and would have done anything for her – she was my weakness.' He glances over, taking in my form. 'Violet would no doubt do the same. She will soon find herself in the same shoes she was when you were children. She won't be able to hide from her feelings forever. Love like that doesn't just fade. If you're serious about wanting her to stay, all you must do is remind her of the feelings you once shared.'

I can't answer, not wishing to get my hopes up. My brother has a romantic heart, always wondering about the meaning of little gestures and if they mean something *more*. But me, I'm a realist. I know for a fact I am not an easy person to love – maybe once upon a time, but not anymore.

'I understand why you kept her a secret from me,' Alex almost whispers, and for once, he does not meet my gaze, he stares off into the distance as if the horizon has all the answers. 'But know that I would have helped you with anything you needed without question. I am always here for you as I know you are always there for me.' He seems concerned that I didn't feel safe enough to confide in him – the only person I do confide in. 'There is nothing wrong with asking for help,' he continues, sounding much like the queen this time.

'I know.' I mutter tiredly.

'Okay,' he replies, but he seems unconvinced as his pale blue eyes study me. And I don't blame him.

A little part of me doesn't believe my words either.

19

THE PAST

Violet's touch is soft as she soothes my shaking body, racked with tears. I have created a list of the boys and girls Fral has killed to give their powers to me.

I mourn them like they are my people because, at the end of the day, they are. I am their prince, and they are mine to watch and rule over with my family. They rely on me to save them and offer reassuring words, but I am helpless. I cannot do anything to rescue them. They must realise the moment our mouths are gagged that we are all doomed – our futures in the hands of a madman.

'What does it mean when they blink three times?' I ask Violet.

She frowns. 'Pardon?'

'Every time I've been experimented on, the other child will look me in the eye and blink three times. It's like they're trying to say something, but I don't know what.'

Her expression changes as discomfort morphs her movements. Violet shuffles closer, her face near mine as she peers around. No one is looking at us and no one is listening, but the hairs on my arms rise at her proximity.

'When Caleb and I first got here, we weren't allowed to converse much. They thought that if we talked, we'd form some grand plan to escape.' I raise a brow and she nods with a humourless laugh. 'I know. It's ridiculous. Two kids against an army of deranged adults? Not a chance.'

Violet pauses, taking a moment to articulate her next words, she's probably trying to make her answer seem less terrifying than it is. She always has a habit of trying to protect me from the worst things, but eventually, they would always come to light. 'We decided to make our own language so if we can't talk, we could convey how we are feeling without the guards knowing.'

I lean back and study her face. She meets my eyes. Shortly after I arrived, they transported Caleb to another tent, ours was too full to accommodate more bodies. I wonder if she misses him.

Violet takes a deep breath and her eyes fade into memory, as if thinking of Caleb and when her days here were just the two of them. 'Two blinks means "you are not alone. I am here with you." Three blinks means "tell my family I love them."'

The words unsettle me as I remember Rigby, the scared redhead, who seemed to know her time was up and that, out of the two of us, I'd be the one to tell her family her final words — words that were stolen from her, words that her family would never hear again from her lips.

I close my eyes, dipping my chin as a new wave of sorrow fills me. How can these men and women who work for the angel of death be so cruel? How can they see the benefit in Fral's operations?

'Ellis,' Violet murmurs, resting a hand on my back. She rubs *in soothing circles while her other hand holds me close to keep me steady. 'We will escape. We will get out of here. I promise.'*

I lift my head and stare. 'Promise me something else.'

'What?' She frowns, and the rubbing on my back pauses.

'Promise me that when we leave – when we are saved – you will still see me and that we will still be friends. Tell me that this won't be the end of you and me.' I motion between us, suddenly desperate to hear her oath. 'Tell me that this isn't some tempo-rary friendship that will fade the moment we return to our different lives.'

Violet tilts her head, appearing to refrain from making a joke out of this. She seems to have a habit of using humour to lighten tense moments. But right now, she considers me with her piercing purple-blue eyes. She runs her knuckles beneath my jaw, and a breath escapes me.

She smiles. 'Ellis Irvine. If you aren't *my best friend once we leave this wretched place, I will bring anguish to your royal doorstep.' I grasp her hand and pull it to my chest, allowing her to feel my racing heart – a gesture we seem to do often – a silent language of our own. 'I have so many things I want to do together when we leave.'*

'Do you?' I ask, enjoying the feel of her fingers splayed across my chest. 'Like what?'

Violet tilts her head to the tent ceiling. 'I want us to bake mermaid cakes in the middle of the night. I want us to watch the stars without this tent in the way,' she says, narrowing her eyes at it. When she lowers her gaze to me once more, her voice soft-ens. 'I want us to live a long and happy life together. Best friends until the real end.'

The real end.

That's what we call it. The end where we aren't stuck in this prison, where we are reunited with our families and free of this cage, where we return to our lives as a prince and baker's daughter.

I smile. 'I like all of them.'

She nods, and a flush of colour brightens her cheeks. 'I thought you would.'

20

VIOLET

I ready myself for fruit picking, something I've become accustomed to doing every week to restock our supplies as Hazel hates going. She prefers to stay in the bakery with our mother and create new desserts. I head for the kitchen, finding Luca kneading some bread, his face covered in flour. I would expect my sister to be helping him, but as promised, Ellis pulled some strings and enrolled Hazel in baking school. I'll be taking her to class on the way.

'I'm going for a walk to Gwenore Forest,' I tell him.

He grunts in answer.

'What was that?' I ask sweetly, but I only receive silence. 'I didn't catch a word you just said.'

He looks up and glares at me. 'Are you really with the prince?'

In seconds, my walls rise and I plant my hands firmly on my hips, staring him down. 'Yes. Is that a problem?'

'He's not with you for the right reasons.'

You don't know the half of it.

'Which are?'

'He wants you for something. I don't know what, but it can't be pure of heart.'

'Okay. Well, when you know, keep me informed. I'm off.' I turn to head for the front of the store, but he wraps his hand around my wrist to stop me.

'Why are you with him, Violet? He is arrogant and possessive and undeserving of you,' Luca states. The bite in his tone has me off guard.

I tilt my head, offering my most patient expression. If he doesn't let me leave soon, I'll be late, and if my mother scolds me because of him ... 'Surely I am capable enough to decide who is deserving or not?'

Luca shakes his head and releases his grip, returning to knead the dough again. 'I only hope he does not hurt you.'

'I appreciate the concern, but I'll be fine.' I nudge him for good measure, earning a slight smile. 'I'm a big girl, and if he does hurt me, you can choose the animal form in which I seek my revenge.'

With a wink to my friend, I exit the kitchen and grab a wicker basket from behind the counter. To my delight, a handful of customers are in the bakery today, no doubt here to buy some baked goods for breakfast.

My mother is busy, Hazel is beside her packing orders into small containers. I ask if they need anything other than the berries on the list.

'Don't be all day, Violet,' calls my mother as I step outside. Hazel holds my free hand as we exit the shop. 'We need them for the jam later this afternoon!'

I drop my sister off to her very first class, her excitement making me feel light and fuzzy, then head for Gwenore Forest, which borders part of Sapphire City. She appears bright and welcoming today as I follow her gravel path to where the strawberry bushes bloom.

What I love about Gwenore is her menacing reputation, she's renowned for being difficult whenever you disobey her rules. For example, if you step off her pathways, she can do what she likes with you, like sending wild animals to chase you or burning a nearby tree to fall in your way or something equally traumatising.

Not me, though, her spirit seems to recognize mine. She understands that I was trapped here once as a child, and we have come to an understanding that she'll never trap me here again.

'Hello again, Gwen,' I greet, gingerly straying off the path.

Even after all these years tending to the same fruit bushes, I feel like today will be the day she changes her mind. But as usual, nothing happens. I bend down and pluck the berries from their branches, whistling a cheerful tune.

While I do it, I try to occupy my mind by thinking of upbeat songs to keep from thinking too deeply about where I am. Growing up, I found that coming back to the place of my trauma helped immensely, seeing the forest in a different light instead of fearing it. But still, at the age of twenty-two, I have days where the terror seeps back in if I think too deeply, as the nightmares I've contained threaten to unleash themselves.

Stay still, my little nightmare, Fral purrs in the depths of my memories.

I shiver.

Fral's time was cut short before he could truly master

the manipulation of magic. He only managed to success-fully transfer magic from one person into another three times. Ellis, myself, and Caleb.

I was born with the ability to shapeshift, but after waking up from one of many agonising experiments, I had gained another's power – the ability to create and control shadows from some poor girl who never made it. I became a weapon. With a single thought, I could send the whole kingdom into eternal darkness.

'My little nightmare,' Fral would call me, and to this day, the name rings inside my head anytime I sense the shadows begging to be used or when another section of my hair has darkened like the night. Day by day, the darkness takes over my soul.

Ellis was always able to create lightning, he crackled with life when he first arrived at camp. But when Fral was done, Ellis could fly just like him, able to escape any situation that turned sour within seconds. Ellis was his protegee – the miniature version of him – the person to continue his legacy when the time came.

And lastly, Caleb. He was the softest and kindest soul of us all, born with the ability to teleport. When we were rescued from the prison camp, Caleb lasted only one full year before taking his own life. His mind was so mangled and manipulated by Fral and his cronies that he left the camp very different to how he went in. I vividly remember the day Caleb had experienced his first dose of dark magic. Fral killing a young boy to steal his magic of mind control and fed it straight to Caleb to use at his command.

'We have a conqueror of the human mind,' the angel of darkness would boast.

That is in the past now. Do not dwell on it. While Caleb may not be here, he is no longer suffering.

A sudden surge of sadness wells inside me, thinking of sweet Caleb. We had become somewhat close in the prison, the two of us naturally drawn together when Fral realised we could sustain stolen magic. That was before Ellis ...

A thunderous boom echoes through the sky and I cry out in alarm. I search the treetops for whatever is causing the noise, but it's gone as quick as it came. Waiting a few moments, I wonder if it will happen again or if Gwenore is hunting down another soul elsewhere.

After a few minutes pass without another sound, I return to work. When my basket is full of wild berries, after visiting a few spots I know with the juiciest fruits, I trail back home, enjoying Gwenore's scenery. The sweet aroma follows me, and I smile without restraint. *This* is why I love fruit picking. Nature and its abundance of beauty. I can't get enough.

A crack of thunder sounds again, and the ground rumbles beneath me this time. I stumble, and a shriek escapes me. I drop my basket, and a whole load of berries roll away, too many are squished from the impact to be saved.

On my hands and knees, I curse and grab my basket and what is left of the picked fruit. When the rumbling sound becomes more frequent, I grow more frustrated. I glance up at the bright sky between the tree branches, yet there are no dark clouds. Here in Tealwaters, rain is unheard of, so when the sky rumbles again, I know it's someone's magic.

My heart races. Only *one* person I know can create lightning hand in hand with thunder.

'Ellis Irvine!' I seethe before deciding to find him. I need answers as to why I must spend more time refilling my basket of berries.

I cast a cloud of shadow around me until I am fully shrouded in darkness. I undress and shove my clothes within the confines of the berry bush, cutting my wrist in the process with a hiss. My basket follows suit, so no one can stumble across it and steal it. Then, I shift into wolf form and command the shadows to fade.

When Hazel was younger, she described my wolf as lethally beautiful with its golden fur and light purple eyes, they reminded her of lavender, she said. But after I was experimented on, any animal form I adopted had fur or feathers of inky black, no longer golden like my hair had once been. No matter how much I tried to shift into my prior golden form, it never worked, the dark magic claimed every bit of colour I used to enjoy, turning it as black as the night.

Using my wolf's heightened sense of smell, it doesn't take long to find the prince. I approach an opening where no trees grow, finding a patch of land where the gravel path expands. The sun beams down across the sparse area, shining upon two half naked men who are fighting.

It is not only Prince Ellis like I expected, but his older brother, too. And I suddenly realise why Ellis is causing such a commotion. He's training.

I hide behind a tree and watch as the brothers swiftly swing their limbs, sweat glistening on their backs as their muscles strain with every attack and act of defence. Thunder rumbles above, despite the beautifully sunny day, and the ground does the same.

'Faster,' Ellis orders and my furry tail flicks in response.

Lightning covers the prince's arms while Alexander disappears, rendering himself invisible, before popping up to attack at another angle.

I take my time to peruse the brothers. I find my temper slowly fading as their bodies become my main focus, with their thick arms and broad shoulders and …

Stop drooling, Violet.

I blink and proceed with my original plan.

Slowly, I morph back into human form, commanding a cloud of darkness around me in case of watchful eyes. When I am decent, I crouch and lay my hand on the ground. Shadows, dark and thick, sprawl along the forest floor, creeping slowly towards the royals and along the edges of their training area. My magic takes its time before coiling around the princes' ankles, their fighting momentarily draws to a halt as Alexander points down at it.

'What is this?'

Ellis quickly searches the perimeter, but the shadow now spans such a large area, making it impossible to discern the source. His sweaty chest gleams beneath the streams of sunlight, and my heart races at the sight. He is toned, and my mind wanders to his muscular arms, remembering when he grabbed me, my eyes lower to the V of his waist that falls behind the band of his trousers.

'Violet?' Ellis calls, wading through the thick cloud. His dark cobalt eyes scan the treeline. 'Violet, are you there?'

I don't answer. It will drive him crazy knowing I'm here, especially when he's unable to find me. When he visibly grits his teeth, I know I'm winning. I can't help the grin that spreads across my face.

'This is all Violet's doing?' asks Alexander, seeming impressed. A spark of pride fills me.

'Wait here,' says Ellis. He crouches and then shoots into the sky. He doesn't come back down, he's no doubt flying above to try to find me. He won't, though. I'm hiding behind a huge tree, its leaves and layered branches are thick without gaps.

The future king stills, his chest still heaving from exercise. He rests his hands on his hips and slowly bends to one knee, touching my shadows with curiosity. I let it coil up and around his arm, so as not to scare him before it crawls away. I smile and create a floating hand that waves. The heir laughs and waves back.

'Hi there.' He grins.

I form words with my shadows, and the hand I created now points to a set of pulsating letters that float above it.

How are you, Your Highness? Recovering from your birthday, I presume?

He wafts away the shadow words and says, 'I said to call me Alex, but yes. Ellis thought we could sweat out the alcohol in my system. I am very fragile today.'

Concentrating hard, I get rid of my shadow hand and replace it with my own shadow reflection, it pops out from the surrounding blanket of darkness. The prince leans back, delighted. He's enjoying the display.

A speech bubble forms above my replica. *We have a special tart that would cure your uneasy state. You should swing by the bakery on your way home.*

'Maybe I will.' He nods, his lips tugging upwards. 'Is Ellis invited, too?

My replica shakes her head and I will shadow horns to grow from her dark hair. *No, I have other plans for him.*

Prince Alexander looks scandalised. 'Is that so?'

Before I answer, a hand grabs my shoulder and twists me. Ellis' grip is firm as he shoves my body up against the tree I'm hiding behind. It knocks the breath out of me. He presses an arm against my bare chest, my shadows hiding not only my breasts but his strong arm, too.

'Violet,' Ellis greets, pinning me with his gaze. 'How nice to see you, sweetheart.'

My heart skitters, threatening to jump from my chest. He looks pissed, but I don't falter, flashing him my most dazzling smile.

'Took you long enough,' I retort. Shadows curl around his bare torso, and I allow my eyes to roam his striking figure. Up close, he's even more impressive, and my shadows tenderly crawl over him as if they yearn for his touch. The prince looks down but doesn't seem fazed by my magic.

'I found you in seconds,' he murmurs, leaning closer. 'But you were too busy talking to my brother to notice me.'

I hum, flicking my gaze back to Alexander. 'What can I say? He's good company.'

'But I am not?'

'I suppose you come in at a close second,' I answer sweetly.

Ellis' nostrils flare as he presses his arm harder against my chest. He closes in as his knee presses in between mine. I am fully naked beneath my cloak of shadows, and the feel of his trousers against my inner thighs makes my fingers tingle with need, my body responding traitorously beneath his hold.

'Is that so?' he murmurs, as if daring me to taunt him further.

I swallow and nod once.

'Well, that just won't do. Will it?' He dips his chin, lowering it above my shoulder. I exhale when his tongue tenderly licks the column of my neck, stopping just below my ear. His next words are a soft caress as they echo in my ear. 'You are supposed to be acting as if you are mine, Violet. We agreed to keep all other parties out of this arrangement – that includes your future king.'

'Sounds to me like you are jealous. There is a lot of that going on with you right now, isn't there?' I question, recalling his behaviour when I admitted to sleeping with Luca.

Something hot flashes in his expression, and I smirk.

'Jealous?' He echoes before smiling back. 'You are mistaken.'

His arm lessens its pressure as he moves slowly downwards, his hand travelling lower. His knuckles graze my skin and draws circles on my stomach.

'Could have fooled me,' I murmur. I'm unable to speak any louder in case my voice cracks, and right now, I must pretend his touch does not affect me.

He lowers his fingers dangerously close to where I want him. I squeeze my thighs together, needing to hide the unforeseen wetness between my legs, but his own leg presses closer until I practically straddle him instead. Slowly, he moves his leg, creating a delicious friction. I bite my lip to keep the moan from escaping. I tip my head back, my eyes fluttering closed.

He will leave you. He will leave you. He will leave you.

I am doing my best not to reach out and grab him, but the sudden need to take him here and now grows stronger the longer he strokes my stomach with his leg between mine.

I am supposed to be annoyed with the prince for being too personal with me last night – not rubbing against him like a brainless fool. I try to stop, but it feels too good, and with his body closing the distance between us, the old feeling of safety and familiarity swarms in, and I breathe easier than I have in a long time.

'Are you enjoying yourself, Violet?' he murmurs, his mouth close to my earlobe. His hand lifts to touch beneath my breast. 'Do you want to touch *me*?'

I shake my head, finding his lips press gently against the side of my throat. Once. Twice.

'I think you are lying.' The rumble of his voice reverberates through his bare chest, which is so close to resting flush against mine. 'I think you are trying to keep your hands to yourself because you know you'll lose the battle if you don't.'

Bastard.

'Says the prince who is pawing at me like a lovesick puppy,' I retort, and his eyes flash with an emotion I cannot discern. I smile demurely, proud to keep my voice from wavering. 'You feel good, but that's all men are good for, isn't it? You and Luca are enough to curb the urges, that's all.'

The mention of Luca has the desired effect. Ellis stiffens, and the reminder of me with another man makes light-ning crackle across his body. Too soon, he backs away, and I shiver without his warm touch. I take him in, his body a mass of muscle and beauty, yet the tips of his fingers are what grab my attention as the ends turn a dark shade of grey. Ellis notices my gaze and curls his hands into fists, leaning both against the tree either side of my head. His face is close enough to mine that I could steal a kiss.

'If that's the case, Violet, I won't touch you until you ask for it. I'll have you begging before I lay another hand on you. Is that what you wish?' He stares into my soul, waiting for an answer. Words seem to have left me, so badly I wish to cave into my desires, but I know what it feels like to have him walk away, and when this arrangement is over, that's what will happen.

'Yes,' I say, my voice breaking. 'I would rather you keep your hands to yourself.'

My heart won't be able to take another round of loss.

The prince stays there, watching me intently, as if hoping to change my mind. But I don't budge. I am protecting myself from him and his tantalising touch, and the strange effect he has on me – even after all this time.

'Very well,' he murmurs, looking away. 'Why are you here?'

I take a moment to compose myself. I swallow and stand up straighter, making sure my shadows around me haven't slipped. Much to my relief, they haven't. Alex is still surrounded by ankle-deep clouds of thick onyx.

'I am here because I was berry picking. That is until the ground shook beneath me, and all my berries fell from the basket.' I give him a half-hearted glare. 'So, I went in search of the person responsible because now I must re-pick All. Those. Berries.'

I do my best not to stare at the faint white lines across his abdomen and avert my gaze, the prominence of his chest makes me want to touch them. Ellis wrinkles his nose in distaste before taking a deep breath. 'Let me walk you home.'

'No, that's fine. You have done enough today.'

Ellis' eyes flash. I smile innocently.

'You'll do as you're told, Violet.'

I quirk a brow in challenge. 'Will I?'

We lock stares in the hope the other will break, but when I remember how much time I've spent in Gwenore Forest after my mother said not to dally, I reluctantly look away.

'I must be going. I have jobs to finish off – *again*,' I emphasise, flashing the prince a look that says *no thanks to you*. 'Maybe shout out a warning next time to help those nearby in case they, too, are petrified to death by your bouts of magic.'

'Let me make it up to you,' offers Ellis, lifting his hand to his chest. The movement makes my eyes run over him again. I swallow. 'I'll help you gather more.'

'No, thank you.' I shake my head and lift a hand in protest. 'Goodbye, Your Highness.'

I quickly shift into wolf form and dash away before he can say much more. I release my hold on the shadows and they encase Ellis in darkness while I make my escape.

☆°₀☾*☆°₀*

When I arrive home, I stalk through to the kitchen, expecting an argument about being late. I halt. Luca is still out front handling customers, which is a surprise in itself, but out back, my mother and sister, who has finished her classes, work hard to make jam with a basket of fruit already sitting on the counter.

'Oh, your home,' says mother with a smile. 'You decided to get double today, I see?' I glance down to where Mum peers at my full basket before returning to the washed fruit in the sink. She motions out front. 'Do you mind helping Luca? It seems word of our tarts at Prince Alexander's birthday have brought in some curious customers.'

I ignore her request, still staring at the fruit she handles.

'I didn't get that basket,' I tell her. 'Where did it come from?'

Mother frowns before pointing to the front door. 'I got them out front. I thought you left them there in search of more.' She seems worried for a moment before revealing a piece of paper. 'Hazel did find this attached to the handle, though.'

There are no words, but a single letter is signed.

I smile despite myself.

E.

21

VIOLET

Time with friends is sacred, letting off steam and laughing with your nearest and dearest are the moments I treasure most. Today, I dine at a place called The Waterway, renowned for its magical drinks and delicious meals.

My best friend Maple orders us both a lemon drink that oozes clouds of pale yellow, which tumbles over the rim of the glass and disappears the moment it touches the table. Maple sips at hers like a true lady while her sparkling ocean eyes hold mine. A lock of reddish-brown tumbles over her shoulder, and her delicate hand is quick to flick it back.

'You've been busy lately,' she says, resting her drink down on the table. 'Have you been taking more shifts with Otto?'

I nod. 'He doesn't need my help, but he's been kind enough to act like he does.'

'Your mother must really appreciate that,' she says wistfully.

I give her a small smile. 'She *is* appreciative,' I agree.

'But I wish it didn't have to come to this. She and Hazel work so hard, and it's as if all their effort is wasted. I'm not sure what we're doing wrong.'

Maple reaches out and grabs my hand, squeezing gently. 'Your time will come, Violet. Something will spark a movement, and everyone will be pushing and shoving to get to Danes Bakery. Just you wait. I have a good feeling about it.'

I give her a small smile. Maple claims not to be a dameer – someone born with magic – but human. I believe her words nevertheless, needing them to be true.

'I hope you're right,' I say, squeezing her hand back. 'Because we really need a stroke of luck right now. But what about you? How is everything at work?' I ask as our meals are served. The plates steam before us.

Maple has worked for the royal family for a few years now. Her mother having been Queen Melody's right-hand lady for years, and was lucky enough to secure her daughter a decent paid job as a maid within Ivory Castle.

'The palace was in disarray for Prince Alexander's birthday. Everyone was losing their heads for nothing,' Maple answers, rolling her eyes. 'Everyone makes such a fuss about rich people, who only care about what they do or wear.' She shakes her head, taking another sip. 'But that's not the worst part. In preparation for our future king's celebrations, I had to polish a mirror in one of the many storage rooms within an inch of its life, as Mrs Grounder claimed I didn't clean it properly the first time round.' Maple huffs, her hatred for her superior having spanned since the two first met.

I pat her shoulder. 'Poor, Maple Syrup,' I coo.

She sighs, leaning back in her chair. 'Who would bother about a mirror in a storage room anyway? I know for a fact no guest invited to the prince's birthday bash would go inside unless it's for activities that don't involve looking at oneself ...'

I smirk. 'Unless you like seeing yourself being ...' I trail off and raise my brows with insinuation. Maple's lips tug upwards, doing her best not to laugh, but we burst into fits of giggles, unable to keep a straight face.

'I can't imagine the wealthy getting into mischief like that. They seem too proper,' says Maple, wrinkling her nose. No doubt she's imagining her employers in precarious positions in the numerous rooms she cleans. 'But back to the mirror story,' says Maple with a wave of her hand. 'I ended up polishing the glass for thirty minutes, and even now, my hands still hurt. The cleaning formula we use is disgusting and I can't get the smell of peaches from my nostrils.' With a show of her delicate hands, she reveals the splotchy stains of pink across her fingers, and I'm hit with the obvious smell of fruit.

'I won't order anything peach flavoured then,' I jest, earning a half-hearted scowl. 'On the bright side, isn't it nice to know the royal family are nice and hygienic?'

The question goes unanswered, though Maple hums in acknowledgement. 'Anyway, I'm not bitter about it, but I thought you ought to know.' She shakes the salt generously on her meal, her strange quirk something I've always admired. 'Salt?' offers Maple.

Suddenly, I taste the gag stuffed inside my mouth, and I swear someone screams in the distance. The sound rings in my ears. I blink, trying to shove the thoughts away. I do my best to stay in the present as my body shuts down. Maple puts the salt back on the table, guilt crossing her features as she moves closer, reaching out with uncertainty.

'I'm so sorry, Vi, I forgot.' She grips my arms, tracing my skin in a show of comfort, yet the smell makes me suddenly need a drink to wash away the taste of salt – the taste of my dark childhood. I reach for the glass jar filled with water, but her hand is there first. She pours me a drink and pushes it to my mouth, watching as I gulp it down.

'Better?' she asks, her bright blue eyes intent. She's an open book as she observes the sudden panic in my body melt to a low simmer of memories I can manage.

'Yes,' I rasp with a shake of my head, dissolving the memories as best as I can. I smile for her sake. I know she will be riddled with shame for having a small moment of forgetfulness. I will never want salt and will be happy if I never tasted the seasoning again. 'I felt overwhelmed all of a sudden, and I needed to get rid of the taste,' I explain, putting my now empty glass down. 'It's gone now. I'm fine.'

By Maple's stare, I know she's unconvinced but doesn't comment. Apart from my parents and Hazel, she is the only person who knows the details of my traumatic past and every nightmare along with it. Yet she doesn't treat me like I'm made of glass, instead, she reminds me of how strong I am for surviving. Though I know she still worries about me.

'Do you want to talk about it?' This is always her first question, deciphering what I want and what I need.

'No, not this time. It's just a minor attack.'

She nods. 'Okay.' Shuffling back into her seat, she continues eating. This is one thing I love about Maple, she knows when to push and when to let things slide. 'So, I heard that the youngest prince brought a date to his brother's birthday,' says Maple, doing her best to change the subject. A small smirk plays on her lips, and my stomach rolls. 'I wasn't able to attend the garden party but there were many comments talking about her appearance.'

'Is that so?' I ask, thankful my voice doesn't betray my churning emotions. Maple does not know about Ellis and I, though not because I didn't wish to tell her, but because *no one* was meant to know.

'I heard she charmed everyone she met. All the servants were talking about them together and how good they looked as a couple.' She dabs the corner of her mouth with a serviette before her brows crease. 'It's strange how no one seems to go near him. They label him as dangerous but can't help but be invested in everything he does.'

'Talking of the prince,' I say, leaning forward to lower my voice. 'I need to tell you something.'

Maple mirrors me, hair falling over her shoulders as her pale eyes narrow with concern.

'Should I be worried?'

'Well, that depends.' I shrug, and she shoots me a look. 'I am—'

A hand lands on my shoulder and I jump, glancing up at none other than Prince Ellis himself.

22

FLISS

My first mission of the day was to persuade my brother to come with me into Sapphire City. It wasn't hard to get him to agree, but when we arrive at Danes Bakery, he tilts his head, confused. We wait in our carriage on the other side of the road, peering out the window together.

He looks perplexed. 'You wanted me to visit a bakery with you?'

'Not just any bakery,' I say, tilting my head to the shop sign. 'It's Violet's family business.'

He nods. 'Right.'

'And I need you to buy everything on the menu.'

He looks my way. 'Truly?'

'But you must only visit the bakery. Nowhere else.'

'Why?'

'Part of the bargain was to help the business bring more customers in. What's better than seeing the charming prince of Tealwaters enter the store and rave about how good the products are?'

'They *were* good,' agrees Alex, recalling the numerous tarts he ate at his birthday.

'Exactly.'

Without prompting, Alex glides out of the carriage, and as I predicted, passersby stop almost immediately. A crowd of people begin forming before I can even step foot onto the street. I stand by the carriage as they wave and point, their curious looks landing on the heir of our mighty kingdom. I am a shadow in the background, and I am glad. The mass of people that my brother captivates is astonishing, but the aggregation of various bodies makes my nerves tingle as I imagine being amongst them.

'Are you coming?' Alex calls, popping his head out of the mass. I shake my head. There are many other things I'd rather do than step into that horde of people. Alex is suddenly occupied with a woman holding a baby, and then a gruff man with a beard, and then a young girl who eyes him like he's buried treasure.

'Don't forget the bakery!' I call out. My brother raises his hand in response as he heads very slowly towards the shop while mingling with the civilians.

When he finally gets to the door and steps inside, a line of people follow him. He orders one of everything on the menu, as requested, and begins to hand things out, offering bags and boxes of pastries, bagels, loaves, and cakes to whoever is nearest.

I hear moans of pleasure as the guests relish the smell, taste, and presentation of the products. Hazel's tarts also appear to be a big hit with their unique flavours. Gratitude for my brother swells inside me that he would be so willing to do this without question.

When he slowly travels back to the carriage, I get back inside, needing its shelter before the throng of people reach me. He finally shuffles back inside and hands me a bag containing a shimmering blue-scaled mermaid cake.

'I made sure to keep this,' he says, smiling.

'I owe you,' I reply, referring to both the cake and his good deed.

'You owe me nothing.'

'I appreciate it nonetheless,' I say.

He watches me, something twinkling in his eyes. 'I'm proud of you, Ellis.' It's sudden and out of the blue. I peer up from my half-eaten pastry with a questioning look. 'I don't tell you enough and now seems like a good time to remind you.'

'You are getting sappy in your old age,' I reply, earning a playful eye roll, but deep down, his comment strikes true. Alex looks at me as if I am not a burden with a dark past but someone worthy of his time. I clear my throat. 'You must travel home without me.'

'Why?' he asks.

'I need to see Violet. I didn't end things well in Gwenore Forest.'

My brother nods. 'I'm sure she will appreciate that.'

'We shall see,' I murmur before stepping out again. Hera is by my side as we watch the carriage return to Ivory Castle.

* ☆ ° ₒ * ☾ * ☆ ° ₒ *

Violet's soul is as easy to find as my own. After spending a considerable amount of time with Violet, when I now close my eyes, I can imagine her essence. The glowing orb that is my childhood friend shines a radiant purple, the same colour as her eyes.

It doesn't take me long to find her. She's talking with who I assume is Maple in a small and cosy restaurant. My breathing deepens at the sight of Violet in her daytime dress with her hair pinned up.

'I will stand outside, Your Highness,' says Hera, motioning for me to enter the establishment.

When I step inside, the staff are stunned by my presence, a slither of wariness coating their features making me feel suddenly tense. I have no patience for their behaviour today, so I order another round of beverages the girls are drinking and pay for their entire meal. The staff rush off when I release them of my presence, probably glad to put distance between us.

When I approach Violet's table, the other girl leans forward with concern etched in her lovely eyes. Perhaps interrupting their time together is unwise, but I'm too close now to turn back.

'Violet,' I say, resting a hand on her shoulder.

She jerks in surprise, shocked by my presence. Violet's gaze roams over me, from my dark blonde hair to my midnight-blue attire. A glint of approval settles in her expression before she suddenly remembers herself.

'Good day, Your Highness,' she greets, her wary gaze flickering between her company and me.

'Violet,' I repeat before facing her friend. 'And you must be Maple. It's lovely to finally meet you.'

Maple appears extremely confused as her bright eyes

bounce between us. However, knowing Violet has kept us a secret from her friend irks me, and the tightness in my chest feels unfamiliar. 'May I join you?'

'Of course, Your Highness,' Maple answers, finally emerging from her stupor. She waves towards a free chair and shuffles in her seat. 'Make yourself comfortable.'

'Please, call me Ellis,' I say. Maple raises her eyebrows at that.

Violet clasps her hands together while her eyes look everywhere else. I smirk. Maple does not know about our agreement, and I intend to make my girl squirm.

'How are you, sweetheart?' I ask Violet. Her eyes flash as if silently begging me not to do this in front of her friend. I move a stray piece of hair from her face, exposing her deep, stunning eyes. 'Are you going to introduce me to Maple?'

'No.' Violet stills beneath my gaze. 'You need to leave.'

'I will if you come with me.'

She shakes her head. 'I know what you're doing.'

'What?' I frown, playing along with the act. 'I am here to see my girl.'

From the corner of my eye, I note the drop of Maple's jaw at my declaration, and I smile, knowing Violet saw it too. I turn abruptly towards Violet's friend. She is beautiful, with long silky hair and kind eyes. I recognise her somehow, but I cannot discern where from. 'I can't help but think I've seen you somewhere, Maple.'

Maple nods slowly. 'I work in the castle.'

'You cleaned my room the other week,' I recall, and she nods again.

'Yes. Annalise was sick, so I stepped in for her.'

I nod. 'How—'

'Can I talk to you outside?' Violet interrupts, her chair screeching against the floor as she stands. 'Right now,' she adds when I don't move.

I dip my chin at Maple. 'Please excuse us.'

The moment we're out in the fresh air, Violet hauls me up against a wall. Shadows coil around her arms as she aims an intimidating finger at my chest. 'What are you doing?'

'I already told you what I'm doing,' I drawl.

Violet looks murderous, which makes my trousers feel extremely tight in a matter of seconds. Does she know how much she affects me? I glance down at my hands, the tips of my fingers turning a dark grey.

Tread carefully, they seem to say.

'She does not know about us,' she seethes, glancing back inside with a scowl.

'I gathered that.'

Violet groans and clamps her hands around her head. 'Are you going to continuously bring every person in my life into this arrangement? How many people do I need to continue lying to, to make you happy?'

When she says it like that, I feel a stab of guilt. 'That was not my intention.'

'Of course, it wasn't,' she huffs. 'It's like you enjoy people knowing I am yours.'

A prickle of something hot and daring settles across my neck and seeps into my skull. She doesn't seem to note my sudden pause, but I can't help but push her limits as she does mine.

'I do,' I answer honestly. Violet's head whips up, her

long gold and onyx hair cradling her flushed face. 'I do like people knowing your mine. You're right.'

She shakes her head, lifting a hand between us as if to keep me away. 'I can't deal with you today.'

'Why? Are you still thinking of me shirtless?' I quip. She slaps my stomach.

'You wish.'

'I do wish.' I allow a tint of amusement through. Violet's face softens as if my glint of emotion is like the rare sighting of a shooting star. Those purple-blue eyes are intent on mine, as if mesmerised. Right now, she looks like the Violet I remembered as a child, always eager for my words and thoughts but impatient for my stories and mishaps. She looks at me like I'm where her world starts and ends, but in seconds, the look is gone, and she is back to being frustrated with me.

'Is there a reason you are here besides annoying me?' she asks.

'No. That was my sole purpose.'

She nods. 'Right. Okay. I need to head back in. Do *not* follow me.'

When Violet turns away, I reach for her wrist, wrapping my fingers around her warm skin. She looks up expectantly, and suddenly I'm lost for words.

'Don't let this feed your ego,' she murmurs, 'but thank you.'

'Whatever for?'

'For picking all those berries for me. My mother was extremely happy with the delivery, and you saved me a good telling off when I eventually got home.'

'So, you owe me,' and though she scowls, she doesn't

move away, keeping her hand in mine. The contact between us is comforting, like being wrapped in a cosy blanket.

'No. You made me drop my pickings in the first place. The least you could do was make up for it. We're *even*,' she says tartly.

I avert my gaze, needing a moment to compose myself. With the way Violet's looking at me right now, I'm surprised I haven't swept her off her feet and taken her somewhere private to do all manner of ungentlemanly things to her.

I shrug. 'If you say so.'

Violet grunts before ripping her hand away. I grab her hair in my fist, tilting her head back until I'm leaning over her. Supporting her back with my other hand, she arches into me, our faces so close I can feel her quickening breath mingle with mine.

'Do me a favour,' I murmur, peering deeply into her eyes. I suspect she enjoys it when I do this, taking the time to look into the depths of her gaze.

'I suppose so?'

'I need a yes, Violet. Not a half-answer.'

Violet clears her throat and nods, forcing her best irritated expression while her hands slowly rise to my arms. She clings to me as if fearing I may let her go. 'Yes, Ellis. I will do you a favour *within reason*. Now, what is it?'

'Never walk alone in Gwenore Forest again. Next time, you will call for me, and I will personally take you. That's an order.' I squeeze Violet close, my chest against hers, as I nip at her chin. Before she answers, I steady her on her feet, keeping my body a safe distance away. I don't wait for a reply as I stalk off, motioning for Hera to follow.

'Wait, you can't tell me what to do!' Violet calls.

I smirk over my shoulder. 'I am the crown prince, Violet. I can do whatever I desire.'

'Jerk,' I hear before she goes back inside.

23

VIOLET

Maple sits on my bed while I hold my head and look everywhere except for her. I've spilled everything about my new arrangement with Ellis. Unsurprisingly, she's very calm about it. She's always abnormally level-headed, no matter how bizarre things are.

'You and Prince Ellington are dating. Who would have thought?' she says cheerfully, leaning back against the headboard. Grabbing a pillow of mine, she holds it against her chest.

'*Fake* dating,' I remind her, shaking my head.

'But you wish it wasn't,' she clarifies.

I sigh. 'I don't know what you're talking about.'

'Accept the facts, Violet. I've never seen you look at someone the way you do the prince. You like him and have done for years. While you say you're over him, clearly you are not, and what's more, he likes you, too.'

'He does not like me. I'm doing him a favour.' I laugh humourlessly.

'It certainly doesn't look like that to me,' replies Maple with a pointed look.

'What part of his demeanour reveals his feelings? The part where he doesn't look at me half the time and seems almost *bored* as if he'd rather be anywhere else but with me?'

She shrugs. 'He's a young man with lots of deep emotions and is likely unpractised in articulating them. Don't forget, he sent Hazel to baking school for you.'

I raise a brow, unconvinced. 'That was part of our bargain. Not something he did out of kindness.'

Maple flashes a bright and mischievous smile. 'Well, let's just say that when I cleaned his room the other week, I noted how many vases of violets were in his chambers, and now I have a theory as to why.'

'Why?' I counter, a glimmer of hope blooming in my chest.

'Because they remind him of *you*,' she says enthusiastically. She sighs happily. 'I've certainly had no partners do that with me.'

'You don't have a name that associates with a flower.'

'True.' She nods. 'But they could have a bottle of syrup by their night table or something ... better than nothing.'

'If you say so.'

'Anyway, we're getting off topic. Why don't you believe he cares for you? What is there not to love?' I smile at where Maple is no doubt going with this. 'You are kind, funny, feisty and incredibly strong. You aren't afraid to stand up for what is right or to put him in his place. He would be lucky to have you, and don't you bloody forget it!' She stands and rearranges my pillows back to how she found them. 'Now, I need to head off. I start work soon.'

'Thanks Maple,' I say, embracing her.

'Anytime. Now, when are you next seeing him?'

I purse my lips. 'Tomorrow. I have been invited as a special guest to watch a game of polo with him and his brother. I hear they are very competitive.'

Maple nods, a sly expression spreading across her beautiful face. 'Well, swing by mine in the morning. I can steal you a dress from the castle to borrow.'

⋆☆°₀⋆☾⋆☆°₀⋆

The game is hosted at the House of Bane, an old private school taken over many generations ago by a blue-haired, blue-eyed army our kingdom calls the Nightshades. The royal family created them as soldiers, who could digest or come into contact with poisonous or toxic substances without harm.

When I arrive, I am not with Ellis but with his aunt and uncle – the princes having left earlier to prepare for their tournament. A young redhead, apparently one of the many dates that the king and queen has arranged for Alexander in hopes of finding him a future bride, is also present, with her bright smile and conversational skills.

When we arrive at our destination, we gather alongside a well-kept field, me and the redhead who I discover is called Isla sitting together. We are special guests of the royal family, so we are situated on a shaded stage where luxurious pastel-blue chairs await us. Along from the dais are several much smaller boxes for the other wealthy patrons.

I feel fairly ridiculous sitting here when the rest of the civilians, who I'd much rather be with – if not for my association with the youngest prince – sit along the lawn on large rugs, roasting in the sun.

'I have attended quite a few polo matches in my time,' admits Isla, her voice quiet as she leans in close to my side. Her cheeks are naturally flushed with a soft pink shade, her emerald eyes glinting with mischief as they roam approvingly over a group of wealthy men who are here to spectate. 'But I still don't know the rules. Absurd isn't it?'

I lean closer, following her gaze with an amused smile. 'Absurd indeed.'

A bell rings loudly across the grounds. Spectators shout and clap as the polo players begin entering the field. Two lines of eight men, dressed in either pure white or dark blue, gallop across the grass and begin to warm up. Many pass the royal box, some casually observe Isla and I, and others are more obvious, studying us with friendly waves and broad smiles.

I vaguely pay attention to them, my sole focus on Ellis. He is dressed immaculately in cobalt blue, the same shade as his eyes. His clothing is tight – tight enough to expose his muscular arms and toned legs, which curl around the stomach of his midnight-blue stallion. He turns in the saddle, a large hand on his thigh as if searching for something. When the youngest prince spots me, he holds my stare, and shivers run down my spine. He gives no other sign of acknowledgment before looking away again.

Hello to you, too, I think with irritation.

'My nephews are both captains. They have a team each, so prepare yourself for some dirty moves,' King Hector says with a chuckle, peering around his wife to speak to Isla and me.

'My favourite kind of game.' Isla smiles.

'I can't wait,' I reply with a grin.

Before the game begins, Ellis and his brother shake hands. Prince Alexander is dressed in pure white, making his tanned skin glow but it's his teammates that seem to make Isla fan herself as if she is feeling particularly hot, and I can't help but smirk.

Another bell rings, and I startle.

'Let the best team win,' the queen murmurs before the teams move into action.

The game is simple. Each male holds a wooden mallet where they must hit the ball into the opposing team's goal, but with magic included in the game, I struggle to keep up. The ball flies from one side to the other, and my neck aches from the series of goals. Ellis is particularly impressive to watch, gaining more points for the blue team than anyone else. Pride swells inside my chest as I watch him. I'm surprised to find myself genuinely enjoying the game, and Isla joins in with my delight.

It seems to be going swimmingly until Ellis and another player dressed in all-white begin shouting. The crowd becomes even more invested, the game no longer their sole focus.

'What is happening?' asks Queen Melody, leaning over the railing for a better look. I follow her lead to find Ellis and the other male, who are now off their horses, shoving at each other. Their words are loud, even from here.

My heart races. I have never seen Ellis so wild before, his usual control unleashed. Even from a distance, I sense his anger as his body language emanates fury.

'Get the Elder Nightshade to separate them,' King Hector orders a servant, pointing to a woman whose long blue hair is plaited down her back.

The Elder, an older but fierce-looking woman, is already heading their way though, outstretching her arms in preparation to stop the fight before it gets more out of hand. Standing in between them, she pushes their chests to create distance while Alexander rides over on his golden steed, jumping gracefully from the saddle to hold Ellis back. He murmurs something to his brother that eventually makes him back down.

It's only when the player in white has the last word that Ellis flings a hand his way, a bolt of lightning shooting through the male in answer. His body shudders, his skin crackles, and when he slumps to the floor, the crowd cries out. I'm on my feet, uncaring of who is watching as I dash out of the royal box towards the youngest prince.

24

ELLIS

'Ellis,' Alex seethes, dragging me by the collar before I can do anymore damage. He pushes me off the field and orders the other team players to continue without us.

We enter the House of Bane's barn before Alex says anything else, he orders the stable-hands to leave. 'What did I say about—'

'I don't fucking care what you bloody said!' I snap, snatching my arm from his hold.

My brother jerks back and shock crosses his features. It's as if I've slapped him. I've never spoken to him like this before – I've never spoken to *anyone* as I have today, not like that. Wild. Savage. Full of uncontrollable hate.

'What did he say?' asks Alex. He knows whatever happened wasn't a typical fight between Castor and me. While Castor is a fucking cheater, it never usually bothers me. We tend to win regardless of his antics, but today ...

I shake my head, unable to relay his filthy, fucking words.

Your girl looks spritely. You're obviously not riding her hard enough. Perhaps I should mount her after we win the game and show her a good time. I think she'll enjoy that.

It was a way to distract me – a tactic he's done before in other games to try and make me falter. But today, his words rang through me and seeped into my bones like they've never done before. All because he spoke about Violet.

'He deserves to have his tongue cut out,' I manage before blowing a harsh breath. I turn away from Alex as the darkness courses through me stronger than before. Too quickly, black veins web across my shaking hands. Panic fills me. I haven't felt this out of control in years, the dark-ness having never seeped past my palms. If I don't ask Alex to leave soon, I may not be able to fight the dark magic inside of me. The monster ripping my resolve.

'Leave me to cool down, Alex. I'll come out when I'm ready.' My tone has returned to normal – calm and in control – but my head spins, hoping and praying he will listen. *'Please,'* I rasp.

My brother steps forward but stops himself. I don't look. I know my eyes will be black, void of all colour as the darkness inside rebels against me.

'Alright,' he says finally. 'If you aren't out by the end of the game, I'm coming back to find you.'

'Fine.'

Only when I hear him leave do I exhale and stumble into an empty stall. I lean against the closest wall and slide down it, suddenly exhausted. Clutching my chest, I press hard to feel my hammering heart beneath my flesh.

'You do not control me. I am my own master,' I whisper to the monster yearning to dominate me. Dark veins creep up my wrists towards my elbows, the speed of it faster than I've seen before. The sight heightens the dread coursing through me. 'You don't own me. You are *mine* – mine to use, mine to control, mine to command.'

It does not listen. My skin darkens by the second, and my mind spins. What will I do if the monster finally takes me as its prisoner? My family is too close. Violet is too close. I won't be able to hold back ...

Suddenly, the stall door crashes open. Violet stops in her tracks when she sees me. My heart hammers at the sight of her. A part of me expects her to scream or run away, but she does no such thing.

'Oh, Ellis.' Those purple-blue eyes wander over me, taking me in from head to toe. Her expression isn't one of judgement but understanding, though she could never understand me. No one can.

Ever so slowly, Violet creeps forward. I jerk away, extending a hand.

'Don't come any closer,' I demand.

She stops immediately, absorbing my words.

Violet wears a long cream-coloured dress that's in pristine condition, though she muddies it as she sits on the dirty barn floor, disturbing the surrounding straw. Her off-the-shoulder dress reveals the bare skin of her neck and collarbone, and I wish to wander my hands over her clavicle, around her throat ...

Her gold and black streaked hair is pinned away from her face, highlighting the beauty of her features – the freckles speckled across her nose, those rosy-coloured cheeks. She is stunning, and to me, she always has been. But seeing how she looks at me now, waiting for my next command, I am enamoured, and I wish to move nearer. Even the monster pauses, intrigued by her beauty.

'Do not be afraid,' says Violet, hands out in reassurance. Slowly, shadows ebb from her fingers and trail along the straw-covered floor. Her magic is careful as it approaches, testing my limits before small tendrils of onyx advance over my outstretched legs, crawling over me. I relish the comfort of its touch as my eyes flicker to Violet, who sits serenely, her eyes on me. She smiles gently.

'Take a deep breath,' she murmurs, voice calm and soothing. Then to my surprise she deliberately blinks twice as if conveying some sort of message. It takes a few moments to remember its meaning.

You are not alone. I am here with you.

Her shadows curl around my arms, pondering the dark veins that cover my tanned skin. They linger, the clouds of magic pressing and massaging my flesh until the small lines across my forearms fade. Violet tends to me, subduing the churning emotions inside as my arms begin to regain their normal colour, shortening the black veins until they reach my wrists again. My fingers are the last to fade until I finally take a deep breath. Somehow, Violet has controlled my inner darkness, and it feels as though the monster no longer has my lungs in its grasp, bending me to its will.

'Better?' she asks, tilting her head.

I nod once, needing to don my mask once more – Violet has already seen too much.

She is fast to approach me, resting a soft hand on my thigh. I instantly put up my mental walls, the need to hold her is overwhelming but I force my hands to myself. Violet shakes her head, suddenly panicked. 'No, don't do that.'

I wrinkle my nose. 'Do what?'

'Hide yourself from me. You have nothing to be ashamed of.' She leans closer, urging my gaze to hold hers as our breath mingles. She is terribly close, but for once, I don't push her away. Right now, I am glad she is here. I want her nearer and her hands to keep touching me. 'Absolutely *nothing*. Do you understand me?'

I don't answer, averting my gaze. I *am* ashamed. I let that bastard Castor affect my emotions enough to lose my usual hold on the darkness, allowing it to consume me so quickly I thought I was ruined.

I must know that I am leaving my legacy in safe hands.

The queen's words ring through me like a warning bell. Who am I kidding? Alex deserves someone – anyone – other than me by his side. I am a threat to myself and others.

'Ellis,' Violet murmurs, scowling. 'Stop thinking so harshly of yourself, you're giving me a headache.'

My gaze snaps up. She is smiling faintly in jest, but I'm feeling far from humourous. Then Violet does the last thing I expect. She makes herself comfortable in my lap, wrapping her arms around my waist and resting her head on my chest.

'Is this alright?' She asks, snuggling into me.

I hum in acknowledgement, unable to speak.

Violet smells like the berries she picks at Gwenore forest. Her long hair tickles my leg as she presses closely against me, and my body instantly reacts. She no doubt feels the sudden growth in my trousers, but doesn't comment. Instead, she wraps her fingers around my wrists and pulls them around her, a silent request to return her embrace.

Reluctantly, I obey, wrapping Violet firmly in my arms until I'm cradling her, surrounding her with what I hope is warmth and comfort. I close my eyes as peace surrounds us.

Violet saved me from myself – saved me from making a mistake I wish to never make again.

Thank you, I want to say, but the words are stuck in my throat.

Instead, I cling tighter, pulling her into me. She tightens her grasp, too, as if answering my silent gratitude. We don't talk – we don't do anything for a long while until Alex comes back and finds us together, sitting on the barn floor.

25

THE PAST

I'm asleep when strong hands grab me and roughly lift me to my feet. I stumble, peering back to search for Violet, but she is gone, and the space beside me is empty. John yanks me outside, caring little about his rough handling of a prince.

'You're hurting me,' I grumble, still coming to my senses. John forces me to my knees. The ground is hard, and my knees crack against it. I try to hide my grimace, not wanting the guards to see me anymore vulnerable than I already am.

'Morning, Ellis,' greets Fral, bending down to lift my chin.

He looms over me, and his warm and genuine smile makes me falter. How can someone I admired so much allow the bodies of children to pile up? Would he be smiling if my body was added to the heap?

'Did you have a good rest?' He wonders with a tilt of his head.

I don't answer. I'm not sure what to say.

No, the chains peel off my skin and the ground is too hard to sleep on. I'm constantly nauseated by the smell and close proximity of filthy and decaying bodies, and I've not had a proper meal in what feels like forever, *I want to say, but I don't.*

Like it would make a difference.

'Are you upset with me?' he asks, his features morphing into something like true concern. 'Have you not realised the true meaning of all of this yet?'

'Power,' I bite back. 'All you want is power.'

Fral shakes his head, his neatly styled hair shining beneath the sunlight. 'I'm disappointed. I thought you of all people would understand.' *He rests a strong hand on my shoulder, and though I try to shake it off, his grip is firm, clenching so I know he's not playing around.*

'You will be better once I am done with you and become the slayer I have dreamed about for years. You will rule over the strongest of armies. You can be the most powerful male in the six kingdoms. I am doing you a favour.'

Right now, it feels like the opposite of a favour. If he truly wanted me to thrive, then why starve us? Why throw buckets of ice-cold water over us as a lame excuse to keep us clean? Why use and abuse the bodies of so many kids to then carelessly dispose of them?

'I don't want your favours,' I say. 'I want you to stop this madness. I want you to stop all this pain.'

'But don't you see?' Fral grins, his eyes alight. 'We have made our first successful transfer of magic. Violet was able to absorb the shadow magic. It was marvellous.'

My gut twists furiously at the thought of Violet on the metal table staring at the child whose power she would ultimately be stealing. My poor Violet.

'Is she alright?'

He nods with obvious pride. 'My little nightmare was

incredible,' he muses. 'Do you wish to see her? She's been upgraded to stage two.'

My nose wrinkles. Stage two?

Yanking me to my feet, Fral escorts me to the largest of tents I have yet to visit. Inside is empty, except for three metal tables. On the right lies Caleb, his eyes closed as if in a deep slumber. His hands rest across his stomach, his features relaxed. Violet is on the middle counter, her golden hair cascades over the edges like a sleeping angel. I move to her without thinking, but a hand pulls me back.

'No touching,' warns Fral, clicking his fingers in front of my face. 'But watch carefully.'

Fral reaches over to touch Violet's ankle, caressing her grimy skin. 'Violet,' he murmurs, and her eyes fly open. 'Come and see Ellis.'

Violet is quick to sit and swing her legs over the edge before jumping off the table. She stops in front of me, looking but not truly seeing. I wave a hand in front of her face, but she doesn't flinch or react. My eyes lower to the gold collar secured around her neck, and my stomach twists.

'You're controlling her,' I mutter, dumbfounded.

'Yes. When a person has too much power, it will be difficult to keep them in line. If Violet was to ever turn her back on me, she will be a dangerous threat. This is a safety precaution so she will never stray from my side.' Fral trails his knuckles down her cheek, and the sight of it has me gritting my teeth. If I had a knife, I wouldn't hesitate to chop off his fingers one by one. 'Violet. Come show us your new powers.'

Instantly, she strides for the exit, pushing the canvas aside to head for the training area. She spins on the spot and waits for her next command.

'Here is fine.' Fral nods.

Violet raises her hands, palms to the sky as darkness ebbs from her body. Her skin turns black and veiny as shadows darken her eyes. Her newfound magic bubbles as if alive, coiling around her feet and thickening by the second. She creates a cloud of shadow that grows furiously with no indication of stopping.

'Send the camp into darkness,' orders Fral.

I cry out with the other children as a tidal wave of shadows approach. I shut my eyes as the fog hits me full force. I fall, scrambling along the floor.

When I peer up, everything is pitch black. I can't see my hands or the ground. Nothing is visible except Violet's dark and terrifying magic. Horror seizes my limbs, and I quake, imagining the world in this permanent state of gloom. Why would Fral want this power in his arsenal?

'When kept in the dark, our enemies will spill all their secrets,' Fral says from somewhere in the shadows, as if reading my mind. 'Humans cannot survive in the dark. They will lose their minds and faith until, eventually, they crumble.'

My heart pumps loudly in my ears, panic flooding my senses.

'Violet!' I call out, wanting her to know I'm here. 'Violet!'

A flicker of something surrounds me and coils around my body, as if in recognition. I shudder at the strange touch of Violet's magic. In seconds, Fral orders the shadows away and the world returns, the colours more vivid than before. My eyes adjust to the sudden burst of green and brown of Gwenore Forest.

'She will not answer you,' Fral says, looking down at me. 'I am her master now.'

26

ELLIS

I lay in bed that evening, the starry night sky shining through my window. Nighttime is when the unwanted thoughts enter my mind, my habit of overthinking everything replaying in my mind until I thoroughly hate myself.

Tonight it's Castor's words.

Your girl looks spritely. You're obviously not riding her hard enough.

My jaw aches from how hard I tense them. I imagine all the ways I would kill the male, how I'd make him pay for talking about Violet in such a way.

Perhaps I should mount her after I win this game and show her a good time. I think she'll enjoy that.

'Bastard,' I utter into my room, not feeling better for letting it out.

My curtains are open, making sure to keep the moonlight streaming in. The darkness is an old foe of mine since childhood. The thought of closing the drapes makes me nauseous, my mind conjuring up images of the gloom sweeping in to take me victim once more.

It's strange how time warps a person's memories. As a boy my nightmares consisted of Fral's face looming over my bed before taking me away – now he is merely a dark figure without a face at all. I wonder if Violet has the same bad dreams or not.

You have nothing to be ashamed of, she had said, her face clear of fear.

I swallow painfully as I stare up at the ceiling.

Fate is a cruel thing. It had brought Violet and I together in a prison camp that experimented and tortured children. It had made me dangerous enough that I was too scared to be her friend in case I hurt her – or worse. It made me the lonely man I am today that cannot fathom asking for help, thinking it will make me be seen as weak – weak like I was when I was a boy.

Fate is a cruel fucking mistress.

I had once promised Violet I would be her friend forever, that no matter how different our lives were, we would still have each other. I broke that promise the day I got home, nightmares of the prison camp and our rescue constantly playing through my mind.

I had hurt someone under the manipulation of Fral and they had made me promise to control my magic – to not be afraid of it. But I *was* afraid.

So I watched day after day, as Violet approached the gates of Ivory Castle asking to see me until one day it was her last time. I somehow knew when she walked away, looking once more over her shoulder, that it would be the last time I saw my best friend. My heart had ripped straight down the middle, knowing she'll always have one half of it.

What hurt the most wasn't that Violet gave up on me – no, I could never fault her for that. But the fact she gave up because she thought *I* had given up on *her*.

'It's for the best,' I had told myself, half believing my words as my cheeks became stained with tears.

I blink harshly, dipping my chin towards the window once more to rid myself of the memories.

Images of Violet readying herself for bed fill my thoughts, making my body react expectantly. She is beautiful, more beautiful everyday I see her. Those purple-blue eyes glow with so much fire – so much compassion for what she believes in – that I know I'm doomed the longer she stays with me, the longer we keep up this ruse.

An owl hoots nearby and I sigh. Escaping the confines of my bed, I walk to my window, leaning out to watch the streets beyond the castle walls. Sapphire City is still alive at this late hour, the memory of flying above it when I was a boy causing my stomach to flip.

Fral comes to mind, his caring face and warm embrace making my teeth grind together. If it weren't for him I wouldn't be in this situation, I could be a normal man with a normal life wanting to court a normal woman.

Without him, you would have never met her though.

I bite my lip. It's true. Without him my path would never have crossed Violet's.

I loathe you, I think into the cool breeze, the smell of the ocean potent, thinking of him and the flight we shared the night he stole me from my bedroom.

I hate what you did to me – and to her. I hate that my life was never the same and you got the easy way out.

I shake my head, my hands gripping the window sill with such strength I wonder why it's not bent beneath my grasp yet. The sound of crackling fills the air, small shots of lightning skittering across my bare arms. The magic I was born with calms me, the energy I use up makes me breathe easier as if the shield of magic will keep me safe – not only from physical threats but mental ones too.

I hate that you involved Alex, that you made my good, pure of heart brother hate himself because of your wrongdoings.

My hands shake as I send my thoughts into the night sky, the stars peering down on me with what I imagine is sympathy.

My older brother had killed the traitor – had slaughtered him to save *me*. I was the reason Alex had blood on his hands, that he had nightmares for weeks after. Back then I had thanked him, over and over again to remind him how I would be forever grateful for what did – for what trauma he ended by taking one life. His usual smile of comfort would be his answer, letting me know he'd do it all over again to make sure I was home safe. But later that night I would hear the muffled crying, the sobs that wracked his body that alerted me to the clear guilt and horror that possessed him.

I blame myself for his agony. That he felt the need to put me before his own mental wellbeing.

Self loathing fills me, my mind spinning 'But I hate myself the most,' I say out loud, letting the soft breeze take my words up to the inky black sky. 'I hate myself that she was there and I was *glad* she was – that in the darkest days of my life it was *her* hand I held and *her* smile I craved for.' I exhale a shaky breath, disgusted by my confession but used to this feeling.

A sudden urge to see her makes my throat bob, breathing suddenly difficult.

Without thinking I grab a jacket and some shoes and jump out the window, soaring towards Violet's home.

27

ELLIS

Uncertainty creeps in as I approach Violet's house. The windows are dark, the moon the only source of light. Taking a breath, I peer around to ensure no one is watching. Carefully, I glance into each window to try and decipher which rooms belong to who. Luckily, the first one I find has a slight gap in the curtains, revealing a bed where a blonde figure lays with streaks of black through her hair.

There is no way I can get inside without waking her, so I knock, allowing no time to second guess myself. Violet stirs and turns to face the window. For a long minute, she stares until realisation dawns on her features. She tumbles out of bed and staggers towards me in her nightgown. I swallow thickly.

'Ellis?' she whispers, widening the window. The evening breeze blows the hair from her face, her luscious body now more obvious than before with the nightgown exposing more skin. I itch with the need to touch her, but her words tether me to reality. 'What are you doing here?'

I motion toward her room. 'May I come in?'

Violet nods before peering at the street behind me. 'Yes, please do.'

I hover until I touch down by her door, away from her bed where Violet sits, her legs tucked beneath her. She's radiant even while half-asleep as she tilts her head in question.

'Do I want to know what you're doing here?' she asks, sleepy but amused.

The need to explain myself stops on my tongue. As always, I struggle to open up, not wishing to surrender the last remnant of my control. She probably knows exactly how I feel and why.

'I came to apologise.'

Violet jerks back. 'Excuse me?'

I lift my eyes to hers. 'Please don't make me repeat myself.'

She considers me before shaking her head. 'If you mean today in the barn, you have nothing to be sorry for. If you mean the behaviour you displayed on the field ...' She sighs before patting the bed beside her. 'It must have been bad given how you reacted. I've never seen you like that before.'

Violet's hand stays splayed out, and when she notices me studying her fingers, she pats again, and I reluctantly surrender to her request. I perch on the other side of the bed, far from Violet and her too-enticing nightgown.

'Castor is a bastard. He always tries to rile me up, but today, I snapped. I shouldn't have given him the satisfaction,' I grumble. Frustration floods through me as I recall his words.

'Your aunt and uncle were very worried,' Violet

murmurs, shuffling closer until she's sprawled along the width of the bed. Her bare legs spread out behind me as she rests on her elbow, her gaze peering into mine. The strap of her gown falls off her shoulder. I burn at the sight of it. I reach and move the strap back up. She smiles softly. 'I was worried, too,' she adds, and my chest tightens.

'You were?' I mutter, unable to comprehend why.

'Of course. Why do you sound like I shouldn't be?' Her brows crease as she rests a hand on my knee, seeming reluctant to confess the following, 'Regardless of whether this relationship is fake, I still care about you, Ellis. I always have.'

My heart races as I meet her purple-blue eyes. She's so sincere. My hand moves at its own accord, wrapping around her cheek before pausing at her neck. I cup the back of her head, my fingers tangled in her hair. A small exhale escapes her, and I lean forward, desperate to be nearer.

'I –' I hesitate, but something in her gaze quells my self-doubt – the voice in my head telling me to keep my feelings locked inside. 'I care about you, too, Violet,' I manage. She wets her lips. It is the most vulnerable thing I've said to anyone in the years since escaping the prison camp, and I think she realises the depth of my words, too, because she tries to cover the moment with humour as a blush covers her cheeks.

'You have a funny way of showing it,' she jests. I realise, not for the first time, I am responsible for her insecurity. Many times in the past, I've told Violet how much I cherished her and our friendship, despite having left her, despite having turned my back when she needed me most –

a sign to Violet that I didn't care anymore. That everything we shared was a lie.

'You don't believe me?' I ask, knowing there's a slither of truth in her answer.

Violet gently shakes her head. 'Not one bit.'

We sit, studying each other in silence, urging the other to make the first move. We're both stubborn, but I sense her need as much as mine. We are two familiar souls, reunited after all this time. We have been playing this game of pretend for far too long.

'Do you want me to show you, sweetheart?' I purr, leaning closer to brush my lips against hers. They are soft – so fucking soft. I want to bite and claim them as mine.

Hunger burns in her eyes as her gaze roams over me with need. If she doesn't answer soon, I'm afraid I'll rip her dress off and have my way with her.

'Yes. Please do,' she whispers, pressing her lips against mine.

28

VIOLET

The kiss is soft and tentative. I am certain I understood him, but just in case, I peck him on the lips. What if his mind isn't as indecent as mine? What if his insinuation isn't what I assume?

You made him promise not to kiss you.

I shove the thought away, relishing the feel of Ellis melting into me. He hums in approval and deepens the kiss, his hand cupping the back of my head. He pulls me closer and wraps himself around my body until I'm comfortable in his lap. Ellis trails his fingers over me with a calmness I'm unable to feel whenever he's nearby, and I shiver at his touch. Curling my arms around his neck, I tug him nearer as his tongue invades my mouth, the feeling making my nails dig into his skin.

'Ellis,' I murmur. I want more but I can't think straight.

He will leave you again.

I bite on his lip, and he hisses. 'Violet,' he rasps, his hands memorising my every curve. I pull him in tighter, the taste of him causing sparks of need to erupt from where his fingers caress me.

How will your heart break this time? In half or into small, shattered pieces?

I pause, and Ellis stiffens.

Neither of us move, and I fear I've lost the moment to my growing fears. But the prince doesn't release me, he holds me, as if only I can keep him anchored.

'Three questions,' I whisper.

Ellis exhales, the disappointment evident as his hold loosens until our faces are at a safer distance. He still cradles me across his lap, and I'm reminded of the times I suffered, when his arms felt warm and steady even then.

When I look up, the boy is no longer there but a man – a man I never had the chance to build something with. Ellis' gaze burns through me, his mouth swollen from our kisses, but he gives no indication of regret.

'Go on,' he says.

'What do you remember about that time?'

It's a broad question – one that could mean anything – but the prince knows exactly what I'm asking, as if reading my mind is still a power he possesses after a decade of being apart.

'I remember everything when it comes to you,' he says, his voice low and rough.

One question down. My heart hammers. I have so many things to ask him – so many things to catch up on in the ten years we've been strangers, but they boil down to a mere few questions I *need* the answer to.

'Why did you ask me to accompany you to all these

events? Why not someone else? Someone with wealth and status?'

'Because they aren't you.'

Scowling, I remove my arms from around his neck and shuffle until I'm perched beside him, our legs dangling off the bed. His warm skin is not as distracting from here. 'Vague answers aren't going to slide with me tonight,' I tell him, and he sighs.

'I thought as much.' Ellis' eyes trail over my attire, lingering on the straps of my nightgown as if wishing to do many other things than have this conversation. 'I asked you because you are the only person I trust besides Alex. And he wasn't allowed to be my date. Apparently it's *unseemly*.'

I scoff, taken off guard by his humour. 'That does seem inappropriate.'

He nods. 'I asked you because I knew you would agree to my proposal.' I lean back, slightly offended he thinks he can so easily sway me. Am I that predictable to him? 'It's not because I knew you would say yes without much persuasion,' he amends upon witnessing my expression. 'It's a matter of I knew you would agree, because no matter what you asked in exchange for helping me, I would say yes.'

My eyes lift to meet his, and to my surprise, he holds my stare, paying close attention to my reaction.

'What does that mean?'

He tilts his dark blonde head, as if silently reprimanding me for being so clueless. 'You could ask for the moon and stars, Violet, and I would make it happen.'

'How can you say that?' I fume, rising to my feet. I need more distance, unable to escape the sudden sensation of his presence creeping over my arms and legs. 'I haven't seen you in ten years, and then you say something like that ... What should that mean to me? Why would you think that way with someone you don't know anymore?'

Ellis shakes his head, his jaw tensed. 'No matter the years we've lost, Violet, I still consider you my best friend. I asked you, and only you, because you're the only person I feel comfortable with. You know what I've been through – you know the horrors I've seen and felt. No other woman, no other *person*, can understand me like you do. There was no debate as to who my first choice was.'

First choice.

I certainly don't feel like his first choice. I haven't for years.

I'm speechless, feeling numb yet light at his confession. While he says he trusts me implicitly, why hadn't he told me sooner? Why am I only hearing this *now*?

One question has swirled inside my head for years, and it tickles the tip of my tongue, urging me to finally ask and demand a truthful answer. I have a right to know.

'If I am your first choice, your best friend, and the person you would gift the moon and stars to ...' I trail off, biting my lip. 'Then why did you refuse to see me? Why did you tell the guards to turn me away when I came to visit you?

Ellis shakes his head again. 'I *did* want to see you.'

'Do you expect me to believe that?'

He breathes in deeply, then exhales his rising frustration. 'We are not having this discussion tonight.'

'Why not?' I step closer, silently urging him to be forthcoming. 'Why not, Ellis? You know the rules of this game. The truth and nothing but the truth, remember?'

'Not tonight,' he repeats, never wavering. He stares at me, willing me to back down.

'I didn't realise best friends kept so much hidden from each other.'

The words seem to strike true as he winces, reaching for my hand. He pulls me onto his lap and wraps his arm around my waist, clutching my side, the other hand strokes circles around my knee. The prince's hard expression contrasts to his gentle touch, handling me like I'm made of something precious.

'I *will* tell you.' He promises.

'Why not tonight?'

'Because you have only stopped looking at me like I'm a stranger,' he says, his fingers trailing over my skin with careful consideration. A shiver runs through me, and all the hairs on my body stand on end. His dark cobalt eyes claim mine, their earnest and softness capturing my breath. 'You're beginning to look at me like the Ellis you once knew, and I am too selfish to change that quite yet.' The words sting but stir my curiosity. 'I have made many promises to you, and I know they mean very little after all this time, but I *will* tell you everything. When the moment is right.'

With Ellis' expectant look, I know I can't fight him. He's asking for time and space to figure everything out, and given the years that have already passed, I can wait a little longer. I huff. Offering no response, I avert my gaze and try not to succumb to the tumultuous emotions threatening to make me cry.

Slowly, he lifts his hand and swipes at my face, where a traitorous tear falls down my cheek.

'Sweetheart, look at me.' I shake my head, refusing for him to see more than he already has. 'Please,' he coaxes. He grasps my chin and turns my head, stroking a thumb over my jaw. His dark remorseful eyes drink in my features like they are something he must never forget. 'I don't expect you to overlook my past choices, Violet. I only wish that, one day, you will forgive me, and I will work my hardest to earn that forgiveness.'

My eyes drop, hating the searing emotion in his gaze, their depths so deep I fear I might drown. This man is going to destroy me, or rather, he already has and will continue to forevermore.

29

VIOLET

My basket is empty as I stand outside Hazel's baking school. A small group of parents surround me, waiting for their children to finish class. The doors fling open, and young girls and boys spill out, glee plastered on their faces.

A prickling sensation trails down my spine, but I don't look anywhere except at the building, waiting for Hazel. Ellis is right behind me, and I hate that I know this without looking.

'Good morning,' Ellis murmurs in my ear.

After our discussion last night, Ellis had lingered long enough where I thought he might kiss me again. He hadn't. Instead, he climbed out of my window and soared into the night, leaving me restless and unable to sleep a wink. So, naturally, I am in a foul mood today.

'Hi.' I keep my back to him yet my grip tightens on the wicker basket.

'I hope that basket does not mean you are heading into Gwenore Forest alone.'

'I'm not,' I grumble. 'Hazel is coming with me.'

Ellis tuts and rests a hand on my waist. I inhale sharply. 'You know that's not what I meant when I told you not to go there alone.'

'Perhaps you should have been more specific, Your Highness,' I bite, enjoying the ensuing silence.

Hazel comes rushing out, and I bolt forward, breathing easier the moment the prince's hand releases me. I bend down to embrace my sister, who wraps her small arms around me.

'How was your day?' I ask, pushing her to arm's length. She is giddy with excitement and beams, her hazel eyes twinkling with mirth. She has been to bakery school a few times now, and the tales she shares with mother and I are always the same – full of excitement and pure joy.

'It was amazing, I was—' She freezes, peering behind me. It's as if her happiness has brightened even more, her expression disbelieving. 'You brought Prince Ellignton!'

'He came of his own accord,' I mutter, but this merely seems to heighten her elation. She releases me and walks straight for Ellis. Placing her hands firmly on her hips, she looks up at the tall figure without a hint of fear or uneasiness. 'Our shop was busy all week because of you.'

'Is that so?' says Ellis, he tucks his hands in his pockets and observes my sister.

Frowning, I stand and watch the exchange. *What is she talking about?*

'Yes. I saw you by the carriage.' Hazel nods merrily. 'I predict you were the one who made Prince Alexander come into our store and buy all our cakes. We were sold out for days afterwards. Mother was so pleased! We've had a constant stream of customers ever since.'

'I'm glad to hear it.'

'What are you talking about Hazel?' I pipe up, watching Ellis carefully but he gives nothing away, his hands sit casually in his pockets, his eyes glued to my sister.

'Prince Ellington came by the other day when you went to lunch with Maple. He got Prince Alexander to buy everything on our menu and gave away all our cakes to the locals – they loved it! Word about my tarts got around, and it was all they could talk about. That's why we've been so busy lately.'

It's true. Recently, our business has grown significantly, but I never realised it was because the heir had been seen at our premises. Hazel's tarts were the star of the show, constantly flying off the shelves that Luca has been having to restock them hourly.

'Is this true?' I ask the prince, who merely shrugs. His cobalt eyes bounce between Hazel and me, and a flicker of something warm unfurls in my chest. My perspective of the prince slowly shifts, as it seems to in every recent moment I spend with the royal.

You could ask for the moon and stars, Violet, and I would make it happen.

I shiver. He appears to sense something in me, and the edge of his mouth tugs upwards. Ellis motions for us to walk. 'Shall we?'

'He's coming foraging with us?' wonders Hazel. Her eyes widen so much I fear they'll pop out of their sockets.

I give him a questioning look. 'Are you?'

'I am.' He nods. 'If that is alright with you, Hazel.'

My sister seems pleased to have been asked, and I can't help but appreciate the way he includes her. She nods.

When we arrive in Gwenore Forest, Hazel takes the basket from me. Today, we are searching for elf blooms – a special flower that grows only under moonlight yet must be picked in daylight. Without a certain skill to smell them out, they are near-impossible to find.

'I choose a fox today,' Hazel says to me, and I nod. Before Ellis can ask what we're talking about, I bring my shadows forth and strip my clothes in the cover of the darkness. My sister loves my shadows, which is one of many things I love about her. She has never feared my darkness – the magic stolen and given to me against my will. If anything, she urges me to use it.

I shift into my new form as the fading shadows reveal the sleek body and fluffy tail of a black fox. Hazel claps, impressed with my shifting, then gathers my clothes and dumps them into the basket.

'What form did you ask Violet to change into last time you went hunting together?' Ellis asks my sister.

She grins. 'A dragonfly, but that didn't last very long. They don't have the capabilities to sniff out elf blooms.'

'Elf blooms? Is that what we're searching for?'

As Ellis silently gestures for the basket, Hazel smiles, allowing the prince to take it. 'Yes. We use their petals in our tarts for one of the flavours. I'm experimenting with medicinal pastries, don't you think that would be brilliant? Our neighbour Mrs Brine said she'd help with ingredients – she's our local healer,' explains Hazel upon noting the prince's furrowed brows.

'I think you're onto something there,' he agrees, flashing me an impressed glance.

We set off. Hazel and Ellis stride behind me as I sniff through the woodland. As always, Gwenore does not harm us when we step off the path, but from the way Ellis holds himself – stiff and alert – he does not know that I, or anyone accompanying me, does not suffer her usual wrath.

Has he not ventured off the paths? Has he always stayed on the tracks?

'Can I ask you some questions? We're going to be together for a while so we may as well get to know one another,' asks Hazel pleasantly. When the royal nods, she ploughs ahead, giving him no chance to ask questions but only answer them.

'What is your favourite food?'

Mermaid cakes, I think.

'Mermaid cakes,' answers Ellis.

'What is your favourite room in the castle?'

The kitchen?

'The cook's kitchen.'

'What is your favourite colour?'

Blue?

'Purple-blue,' Ellis answers without hesitation.

I peer back questioningly, and he meets my eyes. The edge of his lip twitches before he peers back at my sister. My heart stutters.

'Favourite memory?'

'Meeting your sister.'

I snort, though it sounds more like a sneeze from the fox's nose. Ellis' gaze never wavers from Hazel.

'Do you have dreams?'

To anyone else, this may seem like a strange question, but my sister always tells me about her dreamscape and what it means for her future. My sister, unlike me, was never able to shapeshift. Like my mother, she can jump into people's dreams and see their unconscious thoughts whilst sleeping. When I had returned home from prison camp, I had made them both promise never to visit my dreamscape, fearful of what they might find.

Ellis shakes his head. 'If I do dream, I never remember them when I wake up. I have more nightmares than anything.'

'Like Violet,' Hazel hums.

'I'm sure we have similar nightmares,' Ellis agrees.

We walk deeper into the woods, where the birds chirp. The soft breeze catches Ellis' dark blonde hair, and when we share a look, there's something in his gaze, silently telling me something I cannot decipher.

'If you could shift into any animal, like Vi, what would it be?'

He ponders this for a moment, it's the only question he's had to consider. Lips pursed, Hazel becomes impatient. 'I would turn into a parrot, they can fly *and* they're so colourful.'

'I can fly.'

'You can?' gasps Hazel, covering her heart. She looks up to the sky and points. 'Can you fly me up to the tallest branch of this tree?'

Ellis glances my way for permission, and I follow my sister's gaze upward, trying to decipher how far up the tallest branch is. I flash him a warning look, he wouldn't want to know the animal I'd turn into if Hazel is injured in any way. He nods in understanding.

'Sure.' He crouches and extends his arms to her.

With excitement, she practically jumps into his hold, coiling her hands around his neck. He leaves the basket behind, and I stand guard as I watch them whoosh into the air, disappearing into the blanket of green and orange leaves. With my animal hearing, I can vaguely detect their voices. I presume they have chosen a branch to rest on as Hazel gushes about the view. Rustling follows, and I picture her touching all the leaves in awe.

'Do you love your magic?'

'Sometimes,' Ellis offers.

'Was this a power Fral gave you?' asks Hazel. Her tone shifts to one she uses when she's unsure how her question will be received. I've heard it too many times to count.

'Yes it was,' he murmurs. 'He, too, had the power to fly.'

'I suppose when you use it, it reminds you of him and everything he did to you.'

Ellis is silent, and my heart twists. I dread to think of how it must feel to have the same power as the man who captured and abused us. I sigh. Is this why he keeps everyone at arm's length? Does he think he's like Fral?

'I'm sorry I brought it up,' continues Hazel, though she seems unperturbed by his lack of response. 'I know Violet finds solace when she talks to others about her past but I suppose that's not the case for everyone.'

'Violet is very lucky to have your support – your mother's, too.'

Hazel hums. 'Was your family supportive? When you went back home, I mean?'

It's quiet for a beat before the prince answers. 'They did their best, but no, we did not speak openly about my ordeal. They were grieving as much as I was, so we kept our thoughts and feelings mostly to ourselves.'

'It doesn't sound healthy to keep those types of emotions bottled up,' Hazel chides, sounding much like me when we spoke about Ellis no longer seeing a doctor. 'You were a child, and every child needs parental figures.'

He hums. 'Unfortunately, my parents weren't here to witness it. Probably for the best, too. I don't think my mother would have coped seeing me in such a state.'

'They were lost at sea, weren't they?' she asks, breaking me from my trance. I bark, loud enough to echo through the treetops to tell Hazel enough is enough. She goes silent upon hearing my warning. 'I'm sorry, Your Highness. Violet always says I ask too many questions.'

'There is nothing wrong with being curious, Hazel. Your sister is merely protective of you, and once of me. She was the reason I made it out of that camp alive.'

'She was?'

My heart thumps painfully in my chest. I've never heard Ellis be so open with anyone or so softly spoken. While he's always come across as calm, I've come to slowly realise he always has a shield up to keep people out.

'She never let me give up hope. She always told me we would escape, and, after a while, I believed her. She never lied to me before, and that only proved it.'

Oh, Ellis.

I tune out, I'm unable to listen any longer to their conversation. I focus on a buzzing fly and follow it until the pair come floating back down. My sister beams when her feet touch the ground.

'That was amazing, Your Highness. Thank you!'

'You're very welcome.' And he sounds like he means it. 'Shall we continue our search?'

And with that, the three of us walk through the trees of Gwenore Forest. My eyes study the prince to see if I can find a sliver of falsehood – if his words are merely fabrications to please my sister or if they're something he truly believes.

You could ask for the moon and stars, Violet, and I would make it happen.

Perhaps he wasn't lying after all.

30

ELLIS

For weeks, Violet and I attended different events alongside Alex – cooking meals for those in the homeless shelter, walking dogs at the adoption centre, and visiting the House of Bane to maintain relationships with the Elder. In exchange, I went berry-picking with Violet and her sister, helped advertise the Danes Bakery by plastering large signs across the city, and even managed to persuade Alex to visit Violet's home a few more times to bring more customers to their shop.

What really helped the bakery shoot into stardom was Hazel's special flavoured tarts. The city *raved* about them. The wealthy families that attended my brother's birthday had a multitude of orders made for their own parties and events, and thus, word spread of their unique flavours, inviting people to try them to see what the fuss was about.

When I arrive at Danes Bakery, the place is full. Violet's mother is out front rapidly taking orders while I assume Luca, Hazel, and Violet are out back. I head for the counter and wave to Maura, who waves back, permitting me to go behind the workbench and duck into the passageway. I head for the archway, where a waft of pleasant smells hit me. As predicted, the trio are here, working hard as they focus solely on creating Hazel's tarts.

I shuffle past Luca, who barely notices me until his head flings up with surprise. 'What are you doing here?'

I ignore him and sidle up beside Violet. She blows a strand of hair from her sweaty face.

'How can I help?' I ask, her purple-blue eyes look up and meet mine. She frowns.

'What are you doing here?' she echoes while Luca watches us.

'I came to help,' I say, motioning to the kitchen. 'What can I do?'

'You can fill the tart shells with flavouring,' Hazel pipes up, pointing to a counter laden with several bowls of different coloured, sweet-smelling concoctions. She smiles warmly as I move alongside her to the shared counter where the magic happens.

I nod and get to work, spooning ten tarts per flavouring to ensure each baking tray has a good variety. When a tray is done, I put them in the oven, where Luca is then in charge of taking them out.

I stand by Hazel, scooping different shades of red, green, blue, and yellow flavouring for what feels like hours. My fingers cramp from holding a spoon for so long, and when Maura finally comes out back to tell us the shop is due to close, I refrain from sighing with relief. I drop the spoon when the last order is made, making it clatter loudly on the counter.

'Well done everyone! Today was a marvellous day,' says

Violet's mother, waving farewell to Luca who begins packing for home. Before heading out, he waves goodbye to both sisters, but not before giving me a hard look.

'Thanks for your help,' Violet murmurs, patting my back. The touch is nice, and for once, it's something she initiates without me having to tease her. 'It seems your ploy with Alexander has been immensely helpful.' We share a glance, and from the look in her eyes, I know she is grateful for my efforts and appreciates me keeping my side of the bargain.

'I'm glad Hazel's tarts are beginning to be appreciated for the mastery they are,' I say, winking at the young girl.

'So they should be,' answers Hazel. She yawns loudly, and I peer outside the window to find it's dark outside. I didn't intend to stay so long, it was bright when I had arrived. My brother is probably wondering where I've gotten to. 'I'm heading to bed. Goodnight.'

'Night, kid,' Violet chimes, watching her walk out. She waits until Hazel is upstairs before facing me. 'Do you want to stay for a hot drink? Or do you need to get home?'

'I can stay,' I muse, glancing around the kitchen. 'I'll make us some hot cocoa while you get ready for bed. I'll meet you upstairs.' Something changes in her gaze, and a moment of self-doubt creeps in. 'Or you can meet me back down here when you are done?'

'No, my bedroom is fine.' With that, she leaves, stealing a glance over her shoulder at me. Something dark and daring lines her features before she disappears upstairs.

I close my eyes and sense her soul, her violet orb floats upstairs, where she runs herself a bath. It's comforting to watch her movements and study her night-time routine.

When I eventually go upstairs, I puzzle out which one is hers, given that the last time I entered was through a window. When I spot a door that's open just a crack, I peer inside and see a familiar bed. Pushing through with two steaming cups of hot cocoa, I stop in my tracks, finding Violet on her bed with wet hair. This isn't what grabs my attention, though. It's the damp stains where her wet hair flows down her shoulders and over her breasts, her nipples visible from beneath her emerald nightgown.

Breathe, Ellis.

My hands do not shake but I notice they slowly turn black. Violet doesn't seem bothered about the colour changing, she smiles, patting the spot beside her like she did the last time I visited her room.

'Hmm. They look delicious. Come, sit.'

31

VIOLET

Ellis looks dishevelled from his day of working at the bakery. His usually neat hair is messy, and hunger leaks through his calm and calculating expression upon noticing my night attire.

I cross a bare leg over the other, and his cobalt eyes carefully follow my movements.

'Will you be standing there all night?' I ask, patting the bed again. 'Or can I have my drink?'

Ellis silently comes to sit beside me and we silently sip at our beverages. The warm chocolate coats my tongue, and I hum in pleasure. Ellis shuffles, he seems stiff, like he's unsure about something.

'Why do you look uncomfortable? Do you want me to cover up?' I motion to my attire, and only now do I realise this is a lot of skin to be showing a member of the royal family.

'No,' Ellis murmurs, his gaze dropping to my damp locks.

I stand and put my drink down on a side table, twirling my wet hair above my head and holding it in place while looking for something to secure it with. In a flash, Ellis' large hands grab my waist, pulling me towards him. His drink is gone, his features ravenous.

'Why do you torture me like this?' He eyes the patches of wetness that have my gown clinging to my skin and makes my nipples peak. I inhale sharply at the look he is giving me, my desire longing for him to touch me in other places. 'It makes me want to rip it off.'

I swallow. Part of me wants to deny the prince and push him away. But the other part – the part where his warm grip sends tingles through me – wonders how it would feel for him to make true on his word.

'Why don't you then?' I whisper.

He jerks back, surprised. 'The last time you backed away.'

'I panicked.' I shrug, arms still above my head. I release my hair, allowing it to fall down my back. My hands hover, and I'm unsure where to put them. When Ellis moves them to rest upon his shoulders, I say quietly, 'I second guessed myself.'

The prince pulls me close, causing me to straddle his lap, and from his heated expression, I know he feels the warmth between my legs, my need for him evident. He wraps his warm muscular arms around my hips and brings me close, leaning his head against my chest in a brief embrace. The prince can probably hear my thundering heart, but he doesn't comment. He gently strokes the column of my spine as he peers up at me.

'Whatever you want from me, you can have it. You don't need to doubt yourself.' His voice is low and hoarse, as if he's not used it in years, but from the way his cobalt eyes now roam lower – over my breasts, my arms, my legs, my face – I know he's trying to keep himself in control of his emotions. 'What do you want, Violet?'

I yearn to grab him, remembering the memory of him sitting in the hay-filled stall, those onyx eyes of his pleading for help while dark veins crawled across his skin. Yet the trauma of our past is just that – the past. He had spoken to Hazel so candidly about our childhood, what he thought of me, and I have no doubt now he meant every word. Here sits my old friend, the best person I knew and loved.

'From you, I want everything,' I answer honestly.

Seeing Ellis soften, I realise we can conquer our darkest parts together, shining a light on the blackest corners of our souls. Together, we can learn they aren't so scary after all, as long as we have each other.

I run my fingers through his dishevelled hair as the moonlight filtering through the window lights up his hand-some face. I feel nervous, but I want Ellis to know I'll take whatever he's ready to offer me without complaint. I was a fool for him once, and I am again. But I don't care now, somehow, having him this close makes it worth it. Worth every day I felt the pain of his absence.

'What do *you* want?' I ask him.

He smiles a rare smile, and my heart stops at the sight of it. Ellis looks up and closes the distance, stopping just shy of kissing me. His body is hard and steady against mine, I hold onto his broad shoulders as his hand wanders over my arms, then tickles up my ribs. He stares at my gown and growls, peering deep into my eyes. 'I want all of you, Violet. I want your trust, your friendship, your touch, and your attention. I want your laugh and smiles, your anger, your frustration – I want it all. But what I need right now in this very moment, is *this* to be gone.' He pinches the strap of my nightgown between his fingers and scowls like it causes him physical pain.

'Then take it off,' I mutter, as if the answer is obvious.

'So snarky, Miss Danes. Do you know you are talking to a *prince*?' He teases, the glint of mischief in his eyes suiting him.

I smirk. 'I see no crown.'

Ellis' movements are quick as he pulls down my dress strap, revealing my breast. His mouth moves without hesitation, and his sudden sucking and biting has me struggling for air.

'Talking to a royal in such a manner can lead to punishment,' Ellis murmurs, trailing his tongue along my chest toward my other breast. 'And oh, do I have some plans for you, Violet.'

I hum. 'I think I'm going to like this.'

He stops and looks me dead in the eyes. 'Yes, you will.'

He rolls us over, flipping me so my hands and knees are upon the bed. He pulls my nightgown down, and before I can manoeuvre my body, he rips off the garment and tosses it across the room before removing my underwear, too. His body is above me, and he presses his chest against my bare back. I push my arse against him, and he licks the column of my back in answer, tasting my scarred skin like he did when licking the alcohol off my face all those weeks ago.

'Keep this up, and I'll make you suffer more,' he

murmurs, biting my earlobe. A shiver rushes down my spine as he palms my needy arse.

'Don't threaten me with a good time, Your Highness.'

His strong hand snakes across my front to play with my breasts and he pulls me up so we're both kneeling. 'I thought I wanted you to bend over, but I want to use both my hands,' he explains, and the thought of it makes me starve for more of his caresses.

Whilst playing with my nipple and twisting it to the point of pain, I bite my lip to stop from crying out. My family is on the other side of the house, and if I'm too loud, they might come running in – it wouldn't be the first time.

The prince's other hand moves slowly, his fingers slow and careful as they run down my stomach. My breathing hitches. Ellis pauses just before reaching between my thighs. 'Are you sure you want this, Violet?'

I nod eagerly, wanting nothing more than to feel him – to *have* him – even for a moment.

'Use your words, sweetheart.' His voice tickles my neck and I exhale a shaky breath.

'Yes, Ellis. I want you,' I say with gritted teeth, trying to keep my cool. *'Right now.'* I add for good measure.

He chuckles, tantalisingly slow as he explores my wetness, his moan of approval making pleasure strum through me. 'What a good girl. Already soaking for me.'

The hand playing with my breast flicks my nipple until they pebble, and with one hand between my legs and the other on my chest, I can't seem to decide which feels better.

'Oh,' I murmur. I throw my head back against his shoulder, closing my eyes with satisfaction. Reaching behind me,

I grip his legs. 'That feels—' He dips his finger inside me, thrusting in and out at a delicious pace. I whimper. '—so good.' I rasp.

He quickens his fingers and adds another as I sink further onto him, riding his hand, becoming hopelessly desperate as the delicious heat I feel builds inside me. When our breathing becomes loud and haggard, I know I am near the edge.

'Ellis, let me—' I move to touch him. I want to throw his clothes away and pleasure him so we can climax together, but his hold on me is like stone. Immovable and unyielding.

'No,' he answers, licking my neck as his moonlit hand speeds up. 'Let me see you come onto my hand, Violet. I want to see how much you enjoy this – enjoy *me*.'

I have no brain space to argue. I also want to come on his fucking incredible hand like the good girl he claims I am, but I want him to share my pleasure and experience this with me.

'I want to do things to you, too.' I groan.

'Come for me, Violet,' he demands, and the last part of my resolve finally crumbles. My climax is like an inferno of flames, forceful and intoxicating. He pounds his fingers into me as I ride the feeling, gripping on him like a vice as I come down from my high. Nothing but our breathing fills the silent space.

He removes his fingers and lifts them, I think he'll wipe them off, but instead, they move past my shoulder, up towards his face and I watch as he tastes them. Meeting my eyes, he sucks them one by one.

Mother of pearl.

'You taste incredible,' he murmurs before kissing my temple.

I'm speechless upon seeing him taste me so openly without a hint of ... I'm not sure. Awkwardness? Uncertainty?

'Your turn,' I breathe, reaching for his trousers. His hand firmly stops me.

'No. Not tonight.'

My eyes narrow, and I tilt my head, unsure. 'You have a habit of saying that.' He looks determined not to back down, so I sigh. 'Why not?'

'Because I don't want to,' he says, slowly detangling from me. His fingers leave a trail of cold shivers across my skin as he retrieves my nightgown, replacing the straps as he carefully dresses me once more.

'You don't want to, or you are afraid to?' I question without bite. 'Or am I not ...' I trail off, hesitating.

'You are breathtaking,' he says quickly, manoeuvring, so we kneel face to face. His hands roam over my arms before gripping my hands. 'I look at you and sometimes I wonder how I'm able to withstand you looking at me without shattering on the spot.'

I dip my chin, looking up at the prince from below my lashes. 'Really?'

He lowers his lip to my shoulder and tenderly kisses the skin, like I'm precious and deserve the utmost care. His mouth trails along my neck to the back of my ear, and my breath comes out shaky.

'Why do you think I avert my gaze so often in your presence? I am not a man who backs down easily, but with you ... I am a fool for *you*, Violet Danes.'

'Then why don't you want more?' I ask uncertainly.

'Because we are too close to your family, and if I lose control like I did in the barn, I will never forgive myself. You are tempting me in that bloody nightgown, but I cannot afford to make any more mistakes. Not with you. *Never* with you.'

Ellis leans back and peers deep into my eyes, urging me to understand. And I do. He is still afraid of the darkness lingering within, he has his coping mechanisms, and this is one of them.

'I understand, but I'm a little disappointed,' I admit, glancing away, but he doesn't allow me to. Ellis grabs my chin and kisses the corner of my mouth. 'If you want me so badly, sweetheart, I'm sure I can arrange something.'

I roll my eyes, and his arrogance makes me smile before I can stop it. 'You think very highly of yourself.'

'I think you do, too, with how well your body takes me.'

'Oh, don't—' I protest, covering my burning face with my hands. Ellis is quick to whip them away, tangling them into his silken hair instead.

'Don't hide from me. I want to see you flush with pleasure and burn with anger. I want all your emotions and I want them all to be with *me*. Do you understand?'

I bite my lip. 'Do you mean—'

'I want to end our arrangement,' he says, and my heart gallops. 'Since the moment I met you, Violet, you have been *mine*. This ruse was just that – an excuse to get closer.'

My heart blooms with relief and hope for the future. How long have I waited to hear those words? How long have I dreamed of such declarations from Ellis, but to no avail?

'I am yours as long as you are mine,' I retort, and his lips tip upwards.

'I have always been yours, sweetheart. Since the day you slept by my side that first night, I was yours. It was written in the stars, and I have been enchanted by you ever since.'

32

VIOLET

When a carriage arrives at the bakery the following day, Hazel is beside me, seeming as excited as I feel. Ellis jumps out of the carriage and waves at the coachman before approaching our shop. He bows to my little sister, who grins like a child buzzing with sugar-induced energy.

'Hazel. It's lovely to see you again,' greets Ellis, taking her hand and kissing her knuckles.

Hazel bows in her flour-covered apron, but she doesn't seem to care. 'Hello, Your Highness.'

The prince smiles, then peers up at me, taking my hand. His hold lingers as he takes his time to drink me in with his dark cobalt eyes.

'Violet.' He kisses my knuckles and shivers race up my arm.

I want to see you flush with pleasure and burn with anger. I want all your emotions and I want them all to be with me.

His words echo in my mind, and I beam, alight with

happiness. In return, his eyes twinkle, and I have no doubt I've inflated his ego.

'Ellis,' I say. 'We should go. We don't want to be late.'

Ellis nods and returns to his full height, looming over Hazel and I. Escorting me to the horse-drawn carriage, he motions for me to step inside, and I frown at a long, dark-coloured bag flung over one of the seats. The prince follows, sitting beside the mysterious item.

'What is that?' I ask as the coachman closes the door and sets the horses at a steady pace.

Ellis glances at it. 'Oh, that.' He takes me in from head to toe as I arrange myself opposite him. 'I have something for you to change into.'

He hands over the bag and I peer inside. A beautiful gown is tucked inside, the material more extravagant than anything I have ever owned.

'I assumed my own choice of attire would be sufficient?' I frown, motioning to my pale-yellow dress. When I put it on, I thought it looked sweet. Maple had lent it to me – again borrowed from her work.

'You look ravishing.' Ellis peers outside the window, his attention elsewhere. His words fray every one of my nerves. 'But I want us to match.'

Ellis is dressed in a waistcoat of dark blue with fine silver thread, it reminds me of the night sky, adorned with glittering stars. I take in the silky midnight blue dress, noting it has little material at the top. I hum, unconvinced. 'I'm not sure I'll be covered in this. Did you pick this out yourself?'

'Of course,' he answers, taking it from me. He is impatient as he unravels it, motioning for me to strip. 'I'll help you get into it.'

'Right now?' I scowl.

'Yes, right now. We will be there soon.'

Our eyes meet and his mouth tilts, as if doing his best not to grin. I laugh, unable to contain it. *This* is why he didn't send the dress prior.

'You just want to see me naked again, don't you?'

He tilts his head innocently. 'I am a *gentleman*.'

'That's not an answer.'

He shrugs. 'I am a gentleman, but that doesn't mean I won't make excuses to see you nude as often as possible.'

'Fine.' I lean back and fiddle with my current attire, which slips away with the help of the prince, who leaves me sitting in my underwear. His eyes roam over my every curve and bump as he licks his lips without a hint of shame. I burn for him and I itch to reach forward and take advantage of his sitting state.

'Come here,' he murmurs, patting his lap. I do as I'm told, feeling him already hard beneath me. My grin widens. As if sensing my delight, he says, 'No matter what you wear, you will always have this effect on me.'

I hum and allow him to slip the dark blue dress on me. My feet slide into the gap as he lifts it over my hips, his touch licking up my legs and hips before trailing across my ribs. I flush when his fingers pull the single strap of the dress over my shoulder and he plants a kiss on my bare skin. His knuckles trail up my back slowly before rising to massage the back of my head.

'I chose this dress because it matches me perfectly. If people see us together, they'll know you're mine. Make sure you remind them of that when they step into your personal space because I won't hesitate to make a scene.' A small tremor runs through my body which makes him chuckle. 'You like the thought of me fighting over you, sweetheart?'

I nod. 'Strangely, yes. Are you usually this possessive with your women?' I turn in his lap to face him, resting an arm around his shoulders as he leans back in the seat.

'Women? Who said there was ever anybody else?' He raises a brow and relaxes his hand on my thigh. Swiping away the material covering my skin, he is so close to the apex of my thighs that I'm afraid he'll feel the warmth radiating from me. I shuffle away. I don't want him to know the effects his presence has on me. 'Are you moving away from my touch, Violet?' Amusement tints his words.

'No,' I grumble.

He tightens his grip, lifting his fingers ever so slowly to the area between my legs. I refrain from squirming, I can't be aroused before a royal event. I need to look presentable, not lustful and wild beside Ellis, who always looks immaculate and frustratingly handsome.

'Are you trying to hide your arousal from me?' He taunts.

I breathe deeply at the rasp in his voice. I need to calm down – and fast. I shake my head, fixing my eyes on the passing scenes outside.

'Nope.'

'May I see for myself?' he questions, moving before receiving an answer.

I grab his hand to halt his movements. 'You know I want this, but I cannot step out of this carriage with desire in my eyes. Not only will it seem inappropriate, as you are a *prince*, but the king and queen will not be impressed, either. I don't want to disappoint anyone, especially not your family.'

Never did I think I'd ever see Ellis sulk, but his pout at being scolded is almost comical. Not surprising, really, he probably gets everything he wants as a royal.

'Not even a little?' He dips me and my hair tumbles across the seat as Ellis leans in for a kiss. I splay my fingers across his mouth to push his lips away, but he bites down. Hard. I hiss and escape from his lap, sitting back on the opposite side of the carriage.

'No, Your Highness. Behave yourself.'

'Just one kiss,' he presses, his gaze lingering on my mouth. *'Please.'*

I huff and eye the window before nodding. When he's polite like that, I can't seem to find the will to deny him. 'Fine, but make it quick.'

In seconds, he's on his knees, lifting my skirts, and moving aside my underwear.

'Ellis,' I seethe. 'I said one kiss. What are you doing?'

'You didn't clarify which lips I was allowed to kiss.' He smirks, and as his tongue swirls once, something is ignited within me. A soft zap of his lightning bursts through me, and I arch my back, my gasp of surprise echoing through the cab.

'Oh, my—' I grit my teeth, digging my fingers into the seat. Before I can ask for more, the prince replaces my skirt and returns to his seat, peering out the window as if nothing happened. 'Ellis,' I whisper, scorching with need. 'You can't just ...' I'm wide-eyed from the lingering effects of his magic still coursing through my limbs.

'You said only *one* kiss, Violet.' He looks me up and down, and I want to claw at his smug expression. 'Plus, we're here.'

I simmer with anger, my fury slowly replacing my ebbing lust.

He smiles upon noting my expression, and a tinge of pleasure flickers in his hungry gaze. 'Shouldn't have denied me, sweetheart. You could have been finished by now.'

Ellis exits the carriage, not bothering to wait for the coachman. Glancing back, he offers his hand. I tentatively take it, knowing I can't sulk with the spectators waiting outside as we exit the carriage.

'You've started it now,' I tell him, straightening and willing my features into neutrality. I push away the desire to grab him and imagine a wall of ice forming before me.

'Started what?' He asks, keeping my hand in his. His grip is like iron.

'A night of torture.' I smile deviously, as we walk into the event.

33

THE PAST

Four days after losing Violet, I wake up to find myself on the cold table. Fral stares at me with hope glimmering in his eyes, John seeming almost as optimistic behind him.

'How are you feeling?' Fral asks.

I shake my head, my eyes fluttering. What happened? Where is everyone?

'What?' I blurt. I try but fail to move my arms and glance down to find I'm secured to the metal counter, my arms, legs, and torso clamped down.

'I think it worked,' muses Fral, glancing back at John.

'Ellis, how do you feel about having Violet back with you?' asks John, looking suspiciously chipper. I don't answer. Somehow, I know it's a trick. She's no longer my Violet, they would never let her out their sights. She is too precious – too powerful of a weapon to risk.

I tense my jaw and John shrugs, unperturbed by my lack of response. 'Nevermind. I'll keep her in my tent if you don't want her.'

My *tent*.

It echoes in my skull and bounces off the walls. Is Violet really residing with him? The guard who watches her like she's a prize. Fury boils in my veins and thoughts fill my head of John touching her while she's under Fral's control, looming over her body on the cold metal table.

A darkness I've never felt before lingers in the corners of my vision.

What is that?

Sensing my rising anger, the men smile.

'It worked,' *Fral confirms, satisfied.* 'The dark magic has clung to his soul.'

John laughs and the sound feels strange — something so joyous in a place like this doesn't make sense.

'Dark magic?' *I ask, narrowing my eyes.*

'When a person's power is transferred from one body to another,' *Fral explains, patting my hand.* 'There must be dark magic involved for it to work successfully. Now you possess a new power, you will always have dark magic in your veins to keep you alive. The human body can only take so much.'

As if on cue, something slithers inside me and curls in the darkest corners of my mind. I tremble, wondering what it is and why it watches me so closely. Why do I feel like it's living?

'Get rid of it,' *I plead.*

'No. You will learn to live with it. That is the only way you can use your new power.'

I pause. 'Which is?'

Fral grins, his white teeth on show. 'To fly like me.'

Dread fills me, and the thing inside me nods with approval. To fly? Why that gift, and why me?

'I wanted you and I to share this one thing. One day, you'll come to realise I was right and this—' He motions to the surrounding tent. '—is necessary. I hope you'll take over from me when I no longer can. You and I are similar in so many ways, and it seems right to hand my legacy to you.' Horror strikes me with its claws and slices through my panic with something so sharp I'm suddenly breathless. 'Unlike your brother, you have always been clever enough to keep an open mind. You do not judge others, you merely listen and absorb the information – a trait all leaders should have.'

Like you? I want to spit, but I know the insult will roll off him like water.

'I feel so honoured,' I mutter.

'You jest, but wait and see. It will all fall into place.' Fral motions to John with a cocked finger. 'Bring it over.'

The gold collar comes into view, and I jerk away, knowing what's coming. Violet springs to mind, and I think of how she must have felt when it was put on her. Like a dog being leashed.

'I am so proud of you, Ellis,' murmurs Fral, taking no time to secure the gold metal around my throat as I try to fight him off. 'You pulled through as I knew you would. You have a strong soul. You and I will do many great things together.'

'If only I could say the same back,' I say. Any hope I had finally drains from me. I had dreamed of escaping this hell hole – of Fral being discovered and taken away like the criminal he is, but it's a fool's hope. A click resounds in my ear as the collar fits into place. 'You are a disgrace, and I hope the Gods punish you accordingly.'

A slash of heat floods my face as Fral slaps me hard across the cheek.

'Ellis,' he says. His hand on my arm seems to shoot currents of magic through me, and I straighten, my mind fuzzy. I faintly hear the restraints release from my body. 'Kill the first guard you come across outside with your lightning.'

My arms and legs move of their own accord as I escape the metal table. Somehow, my body knows where it's going from just one simple command. As I walk into the open space of the prison camp, I unfurl my fingers as a bright ball of light grows within my palm. I'm screaming, begging my body not to move – not to do anything Fral says – but it carries on, deaf to my pleas.

My eyes find a female guard kneeling over a little girl who cries, asking for food. I extend my hand, and a blinding bolt of lightning shoots through the guard's skull. The shock on her face is permanently embedded in my memory as my strike kills her instantly. The young girl screams, shuffling away from the fallen body.

My heart sinks, but my face shows no sign of remorse. I am a weapon and soldier. I am the slayer Fral has created me to be, and I have no control, no help, and no choice over my actions.

I am all alone.

'Well done, Ellis,' Fral praises.

34

ELLIS

They hold the charity event at the Rhinelanders' residence. The Rhinelanders are a wealthy family with an extraordinarily luxurious home and who are known for being over the top. The event is hosted in their expansive garden, where a small waterfall resides to the left. The crystal clear water glows a soft blue with what I assume is magic. The temperature is pleasant, and the darkening sky brings a cosy ambience as numerous lines of different coloured lanterns hang above us.

Tonight, the aim is to raise money for several families after a ship sank not long ago and killed nearly twenty men. This charity is close to my heart – and Alex's. After the ocean took our parents, we know the importance of looking after the families left behind, especially those who've lost their main source of income.

What I didn't realise is that tonight involves an auction. Alex vaguely mentioned having sorted out something we could offer for tonight's event and to expect that whatever the Rhinelanders and other wealthy guests have arranged will bring in large amounts of money.

'This place is grand,' Violet says, searching the whole garden in awe. Her mouth hangs open in obvious amazement, and I have the urge to slip my tongue in, so she isn't so distracted. I roll my eyes. How has Violet turned me so bloody needy?

'Close your mouth, sweetheart,' I murmur into her ear.

'Or what?' Violet bites, annoyed at my lack of follow through in the carriage.

'I'll occupy it for you.'

She snorts. 'You had your chance. You won't be getting another tonight. You're on my blacklist now.'

'We'll see about that,' I whisper, releasing her hand and resting it on her backside. I squeeze firmly, and I regret the decision almost immediately as my cock twitches. Suddenly, I want to pick her up and carry her back into the privacy of our carriage. But I don't back down. Violet's fiery look makes my lips twitch. Oh, she is *furious*.

A hand clamps on my shoulder, and I turn to find Alex, beaming. He's immaculately dressed, his blonde hair is combed, and he looks ready for business, which tonight, I suppose he is.

'Good evening,' he greets before finding Violet's hand and kissing it politely. 'Nice to see you again, Violet. How have you been?'

'Fine, thank you. And you?' She looks at him expectantly but my brother frowns.

'Oh, I know that look.' He waggles a finger at my girl. 'What has Ellis done to annoy you?'

I frown. 'Who said I've done something?'

He smiles. 'Because it's the same look Aunt Melody has whenever you anger her.'

I glance at Violet, whose eyes still glimmer with lingering fury, she presses her lips together in an attempt to look normal. I refrain from grimacing, and Alex laughs.

'Whatever it is, Violet, milk it for all its worth. I think Ellis would grovel to you, unlike our queen.' He winks, then glances towards the drinks table as someone calls out to him. 'I better go, but I want a dance tonight.' He directs his words at my very beautiful date.

She nods, smiling sweetly at him. 'Of course. I'll grab you when you're free.'

The gesture irks me, but I don't say anything. I know she's doing it on purpose. I squeeze her arse again and lean into her ear. 'Are you going to make me suffer all night long?'

She nods. 'That's the plan.'

I bite her lobe, and she growls, attempting but failing to push me away. I smirk. 'You are a vision when you are vexed.'

'You are intolerable,' she utters, walking further into the garden and leaving me behind.

A bell rings. The auction will start shortly. We're escorted to our tables, with Violet and I seated on a circular table alongside my family. The king and queen greet her politely, and King Hector's growing expression of happiness heightens at the sight of us together.

'Violet. A pleasure to see you again, my dear.'

She curtsies, the picture of practised grace. 'And you, Your Majesty.'

We take our seats, and the queen meets my eye with a

silent look I can't decipher. I glance away. I can't deal with her infuriating moods this evening. Tonight, I'm content, and she will not change that.

When Arthur the auctioneer stands on the stage, he explains the reasoning for the charity and how it came to be. 'Tonight, we will be auctioning off items or gifts arranged by each family. It's something you won't want to miss!'

I peer at Alex beside me, who grins.

'What did we offer?' I ask.

He points to the stage. 'Just wait and listen.'

Arthur waves his hand and motions to the family sitting on the far side of the garden. 'First up, we have the wonderful hosts of tonight's event, the Rhinelanders, who have auctioned off a luxury carriage—'

I immediately lose interest, and my eyes wander to Violet. Her expression is one of polite attentiveness, but her pursed lips show me something else. Judgement? Surprise at the items on offer?

The auction continues with expensive jewellery, fine art, rare artefacts, tickets for upcoming musical concerts, and, lastly, a vintage wine made centuries ago.

'How impressed are we with the selection so far, sweetheart?' I ask. I lean over and wrap my arm around Violet's chair. She leans closer yet keeps her face directed at the stage as people begin to shout and raise their paddles with vigour.

'And here I was thinking people would be auctioning off simple things. If I were chosen to offer something, I would have given a tray of Hazel's tarts.' She scoffs, amusement lining her features. 'I swear, rich people are a different breed.'

'I think you both will like the next one,' Alex pipes up, nudging my side. 'Violet, get ready with your paddle.'

I give him a questioning look, but he responds by dipping his chin towards the stage.

'And lastly, we have a special lot from our wonderful royal family. Tonight, we're offering a weekend at the infamous chalet retreat of the late Prince Alexander and Princess Lucille,' Arthur announces, causing the guests to chatter excitedly amongst themselves. It takes no time for the shouting to begin. I swivel my head to face my brother.

'Mother and father's home?' I murmur, unsure if I'm angry or pleased about him offering up such a sacred place.

'We've not set foot in there for over a decade. I thought it deserved a bit of love,' says Alex, his mouth twisting. 'I don't think mother would want it sitting there unused. Besides, the money is going towards a good cause.'

My mind wanders to the woman who brought us up – her bright smile and beautiful blue eyes. She had always been carefree, and her charm and wit were what melted my father's heart. A pang shoots through my chest.

'Violet,' I mutter.

She turns, frowning at my tone. 'Yes?'

'Win that chalet.'

Her frown deepens. 'You want to win your own chalet?'

It sounds strange when she says it like that, but something inside me tells me we must win it. No other outsider is allowed within that house. It's mine and Alex's family home – a sacred place where our parents' memories shouldn't be disturbed.

'Do as you're told, sweetheart,' I growl, finding a glint of yearning in her gaze as she beholds me. 'I want that place for us.'

A glimmer of a challenge shimmers in her eyes as she turns towards the stage. Violet sits and waits patiently, allowing the men and women to throw their money away. Those present are surprisingly desperate for a glimpse into the residence of the late prince and princess – mine and Alex's childhood home. As the increments of money grow steadily, Violet grows inpatient and shouts the obscenest amount that makes everyone pause.

'Oh no, was that too much?' she whispers, her frame shrinking into the shadows of my body. My arm across her chair coils protectively before her. 'I thought you were all super rich.'

'Well, we were until you threw it all away,' I mutter.

She gapes, horrified. 'Why did you give me this paddle!' She frets to my brother, trying to give it back. Alex moves away as if the item is cursed, and his grin is contagious. 'I'm so sorry, I am such a fool—'

The queen gives me a strange look and my uncle appears as surprised – and amazed – as I do. Violet covers her face with her hands, leaning into my chest for comfort.

'I'm teasing,' I say, rubbing her back. 'Don't apologise. You did as you were told, and I'm thankful we won.'

Violet shakes her head, coming down from the adrenaline. She sighs and meets my gaze. 'I can imagine what the chalet means to you.'

'I don't want strangers traipsing through and staining my parents' memories there.'

She nods. 'I understand.'

'Plus, I think it's time you saw where I grew up.' I purse my lips, debating my next words.

'And?' she prompts.

'I think my parents would have adored you, Violet.'

'You really think so?' She softens, and her prior irritation with me floats away in the gentle breeze.

I smile, and plant a lingering kiss on her temple. 'Yes, I do.'

35

VIOLET

O nce the auction is finished, dinner is served. The dishes are laden with delicious smelling meats and an abundance of steamed vegetables, while the dessert is tooth-rotting sweet, just how Ellis likes it.

Soon after, when the music grows louder, the guests get on their feet to dance. I'm reminded of the time I was invited to Alexander's birthday, where Ellis was slightly on edge, and his brother was intoxicated.

Now as we talk amongst each other, my prince looks comfortable with me and Alexander either side of him. I quietly head for the refreshments table, but Ellis' hand wraps around my wrist the moment I try to step away.

'Where are you going, sweetheart?' His tone is light, but I sense the undercurrent of tension beneath his words.

I lean in close so only he can hear me. 'To find a man who lets me finish.' His powerful fingers unfurl from my skin, and I trot away, knowing he'll follow. When I peer back, Ellis stands at our table, most likely making an excuse to escape. Forgetting the refreshments table immediately, I head for the single gravel path leading into the botanic gardens.

I smirk, weaving through the estate until pausing at a large willow tree beside a small pond. Ducks float across the water and fish swim beneath the surface, their colours of gold and sapphire-blue bright even at night.

A small but intimate bench sits beneath the willow tree and its long leafy strands brush the immaculate lawn in several places. I take a seat and watch my prince walk around the water's circumference, his cobalt eyes solely on me.

'Where is this man you seemed so eager to see?' he asks half-heartedly.

'I was hoping it was *you*.' I raise a brow, and one side of his mouth tugs up, quietly delighted by my answer. 'Unless you aren't up to it. I know being a royal can be tiring and all but—'

He's on me in seconds, kneeling before me to capture my lips with his. He wraps his hand around my neck, his fingers sliding behind to sink into my hair, as he plunges his tongue deeper into my mouth with no hesitancy or warning. The kiss is wild and exhilarating, hot and wet, the risk of being caught making this moment even more tantalising. I find it thrilling, Ellis is being so unabashedly open when, at any moment, someone could walk into the gardens and see us half sprawled along this bench.

'You better not leave me hanging like the last time,' I gasp, pulling away, but we've already gone too far. I won't be able to settle myself now. 'I don't think I can take two rejections in one evening.'

He frowns, the lines on his face deepening. 'I didn't reject you. I followed your wishes.'

'Don't be obtuse,' I blurt. 'You knew my wish was complete and utter drivel the moment you decided to bend the rules to your benefit.'

Ellis' mouth twists, amusement lingering in his eyes. 'Whatever do you mean?'

I slap his chest playfully. 'You owe me, Your Highness.'

'Do I?' he murmurs, nipping at my lips. 'Why's that?'

I swallow but plough ahead. I want to be honest while making him simmer with need. 'Because I've been thinking of your lips ever since I stepped out of that carriage. I want them on me again, but this time, I want them to taunt me to the point I can't help but *scream*.'

Ellis' eyes sparkle, like I've given him the most thoughtful gift imaginable. His beautiful smile turns feral, and his body crowds mine as he lifts me into his strong arms. I wrap my hands around his neck, peering up at him, confused.

'Hold on,' he murmurs.

'No!' I squeal as we shoot into the air.

Beneath the willow tree branches, we settle on one of the highest limbs – thick and covered in leaves. From here, the only way to see us is if you stand in a particular spot right below. My heart races. He's taken me somewhere private.

'If you want to scream, Violet, it's going to be my name,' he murmurs, his mouth by my ear. Shivers run over my arms and legs as he gently lets me down, my legs feeling wobbly. 'Do you understand?'

My head swivels to him. He's serious as he watches

with those probing eyes, ensuring I acknowledge his request. I nod slowly.

Yes. I will gladly scream your name.

In one swift movement, he lifts me again, so I am sitting on a sloping branch that protrudes from the trunk of the tree. It's a large enough space to sit comfortably and tall enough that I am now looking down at him – but only just.

He eyes my gown and reaches over. Slowly, he runs his hands beneath my dress, he touches my ankles first, and the heat from his fingers makes my cheeks burn. He ponders a moment, then cups the back of my legs, tilting his head as he peers up at me with his handsome, hungry expression.

'Tell me how much you want me.'

It's not a request.

'Badly,' I say, not wanting to appease him just yet.

'That's it?' He purses his lips, running his fingers over the soft skin behind my knees, while his thumb trails circles along my kneecap. Ellis shakes his head like he's disappointed in me. 'That just won't do.'

In one swift movement, he flips up my dress skirt so my bare legs are on display, the material barely covering the space between my thighs. My chest tightens at the way he studies me and my breathing shallows. He enjoys the effect he has on me. He enjoys pushing me.

'Tell me what you want, Violet, or else I may never live up to your expectations,' Ellis tries again.

I roll my eyes. If only. He could do no wrong and he knows it.

'Are you that self-conscious that you need me to stroke your ego?' I ask, grabbing the collar of his shirt and yanking him towards me. 'How about this?' I pepper kisses along his jaw, and his eyes close briefly as his hands wander higher along my thighs, touching the tops of my legs. 'I want you so deep inside me, my eyes water,' I whisper, allowing my voice to trail over the bare skin of his neck. 'I want your mouth on my breasts, sucking and savouring until you can taste the desire that seeps from my skin whenever you're near me. I want—' I peer down to where his trousers struggle to contain his hardness. I tenderly touch him and he moans as I massage him through the fabric of his clothing. 'I want to taste you, I want to watch as you come at the sight of me on my knees for you.'

His eyes fly open with surprise and wicked glee.

I smirk. 'Was that what you wanted to hear, Your Highness?'

He hums. 'Everything and more.'

'Then what are you waiting for? Kiss me again,' I order. I lean back and open my legs, showing him exactly what I want before my confidence wavers. He obliges. Ellis' hands are quick as he moves aside my underwear, his deft fingers finding my arousal and moving the pad of his thumb across my clit. I whimper, so tense with need. I reach for his shoulders, holding on tightly.

'I love it when you're soaking for me,' mutters Ellis, gritting his teeth. 'The smell of you wanting me is fucking bliss, Violet. I never want to stop. I never want to stop touching you, feeling you, *needing* you.'

He dips two fingers inside me, playing me like an instrument in a slow, enticing rhythm, and my body moves with him as he moves in and out. I can't get enough of him and what he does to me, or how my body reacts.

'Don't you dare walk away this time,' I warn, throwing my head back as he picks up speed, his fingers curling around my walls and testing my limits. 'Because you'll have hell to pay if you do. I don't care if you're a prince.'

He chuckles, though his fingers pause. I lift my head to meet his eyes, glaring daggers at him.

Don't do it. Don't stop, I plead, my legs quivering as my body sings for his touch once again.

'I would never dream of displeasing you, sweetheart,' Ellis replies. He rips off my underwear and tucks them into his pocket. 'I want to see you pant, gasp, and scream my name. I want to lick off your sweat, to taste your pretty pussy, and to fuck you into oblivion.'

My mouth gapes at his filthy words – words I am certain no member of the royal family has ever said before. But my, oh my, am I wetter than before.

'Ellis Irvine,' I huff. 'Get on with it.'

He bends down until his mouth is between my legs. I lean back against the trunk as Ellis' hand slithers up my dress until resting on my breast, squeezing as he swirls his tongue. My hips buck and I arch my back as pleasure bursts through me.

'You are so demanding,' he mutters, curling his free hand around my waist. He pulls me closer to get a better angle. My moans are loud and my hands grip onto the first thing I find – Ellis' hair. 'You'll make an exquisite princess alongside me.'

I gasp, my heart hammering at his words. 'I – w-what?'

I am near to finishing, my climax growing, as my hands and toes curl from the expert way his mouth worships me. His hand pinches and teases my nipple.

'You think I'll let you go now?' he asks with a lift of his head. His chin and mouth shine with my essence. He squeezes me tightly, and a small, intoxicating bolt of lightning leaves his touch. I gasp, desperate for more. 'You are sorely mistaken. You're *mine*, Violet – always have been and always will be.'

He licks me up, then adds his fingers into the mix, yet the building sensations coursing through me are too much. I close my eyes and cry out his name. My orgasm leaves me limp and heaving for breath.

Slowly, he lowers my skirts, and I wrap my arms and legs around him. Ellis carefully turns with me in his grip until we're sitting on a thicker branch together, he shifts me onto his lap and strokes my hair. I rest my head against his chest, my heart still racing, and I know Ellis is as content as I am at this moment.

'That was nice.' I sigh. Ellis chuckles.

'Nice? That's all you can say about my exceptional mouth? *Nice*?' He scoffs as if offended.

When I look up, he's already watching me. 'I'm lost for words right now. I can get some better ones later, if you like.'

Ellis kisses my forehead and holds me tighter, rearranging himself into a comfier position. 'Nice is fine. From you, it's the best compliment I've ever received.'

I narrow my eyes. He stares back. Suspicion roams his features. I roll out of his grasp, doing my best not to topple off the branch. I mirror him, kneeling in-between his long, muscular legs. 'Do you trust me?'

'Not with that expression.'

I urge him to shuffle forward and tug both his hands

firmly. He does as he's told, but not before stealing a quick kiss. I smile and push him back, so he leans against the trunk of the willow tree, his legs stretching out on either side of me.

Perfect.

I trail a hand up each of his thighs, up and up and up, until my fingers brush the band of his trousers. He stiffens, but I soothe him with my voice.

'Do you trust me?' I repeat. He gulps, and I see the gleam in his eyes – and the fear. He wants what I'm offering, but he's afraid of losing control.

'Yes,' he whispers.

'Then, relax,' I say, before unbuttoning his trousers.

36

XADEN

Violet touches me so tenderly my body vibrates with need, and though watching her come for me was pleasurable enough, to have her hands slowly roll down my trousers and free my erection is even more exhilarating.

'Breathe,' she commands, noting my still chest. I exhale, trying to ease up. 'I will stop if you ask me to, but I want this just as much as you do.'

Violet's eyes burn with need – and hope. I am a man balancing on a fine thread of control, and any moment, I fear it will snap. She notices my hands curl, an instant reaction when I fear my fingers have turned to darkness.

Violet's shadows immediately crawl up my legs, roaming over my arms and neck, and through my hair. One dark cloud forms into a hand shape and pulls my head back. Violet leans in to suck my neck, her delicious mouth firm and greedy as she plants tentative bites along my skin.

'Violet,' I murmur. I rest my hands on her hips, wishing to bend her to my will again. Pressing her onto my erection, she smiles against my throat. She trails kisses along my jaw before pulling away, but the shadows keep me from reaching for her as they pin my hands to my sides.

'No, you are not turning this around to me again,' she muses, gripping me without wasting another second. I tense, and the monster in me stirs. 'Breathe for me, Ellis. *Breathe.*'

I do as I'm told, watching her every move. Violet angles her body over me and tightens her grip. She thumbs the tip of my cock, and I moan. Violet's mouth curls upwards in pride.

'I can't tell you the amount of times I've wanted you like this,' she whispers, a bloom of colour spreading along her nose and cheeks. The sight of it makes me hard, yet the feeling is painfully enjoyable as she continues stroking me. 'The look in your eyes is solely for me.'

'Yes,' I murmur. I lean forward to steal a kiss and take her lips between my teeth. She hisses with the sudden nip but doesn't complain. 'You are *captivating.*'

Violet smiles. I reach for her chin, but she pushes it away.

'My turn.' Violet lowers, wrapping her mouth around me. She is quick and fierce, her tongue like nothing I've ever experienced. I am a puddle of emotions as she presses and sucks and bites, stroking my length as her mouth continues its intoxicating rhythm. My legs build with so much magic I can't help but release a few bolts of lightning that skitter above us. I grip the tree trunk for stability, and the willow tree sparks, the leaves crackling a blinding silver. A few come undone from their branches and flutter towards us. I hear cries of delight from the party – a short distance away – and I have no doubt the tree looks like a light show.

'Fuck, Violet!' I grind out as she ups the tempo. Her head bobs at the same pace as her hands, and my moans grow louder until I feel ready to explode. She surrounds me in shadows, taunting and teasing and pulling at my clothes. I want Violet's hands everywhere, touching every part of me to the point of no return. 'I'm going to come.'

She hums, giving me the go ahead.

'I'm going to come,' I repeat with a rasp.

Violet squeezes my leg, sucking harder. I can't contain it any longer. I empty into her mouth, and those lips of hers gulp down every drop.

'Fuck!'

My breathing is loud in my ears as Violet rises to her knees once more, a vision as she licks her lips. I could get used to this. Taking her head in my hands, I bring her forward and taste her mouth, tasting myself on her lips. I can't get enough of her.

'Was that nice?' she asks, her purple-blue eyes twinkle.

'Yes.' I say, lost for words. 'Nice.'

'Thank you.' She begins re-buttoning my trousers.

'For what?'

'You gave me some control. I know how hard that is for you.'

I touch the edge of her lips, peering deep into that piercing gaze of hers. Fuck, I could quite easily lose myself in them.

'You are the only person I'd allow it with, but also the one person I must be extremely careful around. You drive me mad, and I can't fully relax because of it.'

'We can work on it.' She shrugs.

The thrill of her words makes me smile. We can work on it – together and with time.

Violet glances behind me, tilting her head up to the branch she sat on before. 'You could have left me hanging,' she remarks, flicking her gaze down to me before looking away again.

'I could have,' I agree, loving how pent up she still is about the carriage ride here. She will never let me forget it – not that I'm bothered. I'll keep making it up to her if I must. 'But I would never do that to you.'

'Only when it comes to carriage rides,' she chimes.

My lips twitch as I try to keep my amusement at bay. 'Only in carriage rides,' I agree, before pecking her cheek. 'You did say only *one* kiss.'

She rolls her eyes and moves forward to rest a hand on each of my shoulders. I pull her closer, straddling those gorgeous legs of hers across my lap – right where she belongs. 'I don't care what I said. You used your lightning on me and expected me to be fine afterwards.'

'So, you enjoyed it?' I drawl, enjoying the rosy pink tinge flushing across Violet's face.

'You're insufferable.'

'How can I make it up to you?' My breath tickles her soft delicate neck, and my lips have a mind of their own as they press against the column of her throat.

'I want you to be with me forever,' she whispers, and I pause. I lift my head to find her features schooled into a seriousness I rarely see with Violet. My heart cracks at her beauty and the raw honesty of her words. I kiss the corner of her mouth and snake my hands around her waist, pulling her into my chest so she can rest against me.

'Forever doesn't seem like enough,' I murmur, playing with her strands of gold and onyx hair. 'How about for the rest of this lifetime, and all the ones after?'

Violet mirrors my smile. 'You don't think you'd be bored with me by the second or third lifetime?' she jests.

I shake my head, tracing my fingers along her cheek. 'No. Definitely not. I'd still be captivated by you, even then.'

37

THE PAST

Time moves slower when you lose hope. I look out of my body, but I do not see. I touch, but I do not feel. It is a strange sensation to have your limbs move, but your mind lack all control. A living nightmare. A haunting place of uncertainty and loneliness I cannot escape.

I am a weapon, and my power grows stronger by the day under Fral's commands. He wants to toughen me up and build my agility skills, to fashion and mould my arsenal of magical powers. And he succeeds, creating a slayer he's always wanted. Violet remains by my side the whole time with a vacant look on her face, shadows wrap around her malnourished body every time I see her.

Now I am of more value, I sleep on my own metal table in a tent far from the other boys and girls. Guards line the perimeter of our marquee, ensuring nothing happens to us, but to my dismay, they're always in groups of two or three. I do not complain about the lack of space, nor the smell of dirty skin, nor the terrifying sounds. I cannot open my mouth without an order from Fral. I cannot taste my food without his consent. I am a puppet, and he plays my strings well, holding them breathtak-ingly tight to keep me from straying.

Caleb and Violet are alongside me. They're rarely in their own minds to communicate, but somehow, at night, I come back to myself. At night, I hear the hooting of owls and rustling of Gwenore's trees. I can breathe easier. It's as if Fral eases his hold on me, and only me, when he falls into a restful sleep.

I tilt my head to the side, the only movement I can make with my limbs and torso clamped to the table. I peer over to Violet, who lays peacefully with her hands beside her legs. Even though she's more of an asset now than ever, they do not look after her well. She has only been bathed once this week, and her freshly washed hair tumbles over the edge of the table like a waterfall of sunshine. Even from here, I smell the scent of orange wafting from her. But Violet's fingernails do not match her clean appearance, and it's as if the girl I know is still inside – fighting. As if she finds triumph in keeping one part of herself broken to show the truth of her feelings, even if she cannot show or voice it.

'Violet,' I whisper, surprised when the words come out. I try again, eager for her to hear my voice, to answer me with hers. 'Violet. Open your eyes if you can hear me.'

On bated breath, I wait for her purple-blue eyes to flutter – to move – but she lays as still as a statue. I sigh.

'If you can hear me, please keep fighting,' I murmur, saddened by the sight of her. I look up to the canvas above, focusing on the silver-white glow of the moon through the tent's canvas roof. A tear escapes my eye and trails down my temple, dripping onto the cool table top. The sound of it echoes through my skull.

'Keep fighting for our real end with me, Violet. I'll be there *waiting for you. Even if it means being in this horrible state for years to come, I'll be there with you. Just keep holding on.'*

Again, she does not answer.

I try to sleep. I close my eyes, but I'm never fully resting, my mind whirs with activity – thoughts, dreams, and nightmares. I wonder if my family misses me, if Alex is searching for his only brother, if my bedroom looks the same as how I left it months ago, or if a servant has cleaned it up as if erasing me from the castle forever.

Keep fighting, *I remind myself.* If not for yourself but for those you love and care for. Fight for them.

38

VIOLET

A carriage arrives outside my house an hour before sunset. I frown when I find it's empty inside. I assumed the youngest prince would be present, and my curiosity spikes as I peer outside the window to find us heading back toward the castle. A mysterious envelope had arrived this morning with a cryptic message demanding I be ready by sunset as a royal carriage will be collecting me. Comfortable clothing was recommended.

Only when we approach Ivory Castle does my transportation make a sharp left from the shining pearlescent gates, turning alongside the ocean road to where the waves crash in, the sound calming.

We stop in an unfamiliar area, and when the carriage door finally opens, I step out to endless trees. Searching for a clear answer, I turn in a circle to find only bushland and a road leading to it. It's a dead end.

'Where are we?' I ask the coachman. His expression gives nothing away.

'Bloomsoar Lake, Miss Violet,' he says before snapping

the reins and circling the horse and carriage back the way we came. 'The young prince is waiting for you.' He motions towards a tree with a small star painted across it in white. 'Follow the stars.'

I smile faintly, intrigued.

The coachman leaves me alone to follow the road back to civilisation. Weaving through the bushes, I pass thin and wispy trunks, tree branches pulling at my clothes and the odd offshoot tangling in my hair. I grumble, having dressed in my nicer clothes. By the time I find Ellis, I'll look like a bedraggled mess.

Once I finally walk out into an opening, a large pool of dark blue water greets me.

'Good evening.'

My head snaps towards the prince, who lounges along a rug draped in cushions and blankets. Ellis looks striking in his dark clothes, where the material stretches over his muscles. He seems to know it, too, and when I meet his gaze, a sly smile crosses his lips.

'Hello,' I chirp, gesturing at the scenery. 'What is this place?'

'Bloomsoar. It's a lake hardly anyone knows about, let alone visits,' he explains, rising to his feet. Slowly, he approaches, and the tension builds. A part of me wants to launch myself at him, claiming every part of his body for my own. But I don't. Instead, I wait patiently, though I am not disappointed when he bends down to kiss me, taking his time. I savour the taste of him.

When we break apart, Ellis smiles. 'I hope you like cheese and meat because I brought a whole load of it.'

'I sure do.' I nod as he leads me to the rug. It's arranged

beautifully, adorned with decorations and candles with wax dripping down the sides. We sit amongst the cushions and take a moment to admire the large trays of assorted foods and dips that make my stomach grumble. 'I'm starving.'

'Help yourself,' Ellis says. He takes a knife and cuts me off a slither of orange coloured cheese. I watch as the sun sets behind him, the sky blending into shades of dark blue, purple, and pink. We sit in comfortable silence as we satisfy our appetites. The array of cheeses and finely cut meats are half gone by the time we pause for air.

'I used to come here with my parents and Alex,' Ellis confesses, glancing at the beautiful view. Candlelight shrouds his face in shadows as he turns away to admire the surrounding trees that glow a burnt orange, their green leaves now a fiery red from the sunset. 'We would spend family time together – swimming and eating and just *being*.'

My heart lurches for the loss of his parents. On the way to another kingdom, they had been swept away at sea, never to be seen again. I couldn't imagine such a tragedy.

'I'm sorry, Ellis,' I say, resting my hand on his. Immediately, his fingers curl around mine. 'They would be proud of the person you are today.'

'Would they?' he questions with a subtle shake of his head. 'I'm not so sure.'

'What makes you say that?'

'Some days, I fear I will become like Fral. His twisted way of thinking is how the monster inside me feels, and I can't always control it. I'm afraid it will take over when I least expect it, and I'll be the slayer Fral made us to be – *wished* us to be.'

I press my lips together, hating that he feels such a way. To my surprise, he continues, allowing the words to flow as if they have been in his consciousness for too long and finally need an escape.

'Do you ever think the darkness is so ingrained in you that you can never truly be yourself again? That if you let the focus slip for just a second, you'll lose everything you've worked so hard to control?' Ellis sighs and squeezes my hand. He lies on his side to face me. 'Am I babbling? Stop me if I am.'

I don't know what to say as his words sink in.

'Never stop sharing your feelings with me, Ellis.' I run a hand through the soft strands of his hair. His eyes close at my touch, and he seems to enjoy the feel of my nails along his skull.

'I won't if you keep this up,' he mumbles. His cobalt eyes watch me intently. I want him to realise that opening up or asking for help isn't a weakness. He's allowed to feel anger or fear and share those emotions with others without feeling out of control. He's allowed to be himself.

'Promise me,' I press, suddenly desperate to hear his oath. I hold my breath until he answers.

Ellis nods, becoming serious. 'I promise I won't keep my feelings from you, Violet. I will never hide from you again.'

I nod and lean away from him, and though he purses his lips, he doesn't complain. 'Everyone has light and dark parts in them,' I say, shuffling closer. 'But it's what we *choose* to do with those parts that counts. You may have darkness in you, just as I have.' I raise my hand, and a tendril of shadow curls from my palm. 'But if you fight every day to share the light with those around you, *that's* what matters. Being afraid means you care. If you care, it's because you are a good person.' I offer him my hand and he's quick to take it. 'As my mother always told me, "Only the brightest of stars can shine in the darkest of nights."'

'What does that mean?' He wrinkles his nose, and I repress the urge to touch the lines that form between his brows.

I squeeze his fingers and smile faintly. 'It means, my dear prince, that only in our darkest moments do we truly understand how strong we are and how much we can endure when tested. All these years we have lived with dark magic in our veins – darkness that was put there for us to constantly fight against. Yet not once have you succumbed to its will. You are much stronger than you give yourself credit for.'

Ellis twists his mouth with a show of something unsettling. 'I have.'

'Have what?' I ask, confused.

He averts his gaze, guilt coating his handsome features. 'I have let the darkness out.'

39

ELLIS

Violet has been quiet ever since I opened up to her. After finishing our platter, we go for a walk, and I continuously glance back to ensure she's still there. Trees and bushes conceal the secret I have planned, and as we approach a waterfall in the distance, her mouth widens, showing her teeth. A tiny rowboat rests, unused, on the sandy shore. It takes no time for her to realise my plans.

'You are taking me on that?' She wonders with a laugh. 'I can't wait to see this.'

'You are rowing,' I clarify.

She scoffs. 'You wish.'

She kicks off her shoes, sending them flying to the shore. Mine follow close behind. She clambers into the wooden boat, and I push it out into the water, jumping in before it gets too far. It threatens to topple as we sway from side to side, and Violet grips the sides with white knuckled hands.

'Relax,' I soothe, patting her hand for good measure. 'I will keep us dry.'

She raises a brow doubtfully.

I shrug and pick up the oars, beginning to row us towards the waterfall. 'I suppose if you wish to get wet ...' I flash her a presumptuous look.

'I'll go swimming,' she finishes for me.

'Right.' I nod, as if that's what I meant all along.

The sound of churning water grows louder as we approach the cascade of water. I stop rowing, allowing the boat to float gently towards it. Violet reaches out, and the element trickles through her hands, and the spray makes her clothes shimmer with droplets.

At this moment, I am wholly content with my child-hood best friend, who smiles at the simpler things in life, like nature and the glowing moon above. I sense her happiness, and it mirrors my own as my body relaxes.

'I like your smile,' she says without looking my way.

'Do you?'

She nods and finally meets my eyes. 'It reminds me of the young Ellis I met all those years ago. When you didn't worry so much, and you showed your true colours more often.' Violet seems to notice the shift in my demeanour and crawls towards me to avoid unsettling the boat. 'I don't mean to imply that you aren't *you* now. I just feel helpless when I know you're still suffering. You keep all these things bottled up, and I don't know how to ease that burden.'

I caress her cheek with my thumb, and her purple-blue eyes watch warily. I press my mouth softly to hers. Without a doubt, Violet is my soulmate. She sees everything without an ounce of judgement. She sees me for who I am and is truly untroubled by it. A heavy feeling coils in my stomach, and I know that, with my feelings for her, she needs to know everything about me – including the parts I'm still afraid of.

'I want to share why I refused to see you all those years ago.'

She jerks back, surprised. 'Now?'

I nod. 'If you still wish to know.'

Violet swallows, moving back to the bench. Somehow, the distance helps me to think, avoiding the distraction of her touch. She clasps her hands together, resting them in her lap. Quiet and waiting. I take that as my cue to begin. I inhale, readying for her reaction. I tell myself that, no matter what, she deserves to know the truth. I'll allow her the space and time she needs if she requests it.

'When Fral gave me the ability to fly like him, he told me I would carry on his legacy and continue his work. That's why he took me. Like you, I completed stage one, and gained one more power in addition to the lightning magic I was born with.'

Violet listens intently, looking clueless as to where I'm going with this. 'Alright.'

'When we were rescued, you were on stage two, weren't you?'

'Yes. He wanted another power alongside my shadows and shapeshifting, but it was never successful.'

'Right.' I nod. 'Well, when we left the prison camp, I was on stage three.'

Her piercing eyes widen with alarm. 'You gained *two* more powers in that place?'

'I can create lighting, fly, and sense souls.' I declare. She frowns, perplexed.

'Sense souls?'

'When I meet someone, I can immediately picture their soul. It comes to me in feelings, colours or textures. Everyone's soul is different. Yours is warm like a crackling campfire and a unique shade of purple – the same colour as your eyes.' I reach for her cheek, but drop my hand before making contact. She might be revolted by me once I tell her everything. 'What I didn't realise was when someone senses a soul, they also have the ability to devour it.'

'As in, steal it?' Violet wonders.

'No, as in I consume their soul and they die. Fral knew my ability could bring down hundreds, and by consuming their souls, I would gain their life source and energy, becoming stronger with every person I killed.'

Horror ripples across her features as she covers her mouth with her hand.

'Violet, the darkness you possess is different to mine. Mine is a living and breathing entity that I can physically feel, and it threatens to take control of my entire being. It feeds on my strongest emotions. As a boy, I was always overwhelmed by these feelings I could rarely suppress.'

She quietly studies me, but her thoughts are loud.

Protect him. Protect him. Protect him.

'The first time I consumed a soul was my brother's friend, Naveen,' I admit, and the memory makes my eyes prick with guilt. My heart hammers as I observe Violet's demeanour. I notice her white knuckles as she clenches her hands into fists, her gaze on me unwavering. 'I'd had my first argument with the queen. There was shouting and copious amounts of blaming, and I am not proud of it.'

Violet purses her lips, seeming to have guessed my relationship with my aunt is a tumultuous one.

'So, naturally,' I continue. 'I fled to the one person I knew would cheer me up – Alex. It didn't register with me how dark my hands were, my fingers were completely covered in black veins. My brother was with his friend, Naveen, and they were out in the garden. Naveen greeted me with a hand shake.' My lungs feel painfully tight at the memory as I recall Naveen's kind smile. A wave of remorse crashes through me. 'The moment I laid my hand in his, I felt it – the need to consume and devour. The veins moved along my skin and seeped along his fingers like a spreading disease. His red hair turned black as night, and as I held on for longer, his once green eyes began to flutter and fill with darkness. And believe me, I tried to let go, but the feeling of him – his sweet and pure soul – was *euphoric*. I fed upon him with little effort, and I took all his energy and life force until I finally felt a flicker of myself and could leash the monster once more.' I exhale shakily, squeezing my eyes shut. It still haunted me, even now, ten years later. 'But as I came around, I found Alex knelt before me, sobbing over his friend's body. Naveen's small and frail body was hollow, as if I'd emptied his insides and his once bright eyes were vacant.'

Violet's face flickers with sorrow. 'How old were you?'

'Naveen died not long after I returned home. I was still twelve.' Nerves swirl inside my stomach. My soul sensing was a new power I had gained just before being rescued.

Fral hadn't tested it out fully, and so, I had to learn the limitations of the magic myself.

Violet schools her expression into neutrality, so I can't tell what she is thinking. I wipe my palms along my trousers, ridding the build-up of moisture. 'The next day you came to visit me, I watched on the balcony as you were waved away, but you were relentless, always showing up at the same time everyday, asking to see me.'

She purses her lips, her eyes fluttering with the recollection. 'I was a stubborn little thing.'

'You were,' I agree. 'But I had already made the decision that I was unstable. I couldn't be trusted around anyone – especially those I cared most for. My emotions were my weakness, and you would have no doubt ruined me. One touch, and you would have awoken the monster in seconds. I couldn't fathom the thought of hurting you, of you meeting the same fate as Naveen.' I shake my head. A world without Violet would be purposeless.

'So, you pushed everyone away.'

I nod. 'Yes. I stopped myself from seeing Alex so often, I was horrified that one day it might be *him* on the receiving end of my deadly touch. I stopped seeing my friends and only mingled with my family when it was absolutely necessary. I put a barrier up to protect those around me as rumours of my power made its rounds in the city. People were afraid of me, and I learned that it was best to play along, to put a mask on and pretend to feel nothing. At first, it was difficult not to take peoples remarks and insults to heart, but I soon learned that acting emotionless meant keeping those around me safe. So, I adapted and hid my feelings.'

'But you were only a child,' she protests.

'Yes, but a dangerous one. After Fral, it didn't take long for people to become distrusting of me – the queen included. And why would I blame them? I am filled to the brim with a concoction of evil magic I was unwillingly given. I am different. I am an anomaly. And that scares them.'

'You may be in the limelight as a royal,' Violet protests. 'but that doesn't mean you deserve to be cut-off and secluded from reality. You deserve a happy ending – a *real* ending.'

My heart gallops at that. *A real ending*, like we spoke about as children.

I tilt my head, curiosity blooming at her expression. She looks anything but disgusted. 'Do you really believe that, Violet?'

She leans forward and reaches for my hand. I hold on tight. Carefully, Violet climbs into my lap, the smell of berries filling my senses.

'You confessed,' she starts, making herself comfortable in my embrace. 'that as a twelve-year-old boy, you isolated yourself and gave up your reputation and relationships for the sake of those around you. How could you *not* be deserving of that?'

I smile, and though my heart swells with relief, the guilt still lingers. Somehow, Violet does not see me as a monster as she holds me tightly, her concern and protectiveness glowing.

'*You* are my real ending,' I utter, bringing her close. She wraps her arms around my neck, and my body folds into hers like it's the most natural thing in the world. 'Like we discussed, remember?'

'I remember,' she says gently. 'I remember you telling me to keep fighting for our real end.'

I gently push her to arm's length, remembering so vividly the loneliness of that time – when Violet and Caleb were caged inside their own heads while mine was free – and how miserable I was without her. 'You heard that?'

'I heard every declaration from you, Your Highness. Even when you thought I couldn't hear you back. Even when you revealed every piece of your soul to me. I heard it.' I scratch the back of my neck, and Violet smiles. 'When I was turned away from the castle, that's what kept me coming back. Not only had we promised to be best friends, but you had told me to fight. Fight for the real end, and my real end was always going to have *you* in it, Ellis. That's why I'm here. Because you asked me to fight for us, and I did.'

My heart soars at her confession as pride glimmers across her expression. Something else hits me, too. Love. Love as vibrant and as dazzling as the stars above us floods me, consuming my thoughts and filling my lungs. For a moment, I struggle to breathe and find the right words.

'I know how you feel about me,' Violet whispers. She presses her hand hard against my chest as if she wishes to dig inside and grab onto my thumping heart that beats solely for her. 'Because I feel the same about you. It hasn't changed since that day you held me, all battered and bruised.' Her mouth twists, as if the memory is a happy one rather than a nightmare. 'And my feelings will never change until the day I die. Will yours?' she asks tentatively. Her confidence sways for a moment, but I don't allow her to feel it for long. I tilt forward, resting my forehead against hers.

'Never,' I whisper. 'I will never feel anything but devotion for you, Violet. True and wholesome adoration for my best friend, my lover, my *everything*.'

Violet closes her eyes, and the smile upon her beautiful face makes my heart pound beneath my skin. If I can make her look this way for the rest of my life, I'll die a happy man.

Only the brightest of stars can shine in the darkest of nights.

If I am the night sky, Violet is my shining star, sending light into every dark corner of my soul. She will be my salvation, my love, my strength, while I will be her shield, her supporter and devotee. Together, we can move mountains. Together, we will finally be content.

'I forgive you for sending me away,' she whispers, eyes still closed. 'I will always forgive you for putting your needs first. I can never fault you for that – for keeping me safe without my knowing.' Violet kisses me softly. She takes my head in her hands, exploring my mouth with a tenderness I enjoy too much. Her shadows curl around us, considerate of the darkness swelling within me.

We stay in the boat for hours, floating and lying beside each other as we watch the stars. They are brilliant as they twinkle and dance above us. It's one of the best nights of my life.

The other being the day I met Violet.

40

ELLIS

In three days' time, it's Violet's birthday, and I plan on bringing her to my family home – the chalet we won at the charity auction. My girl is ready and waiting outside the bakery when I pick her up, her packed bag by her feet.

The journey is tedious, and my nerves only grow the closer we are to the chalet. Violet seems to sense my tension as she places a hand on my knee, the soft gesture giving me a burst of courage.

When we arrive, I take a deep breath. The outside of the building is made of sandstone, and the windows are open to air out the inside. The front door is the same dark purple Alex painted it twelve years ago - my brother chose the colour, knowing it was our father's favourite. The gardens leading up to the entrance still bloom with an array of pretty, colourful flowers. It's as if my mother still tends to them as the smell of bluebells – her preferred flower – lines the pathway to the front door. My heart jumps in my throat at the sight of it.

'It's beautiful,' Violet murmurs with a look of awe. 'It's so peaceful here.'

Bird songs echo around us, while the faint noise of crashing waves in the distance make me peer around. The chalet sits on the crest of a hill, where a small cliff is but a stone's throw away before dipping to the tide below. It's the perfect place to be near the city – close enough to the royal family, but far enough to have a private life away from the hustle and bustle.

'It was my favourite place in the world,' I say, wrapping my hand in hers. I need bravery to enter my childhood home, and Violet helps with that as her small fingers close around mine in encouragement.

We stand in silence, looking at the door. Violet makes no move to open it. Instead, she seems to wait for a sign I'm ready. I nod and grasp the handle, swinging the wooden door open. The foyer is small and cosy, furniture fills every space, book piles are found on every surface, and flowers in vases decorate each table. The smell of freshly baked pastries fill the space.

I follow the scent to the kitchen, where a tray of what appears to be mermaid cakes cool on a rack. My eyes water as memories of my parents making my favourite pastries fill the crevices of my mind. My mother flinging a towel over her shoulder as she brings the hot tray out of the oven, grinning at the sight of her creations. My father hovering nearby, watching intently, as if ready to step in the moment she asks – always the protector, always the shield for our family.

My throat suddenly feels constricted and my eyes hurt as emotions bubble up. Instinct has me letting go of Violet's hand and shoving my fists into my trouser pockets. Violet frowns but doesn't comment as she notices the pastries.

'Your favourite,' says Violet, pointing to the tray. 'How lovely of them to do that for us.'

'Hmm,' I mumble. 'Let's explore the rest of it.'

I step out of the kitchen, needing space from the heart of our home. I tread carefully along the wooden floor, my steps echo along the passageway. I come to a door I know well – my old bedroom. I fling the door open to find a small bed, a teal-coloured rug covered in marine animals. My windows are wide open, and the view makes my throat bob.

I back up and head for the back door. The breeze caresses my hair as I study the rear garden. Outside is a fresh-cut lawn, where an old cedar tree stands alone, with a wooden swing hanging off a steady branch, secured by two coils of thick rope. Alex got it for one of his birthdays, each of us taking turns to push the other.

'I broke my arm over here,' I tell Violet, pointing to the spot as we approach it. I touch the thick and weathered rope holding the rotting wooden seat. 'I decided to jump off the swing at its highest point then landed on my arms. Good thing, too, because otherwise it would have been my head.' I give a tight laugh.

Violet smiles in answer, observing the scenery like a stranger would – with no history of this place, no memories tied to the small things scattered about it, clueless to the significance of the flower pots we painted together as a family and the rabbit holes we dug in the lawn to find the wildlife nearby.

'I can imagine the upbringing you had here.' Violet

takes in the landscape, she seems relaxed here, which is how this place made me feel growing up. 'It's a shame you moved out.'

I nod, even though she's facing away from me. 'After my parents died, the king and queen took us in. They didn't want Alex and I living here alone – my uncle insisted we were too young. So, we moved to the castle where we would be safe and cared for.' I scoff at the irony of my words. I peer to the pearlescent castle to my left. It shimmers beneath the sunlight, huge and demanding compared to the surrounding city dwellings.

'I don't think that's unreasonable,' Violet acknowledges with a brief glance. 'You were only eleven at the time. I'd do the same if I were in your aunt and uncle's shoes.'

I nod. 'Me too,' I answer honestly.

Hand in hand, we return inside and head to the upper level of the chalet. I don't dare go into my parents' room, so instead, I head for one of the spare chambers that mean very little to me. The window is open already, like everywhere else, and it overlooks the ocean. The sun is much lower than it was when we left Sapphire City.

'I don't think you could get tired of a view like that,' Violet muses, coming to stand beside me as I peer out. I glance sidelong at her. The warm sunlight smooths her features as those piercing eyes lift to meet mine. I can sense the peace in her – in me, too.

'I agree,' I whisper. Seeing Violet in my childhood home is a memory I'll cherish for as long as I live. I reach for her neck, grabbing a handful of gold and onyx hair.

Violet is a vision in her dress, a slither of bare leg peeks out beneath her skirt and all I can think about is what I will find underneath.

'You look hungry, Your Highness,' Violet purrs, tracing the top of her dress where the design cuts away. 'Is there something I can do to feed your appetite? Perhaps a mermaid cake downstairs?'

I narrow my eyes and my body turns to her like she's pulling an invisible string. 'We are going to keep the windows open,' I say, voice low and husky. The way she's studying me ignites my desire, I need her and I need her *now*.

'Keep the—' She frowns. 'Why do you want them open?'

'I want the whole kingdom to hear what a great fucking time we're about to have.'

Pink flushes her cheeks in seconds as her hand rests on the ledge before us as if needing stability. Questions linger in her expression.

'Sit on the ledge,' I instruct, removing my shirt in one smooth motion. Violet glances down the chalet walls with an uneasy look in her eye. It's not a long drop, but for someone who can't fly, I suppose the second level is a long way down. I stroke her shoulder to ease her concern. She shivers and the sight sends a bolt of pleasure through me. 'I won't let you fall, and if you do, you know I'll catch you.'

Violet grimaces but her eyes light up at the sight of my bare chest. 'Strangely enough, that doesn't make me feel better.'

I grab her hips and spin her around, eliciting a gasp as I sit her onto the window ledge. 'I am going to make you think of everything else besides the height,' I grumble, running a hand up her skirt and ripping off her underwear. I growl. 'Why do you bother with these?'

'Because normal people wear them,' she answers tartly, holding onto my bare shoulders for purchase. She's still fearing the drop below if her tight grip is any indication. 'And I enjoy your frustration when taking them off.'

I lean forward, and she bends back, gripping my body even harder.

'I will not let you fall,' I murmur, before giving her a kiss. 'Do you trust me?'

She nods, watching my mouth intently. 'With my life.'

My fingers trail up her leg that's curled around my back. Her body trembles under my touch. 'I'm going to see how wet you are, even under duress.' I wink, and to my delight, she's warm down there as I brush my knuckles between her legs, her whimpers making my cock twitch. 'Oh, sweetheart,' I drawl, touching her with the pad of my thumb and circling the wetness with satisfaction. 'You are always ready for me.'

Violet nods and closes her eyes as I press into her. Her clit is my main focus. She begins to move her hips as her breath quickens. I know I've successfully gotten her mind off the tall ledge she sits on. So, I lean further forward. With the ocean breeze now in her hair, I dip a finger inside her, and the moan sends shocks of lightning to my erection.

'Ellis,' she rasps, exploiting my hand like the good girl she is. 'I do enjoy your touch.'

'And I like what my touch does to you. Look at you. Fucking stunning.' I lick her neck and bite her earlobe before increasing the speed of my fingers, bringing her nearer to my body so I can get deeper. Violet is in her own world and bites her lower lip to keep from whimpering incoherently.

'Don't come just yet,' I order as my fingers stop their torture. Violet's eyes fly open, her anger evident. 'I want to tease you some more.'

I grab her, wrapping her legs firmly around my hips and sliding her arms around my neck. I have no qualms throwing Violet onto the large four-poster bed, set with crisp white covers and fluffy pillows. Her eyes light up, a smug smile having replaced her scowl.

'The swiftness of your emotions fascinates me,' I remark, crawling between her legs. I push her thighs to the sides roughly, her pretty pink pussy ready and waiting for me. 'I feel the instant heat of your stare.'

'I am not a woman to be trifled with,' Violet answers, watching me intently. 'Remember that.'

'Indeed, I will,' I mumble before tasting the spot between her legs. Her body bucks in answer. I lick again and again, like she's my personal feast, and she cries out without restraint, burrowing her fingers into my hair, my locks being used as a hold. 'Come for me, sweetheart.' It doesn't take long for Violet to obey as her body quivers with her climax. Her breath shudders at the release, and I grin down at her. 'I will never get tired of this.'

'Me either,' she says with a sheepish grin.

A thrill shoots through my chest as lightning crackles along my shoulder blades. Her purple-blue eyes trail them, entranced by the sight. She tentatively reaches out, and I allow a small spider web of lightning to touch her finger, giving her only a small shock. She gasps, her nipples hardening through her dress.

'I want to have *all* of you, Violet,' I murmur, watching for her reaction. 'Every piece of you. What do you say?' Her eyes widen.

'Do you trust me?' she asks, and I nod without hesitation.

'Yes. With my life.'

41

THE PAST

My eyes are closed but I sense movement in the tent. My senses prickle as footsteps draw closer, someone standing between the tables Violet and I lay upon.

'Thank the higher powers,' a voice mutters, no doubt female. The sound is melodious, unbefitting in a place like this. 'They aren't dead.'

'No,' another voice confirms. A male. 'Their pulses are faint, but it's there.'

I wonder for a moment if I recognise them. Perhaps they are one of the guards I rarely see. But from the quiet way they potter around the tent, I sense they're not supposed to be here.

Hope blooms in my chest, hard and painful, as it claws hungrily at my lungs. I try my hardest to open my eyes and use my words to warn them, but as expected, I don't move – my body is a traitor to my wishes.

Suddenly, wind wraps around me, and night air envelops the tent. The sounds of Gwenore Forest grow louder as Fral's *commanding voice greets the strangers from above me. He is flying, I realise.*

'You have made a grave mistake coming here, Scarlet Seraphine,' he says, distaste lining his words.

The name sends a flicker of recognition through me. Why? I'm not sure. But from Fral's tone, she's a threat, and if she's a threat, she must be here to save us.

Remove this collar, *I want to shout.* Save me from his control!

My body vibrates as Fral speaks. His command is clear in my head as it echoes through my skull and bounces off its walls. The collar constricts my throat as if sensing my treasonous thoughts. 'Come, my little slayers.'

My eyes open as the restraints around my torso and legs unlatch themselves. My body slowly sits, willed by its master. I take in the female closest to me. She has long crimson hair reminiscent of dried blood. Her eyes match in colour, and her wariness and determination makes the hair on my arms stand on end. She observes not only me, but Caleb and Violet, who also sit patiently upon their own tables with vacant stares.

In a flash, they disappear. Caleb's magic has teleported them from one location to another. For a moment, I wonder why they didn't take me, too, but it doesn't take me long to realise why. Fral extends his arm, and I jump off the table to approach him, coming to his side. Internally, I yell and scream at him to step away and not touch me, to finally let me go. I am so consumed by hatred I almost miss the female's utterance.

'Ellis?'

I'm silent. My mind and body still. The male who accompanies her is shouting and calling Fral a monster, but all I care about is why she uses my nickname – a name only a select few call me.

Suddenly, Caleb sends the male companion flying with an invisible force I didn't know he possessed.

'Jack!' Scarlet cries. When she goes to his aid, I direct a ball of lightning at her, and she hisses when it finds her outstretched hand. Even from here, I hear her pale skin sizzle and her face morphs from agony to determination.

'You have your own problems, Raven,' Fral warns, and finally, I realise who she is.

The Raven. A vampire hybrid trained to save and serve the kingdoms. A figurehead for maintaining peace throughout the lands. A member of the Hex, the most prestigious group of supernatural beings ever to exist. She comes from the House of Raven, an army from the north, and she's a figurehead like our Nightshades from the House of Bane. That's why she looks so familiar. Her name was plastered in every newspaper throughout the kingdom before I was kidnapped. She must have been hired by my aunt and uncle to save us – to save us all.

Scarlet Seraphine.

The new Raven of the Hex. The half-blood Raven, and my salvation.

I do my best to fight the collar and prevent my arms from rising once more. Potent-smelling magic sparks along my hands. Fral's voice is soft as he barks instructions, his fear evident.

Save me! *I try to scream.*

As if reading my thoughts, the Raven shouts, and one name piques my interest.

'Ellis! I'm friends with your brother, Alexander!'

My heart falters as the image of my carefree sibling springs to mind. He befriended the Raven to rescue me? A part of me is surprised by this revelation while the other part is not. Alex could charm anyone with a pulse.

'Incinerate her!' is all I hear, Fral spitting the command with growing panic. I attack the Raven. My small body sends numerous bolts without my permission. Scarlet seems hesitant, her frown deepening as she decides whether to retaliate my strikes.

Fight me! I want to scream at her. Take me down before I hurt anyone else!

Finally, one of my bolts collides with her body and sends her spiraling. I don't stop, I keep up the assault, blast after blast, and she takes every one of them in her stride.

She must be strong to still be breathing, I think as smoke wafts off her gold and garnet fighting suit.

'Ellis, this isn't you! Stop this!' Scarlet tries. She must think I can overcome the collar. I can't. I've tried. I've tried so many times and failed. I'm not strong enough. I'm weak – a prisoner in my own body and mind.

The Raven motions to the surrounding scene, hoping I'll see reason and do as she asks. Though it's a lost cause, I heighten my awareness until I sense Violet in the distance. Her and Caleb are overcoming the male, Jack, and another much larger companion.

I realise with dread, the Hex is no match for us. What has Fral made us into? The Hex are the most powerful beings in the land. If we can conquer them, we can conquer anyone.

Monsters as well as slayers, says a voice inside my head.

'Stop playing with her. I want her gone.' Fral scolds me. A ripple of trepidation runs through me, as it always does when he wishes for me to end my target.

My body lifts slowly as I hover from the ground, my new

power kicking in. Scarlet gapes and her dark crimson eyes widen in horror. It's the flicker of doubt in her expression that makes me panic, uncertainty upon a warrior's face is never a good sign.

Then, my body spins, something I've never done until now. My legs and arms lock firm beside my body as I become a blur, a tornado of dark magic.

'You cannot keep doing this. They do not belong here,' Scarlet shouts, arguing with Fral.

'They belong to me!' Fral snaps. His grasp on my magic and body makes it hard to breathe. 'They'll do as I wish. They do not have a choice.'

And with that, my magic explodes. My hand lashes out, releasing a strike of three lightning bolts so strong and so bright it arcs from me. Three crescent moons of burning light attack the Raven, slicing through the air and her body. Scarlet kneels, and her face is proof enough of the unending pain I've caused. She falls to her side, armour scorched yet glowing a bright silver from my magic. She appears like a broken bird, three gashes rest upon her, bubbling with blood – one from her temple to jaw, one from her shoulder to hip, and one from thigh to calf.

I'm sorry, I want to say, hating my actions and my inability to fight for what is right.

'You will die because you did not heed my warning,' says Fral with more confidence in his voice now. I know then I am doomed. My true hope of escaping this prison was in this female, in this suffering Raven on the brink of death. And I was the one to stop her. I've stopped everyone from going home. 'Your team will be slaughtered because of your pride.'

It's only then I notice the rest of my surroundings. Dead bodies scatter along the camp's floor. Some with bright blue hair, indicating that our own army – the House of Bane – fought for us. My heart twists at the sight of how many came to our aid and how many lost their lives.

My eyes travel back to the Raven, and the pleading in her voice shakes me to my core.

'Ellis. If you can hear me, Alex is waiting for you. He has been searching for you. He's never stopped.' Something cracks inside my chest, hard and brutal as I feel it bleed. I shake against the bars of magic that lock me away and batter them with all the energy and will that remain. I want to see my brother again. I need to tell him I love him, that I miss him, and I want to go home. I manage to make my mouth twitch, the only movement I've been able to make while under Fral's thrall. 'He would want you to defend yourself. But not like this—'

'Ellis! End her now!' Fral orders.

A ball of crackling light bursts from my palm, brighter than a star. I lift my arm to aim and make the killing blow. I desperately want to close my eyes, but I'm unable to look away from the horror soon to unfold. Scarlet looks afraid, like she's watching her life flash before her eyes. All because of me. I am a monster, unleashed and dangerous. I am a killer and a weapon.

I move as Fral commands it until suddenly the Raven is gone. Vanished. Non-existent. My arm freezes mid-air, aiming for a target that's no longer there.

Understanding dawns. Only one person I know can render someone invisible but also undetectable, too.

Alex.

My heart thumps, hoping with all my might he is here to save me from this nightmare.

'Show yourself, Alexander!' Fral seethes, confirming my suspicions. 'Come out and face me like a man!'

42

VIOLET

Ellis looks down at me with such adoration and desire, I feel my heart bloom with happiness. Those cobalt eyes study me, as if I'm the reason he's alive – the air he needs to breathe.

I reach up and pull him forward. Ellis leans between my legs and guides himself into me. The feel of him – the *size* of him – makes me lose my breath and my body shudders with need. I lift my hips instinctively, craving more, more, more.

'I don't want to hurt you,' Ellis says, meeting my eyes. He pauses, allowing me to adjust before pushing a little more in. I appreciate the slow and steady pace, and my breathing hitches when he's fully inside of me.

'You won't,' I manage, relaxing around him. He thrusts gently, and a ripple of pure bliss shoots through my arms and legs. My toes curl as he drives in again, pinning me down with his eyes. Fire blazes within them, burning but patient, as if waiting for permission to push further. I grab his shoulders. 'You feel incredible. Don't you dare stop.'

He smiles. The feeling of him filling me is completely and utterly wondrous. 'No chance of that happening.'

I don't realise my shadows are present until they coil around his neck, caressing and stroking his bare skin. The hair along his arms stand on end where they grab and tease him, and he exhales with a shudder. I command them to cup his brilliant arse and I moan as he thrusts deeper than before.

'Tell me what you want, Violet.' His voice is hoarse, but filled with yearning. He's trying his hardest to stay in control and hold back for my sake.

I grin at him and kiss the tip of his nose. 'I want you to fuck me so hard we break the bed.'

The wicked delight that morphs his features sends a thrill through me. Ellis readjusts himself, his muscled thighs widening as he places both his arms beside my body and licks the centre of my chest. He swirls his tongue over my nipples before biting one.

'Your wish is my command.' He pounds into me, taking no precautions as he uses all his power and strength. I cry out as the burning sensations of my longing and craving for this man rise to the surface. It's like he needs me as much as I need him. He clenches his hands into fists and buries his head into my neck. 'You are mine, Violet. Mine and only mine,' he says gruffly. 'I will cherish you the way you deserve to be.'

Even with the window open, I can't keep quiet. Our moans are loud and obnoxious – unleashed and animalistic. Our bodies move together and our limbs tighten around one another as the tempo becomes quick and erratic.

Ellis lifts me up, still inside of me as he crashes us into

the closest wall, hoisting me up and using the wall as support to thrust deeper into me. The new angle makes me cry out, and I'm screaming for more, screaming for release, screaming for *him*.

'Ellis!'

'Fuck,' he groans. Our impending orgasms are like an inferno, my shadows swirl around us, caging us in a wall of dark clouds. My nails become sharper as they dig into his skin. Ellis thrusts harder and faster in answer, as if the pain is a sign of encouragement. 'Violet, sweetheart, I can't hold on any longer—'

My eyes close with my climax as my walls squeeze around Ellis, enough for him to tumble over the edge, too. Our cries entwine, and his breathing is the only thing I hear. I lean back against the wall as I try to calm myself, closing my eyes as he slowly lifts me off him. I hiss at the sudden loss.

A prickle of something odd makes the hairs along my arms rise, but I can't move, my mind groggy. My shadows dissipate at once, as if something has scared them off. My head lowers and my eyes flutter open. Ellis stares back, his tanned skin now covered in inky-coloured veins, his cobalt eyes now black like the night. But that isn't what scares me. What scares me is that it's not Ellis watching me back – it's something else, something more sinister. Its lip curls upwards, reminding me of a predator watching its prey.

'Ellis?' I whisper.

But the moment his gaze lowers to my mouth, I know the monster has taken his place. My prince is no longer with me.

'Hello, my little nightmare.'

43

VIOLET

My little nightmare.

I swallow. The nickname is terrifyingly similar to Fral's.

'Release me,' I order. I reach down to unwrap his arms from my body while my legs slowly attempt to unravel from his hips. Ellis' grip is iron-tight, amplifying my panic. I try to touch his face and gently stroke his jaw, to try to coax my prince back. 'Come back to me, Ellis. *Please* come back to me.'

Lightning skitters along his face, and the rim of his eyes glow silver – the magic is far from the earlier teasing. Instead, it's powerful eruptions of potent power. My right hand still holds him, and I cry out as the monster inside my prince sends bolts through my arm. Pain slices through my limb as my skin rips open, oozing blood. Tears spring to life in my eyes as agony tears through me.

'Let me go! You're hurting me,' I whimper, wriggling to try to loosen his grip.

A flicker ripples through his face, his next words are quiet.

'Violet.' I stiffen, cradling my wounded arm. Ellis' eyes swirl with shades of onyx and cobalt, as if the monster and Ellis are battling one other for a chance to speak. I wait with bated breath. I sense more is coming. 'You need to *run*.'

I know then the monster is too much for him. The darkness in my prince has grasped all control, and he's trying to fight it.

'Ellis, you can fight it. Take control. Do it now!' But the darkness holds firmer. Lightning surges through me again from where he holds my legs in place. I howl, I feel caged in as memories of my captivity return.

Violet. Run!

I don't hesitate as I form a wolf's claw once again to swipe at his face. He bellows as I knock his jaw to the side. He does not let go, though. With adrenaline coursing through my veins, I shift into mouse form – so small the monster's grip slackens. The moment I painfully thud to the floor, I am running, not bothering to look back. My little legs scurry under the bed. My only escape is the open window.

Don't look back, I tell myself. If I see a flicker of Ellis remaining, I may stop, and right now, I need to warn someone. I need to get as far away from him as possible.

'Violet, come back and let us play some more!' He laughs, and the sound is vile and menacing, making dread and fear coil in my stomach.

When I finally reach the other side of the bed, Ellis stands there. I transform into an eagle, flapping my wings in his face as a distraction. I lift my clawed feet to scratch at his eyes before soaring over his head and into freedom.

I breathe deeply, thinking the worst is behind me, but when I peer back, he's there. The monster flies, shooting like a star towards me. I flap erratically for the cliff, my right wing throbbing from where the lightning scorched my arm. I sense my speed slowing, my pace unable to remain steady with the agony that lingers. He will be on me any second now.

Think Violet.

I glance down at the cliff, the ocean waves crashing onto the sandy shore below. Peering further out at the frightfully dark waters, I propel forward as an idea forms.

'You can't run from me!' taunts the monster. My prince's voice is rougher and darker than I'm used to. The distance between us makes me panic as I glance back for his whereabouts.

Execute the plan right now, Violet.

I lower my eyes. The inhabitants of the ocean are unknown this far out, but before I can second guess myself, I dive. The dark blue depths welcome me with a wave of sudden cold. My body shifts once more, my feathers turning into fur and blubber, and my wings turning into fins. I am glad that my sea lion form can hold its breath for long periods of time.

Swimming to stare up at the threat, I find the monster hovering. Its dark-veined face and evil eyes study the water, before something in the monster stutters. Its hands fly to its head, its face morphing from carnivorous to sorrowful, wicked, and then disgust.

'Violet!' It yells my name like a cry for help. My heart

stutters at the sound and the fear present within it. I don't move closer, unable to figure out if the monster is trying to force my hand and trick me into breaking the barrier of water protecting me. 'No!' it cries, the word long and tortuous as I watch beneath the waves.

Its head falls and arms loosen – resembling my prince once more. Midnight black eyes return to their cobalt colour, but the veins linger, and his neck pulses like he's trying to catch his breath, his chest heaving with effort. Ellis' ocean blue stare searches for me as his body hovers close to the water. He dips his hand in the water to see if he can feel something. I don't move, knowing he won't find me, even if his whole body submerges.

I am safe. I am safe. I am safe.

'Violet, sweetheart,' he calls out. 'It's me. I'm here. Please come out. I'm so sorry.'

My heart races, and my fin aches as blood seeps from numerous gashes. My adrenaline slowly ebbs, replaced with lingering terror, grief, and sorrow.

I stay where I am, unable to move towards him. Of course, I want to, but I can't talk to him like this, I need my energy for the swim home. There will be no way I can return in bird form, the exertion of shifting from water to air will be too much with my injuries.

'Violet, please. Come back to me.'

Finally, I allow myself to swim slowly closer, my energy spent, and my body in agony from his magic. But when his hand disappears, and his body rises, I watch his face harden to the mask I know so well. In one swift movement, he is gone, flying back to land. My head breaks the surface as his figure glides away. Not even the castle is visible at this distance, and when I know I am finally alone, I realise my dilemma.

Fear washes over me at all the creatures that might be lingering beneath the water. What things could be watching, knowing I am not the animal they think I am? Crimson blood surrounds me, and sudden panic propels me forward. Predators roam in the sea, renowned for eating creatures like the one I've shifted into. I swim hard and fast, urging myself not to stop until I hit the shore.

When I finally reach the land of Tealwaters, I collapse. All I can do is close my eyes and hope for my energy to return sooner rather than later, so I can go home to Ellis and ensure he's alright.

44

ELLPS

I wait near the cliffs, the monster trying to claw to the surface. With Violet, I had allowed myself to feel everything wholly and completely, making me lose control of myself and my emotions. But alone with my thoughts, and the memory of Violet's skin tearing from *my* magic, I am riddled with guilt and dread. The monster can feel the power I have over it now, and the hatred I possess for what it's done to my love.

I hover near the Tellian shore in hopes of finding Violet – to know she's alright. But hours pass without a sign of her. With every ripple of water or splash, my heart spikes with the hope that it's her, but disappointment and fear creeps in when it turns out to be something else. Had the monster hurt her beyond repair? Wounding her badly enough she was unable to come home to me?

You are a danger to everyone.

I grit my teeth and shout her name, desperate to hear her voice. What will I do if she's badly injured, or in the water with no way back? I tried to give her space and the time to make her own decision, but what if leaving her was a mistake?

You are going to send your loved ones to an early grave.

I soar over the surface of the darkening blue waters, alert to all movements that may be Violet returning to the sandy beaches of Tealwaters. I close my eyes and try to find her soul – the purple orb that brings me warmth anytime I think of it. Nothing happens, and the inability to feel her wrenches at my heart.

Violet will die under your hand.

I halt, gazing out into the distance. The sun begins to lower in the sky as yellow and orange spans the horizon. I conjure up every possible thing that may have happened to her, and there is no room in my thoughts for her being anything but *alive*. She must be underwater, exploring.

Exploring? In those dark depths? Think again.

I don't waste another second. I head straight for Ivory Castle and fly into the first open window I can find. Even within the stronghold, I don't bother walking, my magic is the quickest way to travel. I shout at every guard I come across to gather in the courtyard, demanding they bring every soldier they meet on the way with them.

It does not take long for a mass of curious men and women to meet me. I shout orders, my voice louder and fiercer than ever before. The soldiers seem alarmed by my outlandish behaviour but they understand their orders. They run off in all directions – magic potent in the air as they search for the love of my life, combining their powers to comb the ocean waters better than I ever could've alone.

'Ellington!' The king strides outside to meet me, confusion and worry on his face. 'What is the meaning of this?'

'Violet is missing,' is all I can say. I run back inside with my uncle close on my heels. 'Where is the queen? I need to meet with her immediately.'

'Your *aunt*,' he says pointedly, 'is in her chambers.'

I leave him behind, sprinting up two levels of the castle until I crash into the queen's room. The guards protecting her wing of the castle are quick to pull out their weapons, but my expression is enough to give them pause. My demeanour clearly shows I'm in a panic.

'Ellington,' says the queen, getting to her feet as the chamber doors bang against the walls. She jumps at my forceful entry. 'What are—'

'You were right,' I blurt out.

Right now, I care little for the games we usually play – the hard stares and sharp quips we share. She, too, seems to understand now is not the time for masks and manoeuvres. For once, I do not talk to her as my sovereign, but as the woman who grew up with my mother, the woman who took me in because her younger sister died, leaving behind her two orphan sons.

'I am?' she asks, eyes roaming over me as if checking for injuries. No wound I hold is visible to the human eye. The queen appears stunned and for good reason. I would never usually allow her to gain the upper hand, but right now, I suppress my pride. For Violet – for everyone around me – I will allow myself this moment of weakness.

I hear quick footsteps as my uncle arrives, slightly breathless. The queen's concerned gaze darts to him as he comes to her side. The king stares at me with questioning.

'I need your help.' They stand silently, both of them showing a variety of emotions. 'I hurt Violet,' I admit as the memory of her face, her terrified yet determined expression, flashes in my mind. 'I hurt her, and now she's gone. I can't find her and I'm ...' I swallow, my throat so tight I struggle to breathe. My legs feel suddenly weak as the tips of my fingers turn a dark grey. The sight panics me as I curl them into fists, hiding the rising monster within me. 'I'm *scared.*'

The queen's pale blue eyes are sharp, but when they rest upon my shaking fists, they soften just a fraction. Slowly, she steps forward and I step back. I glare at her, a sign not to come any closer. She swallows but does not push.

'Have the guards—'

'They are already searching for her.' My voice feigns steadiness, though my heart thumps so forcefully my ribcage aches. 'But *I* need your help.'

'What do you need?' The king asks with a frown.

'I need you to send me away. I need to be as far from our kingdom as possible. I am a threat and a risk to everyone around me. I cannot be trusted.' I show them my hands and the black veins creeping up my wrists. If I don't leave soon, I may kill them all. There is no saying what the monster will do if it takes over again.

The queen stares. She's as still as a statue while absorbing my request. Her husband's hand finds her shoulder. 'I don't believe—'

'You were right in saying I am not worthy to stand by Alex when he is crowned king. He needs stability, and I am far from that. You must find another to replace me, and I shall keep my head down elsewhere. I swear I will not embarrass our family, but *please* send me away,' I urge, raising my hands to her as a sign of my desperation – my *anguish*. Darkness coils around me, tickling my senses. It knows I am upset and frightened for Violet. It knows I am trying to run away from the people it wants to ensnare.

'You are not an embarrassment to us,' says the king, furrowing his brows. 'You never have been and never *will* be.'

The queen shakes her head, lifting a hand to cover her chest that rises and falls to a frantic rhythm. 'I am so sorry, Ellis.'

My name rings inside my ears, and I jerk away. She never calls me by my nickname. Always Ellington. My eyes roam her stern features, wondering if I heard her correctly. The queen holds her trembling hands. I frown. The king grasps one and pulls it close to him.

'I don't understand,' I murmur.

'I know our relationship has not been exemplary.' The king glances down at his wife, whose mouth thins. 'We know you have erected walls around you to keep out those you care for.'

'For good reason,' I say.

'But that does not mean it is the solution. You have encountered some awful things – things no child or adult should ever have to experience,' he continues. The sovereigns stand so close I imagine them to be Violet and I, holding each other for comfort. 'When ...' he struggles with his next words, and when he finally blurts it out, I understand why. 'When Fral was killed ...' His voice breaks, the pain clear in his eyes.

'When you returned home,' the queen pipes up, earning a grateful look from the king. 'We were all grieving. We thought it best to let the past die, and instead focus on the future rather than wallowing in things that could not be changed. Of course, as the years passed, we realised what a fatal oversight that was. It pushed you away and you no longer came to us for support.'

'That's because you didn't bother looking for me when I was taken,' I say coldly. 'I only remember Alex, the Hex, and our Nightshades that night fighting for the lives of those children stolen. There were no royal guards to be seen.'

The queen twists her lips, but to my relief, she does not change the topic, as she would have previously. 'Our son had his teenage years of rebellion, and having lost your mother the year prior, I thought perhaps this was something similar. We did not think it necessary to use more guards to aid in your search.'

My eyes lower to the white carpeted floor. For years, I knew the sovereigns did not use their entire army to search for me, and it was why Alex saved me alone – they had enough on their plates. My brother knew he would find me sooner if he befriended the Hex and worked alongside them. My family thought I had run away, and thus they only sent out a few guards in search of bringing me back to the castle. Of course, they never found me, having been caged within a magical camp where I was experimented on and abused.

'But that does not excuse our behaviour,' the queen says firmly. 'You needed us in a time of grief and loss, and we failed you. We should have consoled you, cared for you as your parents would have – as your parents would have *expected* us to do.' The memory of my mother and father makes her pale eyes water. 'To know you have suffered for so long by yourself and have learned to control the dark magic on your own ... You are stronger than any of us, Ellis. They would be so proud of your strength.'

I am speechless. Never has she been so candid with me. I suppose as we always played a game of power together, neither of us wanted to reveal our weaknesses.

'When I tried to talk to any of you, it was like you wanted me to forget,' I admit, and the pair wince. 'It was like everything I had endured, everything I had suffered, meant *nothing*.'

They nod in unison, but it's the king who speaks. 'There are not enough apologies for what we put you through.'

Silence ensues. Frankly, I have no clue what to say. I have never been close to either my aunt or uncle, and after losing their son and many of the kingdom's children, it had sent the whole city into disarray. I had coped with the dark days alone. After taking Naveen's life, I learned to rely on no one to save me, having never wanted to be a burden or a danger to anyone else.

'I need to leave,' I say, my black-tipped fingers all I can focus on. 'I need to go before I hurt anyone else.' They look ready to protest, but I have had enough. Violet is somewhere out there, likely scared and hurt, while I am here trying to convince the rulers of Tealwaters that I am a threat to everyone in the castle. 'I am asking for your assistance. Either behave as you have for the last ten years and ignore my request, or start proving your apologies are sincere and help me.'

'I will organise a portal for you,' concedes the queen, exiting her chambers. The king comes to my side but does not touch me as he escorts me to my room. Together, we pack a bag, my uncle promising to send anything else I need later. I peer at my desk to scribble down a quick note.

'Where will you send me?' I ask, peering over my shoulder to where the king shoves trousers into a travel bag.

He gives me a half-hearted smile filled with mourning. 'A place we should have sent you a decade ago. A place your aunt found in the kingdom of Whitlocke for those who have suffered under the hand of dark magic. It's where people go to heal.'

Heal, not cure.

A guard comes rushing into my chambers, and we both turn. 'Your Majesty. Your Highness,' greets the soldier, his silver-lined uniform shines beneath the lanterns as he bows. 'Miss Violet has been found. She is heading back to the chalet, we are keeping tabs on her as we speak.'

'Good.' The king dips his chin in approval. 'Bring her here to the castle. Make sure she has everything she needs and get a healer ready for her arrival.'

The soldier nods and rushes away to relay the order.

'I must go before she arrives,' I say.

'Do you not wish to see her?'

I pause my packing. 'Of course, I do. But if she is wounded, she will most likely not want to see me. I saw the havoc I caused, her skin was torn open, and blood covered her arms and legs. The monster in me did not hold back, it enjoyed her fear – enjoyed her retaliation. That is not something a person simply forgives.'

'You may be surprised,' retorts the king, my bag now full.

We head for the portal room, a large chamber with

nothing inside except high windows that show the darkened sky. All royal castles have a room like this, but as I behold the large, rippling portal – that smells of sea salt and fresh air – I suddenly feel very nervous to go.

You must leave for Violet. She is not safe with you. Nor is anyone else.

'You will be safe here,' says the queen, motioning to the large floating orb. On the other side, I can see the expanse of a huge grassy hill, tilting up to a mansion at the top. The sky is dark, and it smells different, but I don't hesitate as I step through. The sudden drop of temperature makes me shiver. I turn around to find the king and queen watching me, their expressions forlorn.

'You were right,' I say to the queen. 'I have run at the first sight of difficulty like you predicted.'

'No.' She shakes her head. 'You asked for help. That is different.'

'Only a true prince can discern when he needs support,' offers the king, curling his arm around his wife's shoulder. He once had to step up from his life as a blacksmith to learn the ways of royalty for his wife. I somehow see the man he was before wearing his crown, the pressure and weight on his shoulders. He does not look like a man who regrets his decision though, but a man who accepted the challenge, who stands by his partner with strength and honour. I vow to myself I will be like that one day. 'A true prince knows when he can fight alone and when he needs those around him to keep him steady on his feet. It does not make us weak, Ellis,' he says softly. 'It makes us *stronger*. We are not a mighty kingdom because we do everything ourselves. We are mighty because we have the support of hundreds – the responsibility, the power, the peace. We thrive because we allow ourselves to share our duties. Asking for help only means you are ready to stand by Alexander's side when he becomes king. But you must help yourself before you can help your brother. He will be waiting for you. As will we.'

'Tell him ...' I struggle for words. I regret not finding Alex before leaving, but my black-stained hands do not let me waver or step back through the portal to the place I call home.

'We will,' says the queen.

The portal closes, and I stand there, staring at where the orb once was. The sovereigns' words swirl inside my skull. But what stays with me are the words from my uncle.

He will be waiting for you. As will we.

But what about Violet?

45

VIOLET

I am naked on the expanse of sand, the sun near to rising when I realise it's early the next morning. Having been stripped of clothing last night, I am lucky no one has come across me in this state. Rocks surround me as the cliff looms above, caging me in so passersby won't notice my presence – no doubt something I thought of before collapsing into a heap.

When I sit up, I hiss as I try to move my limp right arm. It doesn't budge. I poke it tenderly and grit my teeth as pain bursts through my shoulder. It's covered in dried blood and clumpy red-stained sand. When I peer down, a similar sight appears on my legs, where the lightning has left numerous lesions along my skin.

'Mother of pearl,' I curse, wondering what I'm to do with no clothes. I search the area to figure out my location, and the hairs on my neck rise. I feel like I'm being watched, but as I peer at my surroundings, there's nothing but sand, sea, and cliffs.

Forgetting the feeling, I search for the familiar sight of

Ivory Castle down the coastline. It will be quicker to head back to the Irvine family chalet than to Sapphire City. Ellis will be worried about me by now, having not known where I've gone all night. Hopefully he forgives me for being unable to go to him, instead needing time to absorb everything that happened once the monster reared its ugly head.

I straighten my back with determination and rise shakily to my feet. My legs ache and wobble but the pain doesn't compare to that in my arm. Cradling it gently to my middle, I head up the large hill, yet the strange sensation follows me as I keep to the bushes and trees, afraid someone may catch me in my vulnerable state.

I finally reach the chalet, dashing towards it, hoping it's unlocked. Thankfully, it is, but all the windows that were opened for our arrival yesterday are now shut when I walk in.

'Ellis!' I call, hurrying upstairs to our bedroom, where our bags are. I rummage through them and grab a dress, but I am near to tears as I try to get my arm through the sleeve. I take one of my prince's shirts instead, needing the loose fabric.

'Ellis!' I try again, searching the rooms one by one until I am utterly stumped about his whereabouts. I head into the kitchen and find a towel, wrapping it tightly around my wounded arm, the lesion having reopened as I changed. 'Ellis! Where are you?'

Heading outside, I shout again and again, his name echoes, taken by the wind. It's only when I notice a royal carriage racing down the road that I run to the front of the property. Dread makes a home in my heart.

It stops outside the chalet. I recognise the coachman,

it's the same man who dropped me off at Bloomsoar Lake for my date with Ellis. Yet today, he looks grim, and his strides are long and hurried as he approaches.

The man bows low before addressing me. 'Miss Violet, you are needed at Ivory Castle immediately.'

'By Prince Ellington?' I ask. He shakes his head.

'No. King Hector.'

My mouth forms a thin line, and my brows crease. 'Where is Ellis?'

The coachman averts his eyes, seeming to debate his next words. Finally, he meets my gaze. 'He's gone, Miss. He left not long ago.'

* ☆ ° ₒ * ☾ * ☆ ° ₒ *

I feel sick to my stomach as we travel towards the royal residence, where the king waits for me at the entrance. Impatience is my companion as I swing open the carriage door before the horses have halted. I stumble out and rush towards him, but the sovereign meets me halfway, concern etched across his features.

'Violet,' he greets as I frantically bow. He waves me into the castle. The queen and Alexander wait inside. 'You must have many questions, but please, wait until we're inside.'

I keep my mouth clamped shut, wondering why Alexander looks as frantic as I do. When we are escorted to a large bedroom chamber, I am told to sit in a velvet chair. I sink into it, my muscles and bones seeping with fatigue and throbbing with a dull ache. A healer comes in not long after.

'Hello, Miss Violet,' says the healer, pointing to my arm. 'May I?'

I nod. Alexander, having taken an armchair near the window, watches me, his ocean blue eyes etched with worry. He looks tight with tension and his leg jiggles with nerves. He, too, appears not to know anything about Ellis' departure.

'So, where is he?' The prince asks, his tone clipped, confirming my suspicions. It's nothing like the charming heir the kingdom is so used to. 'Where has Ellis gone? And why did he leave without seeing me?'

The queen sits down, closest to Alexander, while the king perches on the side of the spacious bed that takes up the majority of the room. There are no more chairs available.

'As you can see, Violet has been wounded significantly,' begins the queen, gesturing to me. The sorrow in her face makes me avert my gaze. I do not need her sympathy, I only need answers. 'Ellis came home frantic, shouting at guards to find her, he was fretting about needing to be sent away.'

'Sent away?' Alexander says, leaning forward. 'And you did as he asked? How could you—'

The queen raises a hand, stopping him mid-sentence. 'Your brother has been suffering for far too long, and we all know it. He needs time to heal properly from past wounds. He needs the help he deserves, and I was no longer going to keep that from him.'

The king gives his nephew a firm look. 'He wanted to say his goodbyes, but he was afraid. If you had seen the state of him, you would have fulfilled his wishes without question, too.'

The prince leans back in his chair with a heavy sigh, he closes his eyes and grits his teeth. 'Was he alright?'

'No, far from it,' the queen admits. 'I've never seen him so distraught.'

Alexander's eyes pop open and his eyes land on me. 'How much did he hurt you, Violet?'

'Not enough for him to run away,' I mutter.

'My nephew is not to blame.' The king directs his words to me. 'We are. We have let him struggle with his fears for far too long, and now he is suffering the consequences. Where he is heading will help him recover from the trauma he has faced.'

'And where is he heading?' Alexander asks before I can.

'To kingdom Whitlocke.' The queen gives him a long look. 'You will let him have the time he needs, Alexander. Do not make it harder for him than it already has been.'

Anger shines in the prince's eyes as his jaw tenses. My heart drops, my skin ice-cold in seconds.

'Tell me he's coming back,' I whisper, my voice wobbling with dread.

'He will take as much time as he needs to find confidence in himself and his abilities,' answers the king.

'But will he *come back*?' I press. I find only sympathy in his gaze.

The king glances at his wife and nephew. 'May you give Violet and I a moment?'

My chest tightens as both the queen and Alexander stand. The prince gives me a quick look, his lips tugging up in a forced smile. 'I'm glad you are alright, Violet. I am always here if you need anything.'

When we're alone, the king brings out a piece of parchment and hands it over. I tentatively reach for it with my good arm as the healer peers up briefly before returning to her work. 'Before Ellis left, he requested I give this to you.'

I suck in a breath, a small flicker of hope setting alight within my chest. On the outside is the address '*To my brightest star.*'

I begin to sob as everything hits me all at once. My cheeks hurt and my head throbs with what this could mean. I can't stop myself from shaking. I lean forward, my stomach threatening to empty itself. The healer peers at me with clear concern.

He's gone. My prince has left, but this time, I don't know how to get him back.

46

THE PAST

My brother flickers into view, his face dirty, his golden hair skewed, and his filthy clothes ripped. His expression is nothing like I've seen before. The usual happy and cheerful sibling I grew up with now exudes fury and betrayal.

Fral finds a discarded sword and directs it towards him, though my brother holds no weapon. Trepidation coats my tongue and makes me nauseous. I want to scream at Alex to arm and defend himself. Fral will not back down. He will swing until he is the last man standing.

'Here to come save the day?' asks Fral, his lips curling.

'I'm here to bring my brother home – to bring all the children home.' Alex stands tall, his hands clenched. His jaw tenses and his pale eyes flicker between Fral and to where I stand behind him. 'Ellis deserves to come home. You've done enough to him – to all of them. I demand you let them go.'

Fral shakes his head. 'No. I am creating something that will blow all other kingdoms out of the water. I am—'

'You are destroying our youth. You are manipulating them,

controlling *them.' Alex motions to me. The collar feels tighter around my neck, but to my surprise, I don't move or attack, it's as if Fral has forgotten about me, or perhaps he wishes to fight this battle himself for once.*

'You never could see beyond your own nose, Alexander,' spits Fral. Then, he pounces. Alex disappears, reappearing beside me seconds later.

'Can you hear me, Ellis?' he asks, taking my face in his hands. His grasp is tender as his eyes roam over me. My own eyes, though, are glued beyond him to where Fral shouts and screams, distracted and searching for my brother. He swings his sword like a madman. 'I'm getting you out of here if it's the last thing I do. I promise.'

I blink, hoping to communicate with him but unfortunately he does not understand my silent language. Alex's hands flutter over me, studying my skin for wounds. There are many, and he winces at the scabs and scars I've accumulated. But over his shoulder, having finally realised he is fighting a non-existent foe, Fral spins to face us, his expression one of pure hatred. He raises his sword, gaze pinned on my brother as he throws the weapon like a javelin, the blade glinting in the moonlight.

Look behind you, Alex! Look behind you!

I fight with all my power as my mind thrashes against the prison of my collar. I need to warn him, I need to save him before he meets the same fate as the Raven.

Alex. Alex. Alex. Alex.

I reach and touch him, sending shock waves through his arm. I hope it's not enough to kill him, but to merely send him off balance. Thankfully, it does. He falls as the sword spears the space between our bodies where Alex was moments before.

My brother is quick on his feet as Fral flies for him. They're a tangle of limbs and flying fists and kicking legs. All I can do is stand as still as a statue, waiting for a command, as I observe the fight between good and evil. Without weapons, they're evenly matched, yet their strength wanes the longer they fight, knuckles connecting with jaws, boots connecting with stomachs.

Keep fighting! *I yell at my brother, eager for him to end this.*

They tumble to the floor. Alex is on his back with his arm clenched tight around Fral's neck. The latter wiggles, trying to loosen my brother's grip, but he doesn't. Alex's pale eyes find me, as if needing the reminder as to why he is here, and why he is hurting someone.

'I will let go if you promise to shut down this operation,' Alex *says through gritted teeth.* 'We will negotiate your punishment, but at least you will live.'

'No,' Fral *spits.* 'I will never back down.'

Alex's eyes briefly close. He turns his head, the gesture slow and mechanical as if it is not my brother but someone else in his body. At arm's length, a dagger lays unused. It glimmers, and I realise what my brother is about to do.

'Promise me you will walk away from everything, and I will let you live,' Alex *tries again, eyes on the weapon. Fral shouts and thrashes against my brother's arm constricting his windpipe.*

'You claim to kill me, but you won't. You are weak and spineless like your brother. Because of me, he will go on to devastate kingdoms and make them kneel to our every whim. He and I will rule over them all.'

That seems to break my brother's resolve.

In a flash, his arm snakes out and clutches the blade, silencing Fral's next taunts as he slides the knife across his throat. A thick trail of blood streams down the angel of death's neck, dribbling over the knife and my brother's hand. Alex sits up and pushes Fral away.

Fral gurgles and clutches his throat as if to stop the bleeding. But to no avail.

My brother moves to stand over Fral with a grief-stricken expression. He holds the dagger still, his fingers dripping crimson on the floor. We watch the life leave Fral's eyes as his body slumps, his soul escaping into the sky.

A whoosh of air leaves my lungs, as if someone has loosened their grip on them. Now my master is dead, the collar feels like a simple band of metal.

'Alex,' I murmur, my voice hoarse as I fall to my knees. Gravity pulls me down as if all this time Fral's puppet strings have been holding me up on my own two feet.

Violet and Caleb stop mid-battle, peering around with confusion. They dodge attacks as they find their footing, their bodies and minds now their own again. I sigh when Violet's familiar expression rushes back.

I turn towards my brother, who stands and stares unblinkingly. Before him, Fral does not move nor twitch. I feel a twist of sympathy for Alex.

'You came for me,' I say, finally gaining my sibling's attention.

He is suddenly there, holding on so tightly and stroking his non-bloodied hand over my hair. I lean against him, and he soothes me, his voice full of that comforting, familiar warmth.

'Of course I did,' he replies, his brows furrowed. 'I will always come for you.'

'I'm sorry,' I blurt, crying now, my tired body wracked with tears. 'I'm so sorry.'

And it's as if he can read my mind. My brother's eyes trail to the person he killed, and I know then that he will never be the same, his pure heart now tainted in darkness — something Fral has done to all of us.

'No need to be sorry, Ellis. I'm just glad you're safe now.'

47

VIOLET

Dear Violet,

I have made the difficult decision to leave. I cannot put into words how sorry I am for hurting you. I cannot fathom the thought of putting you in harm's way again, so I will be heading to the kingdom of Whitlocke, where I will gain professional support for those who have suffered under the hands of dark magic.

The queen was right. I struggle to ask for help because I believe people will deem me weak. If I present myself as disinterested and capable, everyone will forget the time I was taken from my bedroom and made into a weapon – a prisoner. I had hoped they would forget that, once upon a time, I was a young boy stuck in his own body, a body used against him time and time again to do terrible, terrible things no child should see, let alone perform.

I tell you this because I know you understand.

I know you have felt the same way, too. However, you are stronger than me, Violet, and you always have been. You are brave and full of the courage I lack. You have never viewed our past as a weakness but rather something that's made us stronger. And I admire you for that. However, my admiration for you will not liberate me.

To possess your frame of mind, I must leave to better myself. To mentally and physically recover from a trauma I have never fully let myself get over.

If I could do this with you by my side, I would in a heartbeat, but you deserve a man who will be there to protect and shield you from the dangers of the world — not someone who threatens that.

So, I hope you can forgive me, sweetheart. I will think of you every day as I navigate the darkness until it is safe — until I am confident I will never bring harm to you again.

In the meantime, I don't expect you to wait for me, but I need you to know you are the star I'll search for every evening to get me through this. I will look upon the brightest of them all and know you are with me every step of the way.

Until we meet again, my love, I will be fighting for our _real_ end.

Always yours,
Ellis

48

VIOLET

The Tellian Times

YOUNGEST PRINCE ABSENT FROM ROYAL EVENTS

By Lorna Nova Rey

The sovereigns of our mighty kingdom, and the heir to the throne, Prince Alexander, have been busy making the rounds this month, but the youngest prince has been noticeably absent from all public royal events. It has been rumoured that Prince Ellington has been carted away to a neighbouring kingdom, with King Hector and Queen Melody having dusted their hands off their youngest and most aloof nephew. Ever since his kidnapping back in—

I toss the newspaper aside, sick and tired of their foolish narrative. The list of inconceivable and inaccurate rumours being said about Ellis make me seethe.

Distant. Callous. Arrogant. Hostile. Uncommunicative. Dangerous. A threat.

'Why did you do that? I've yet to read it today,' protests Hazel, pinching the newspaper with her thumb and finger as if it's contracted a disease from the mere seconds it's been in the bin. When she flicks through it, she notably skips the front page, on which there is another story about Ellis. She, unlike some people, doesn't care for the articles written about him. She's adamant they are all lies, and I adore that she is as fiercely loyal to the prince as I am.

My mother peers up briefly as she washes the basket of fruit I gathered, while Hazel leaves us to it. I meet my mother's gaze, who appears worried, and though I give her my best smile and reach for a mixing bowl, my mind goes elsewhere.

Is he alright? Is he gaining the support he needs? Does he miss me?

'How are you holding up?' asks my mother.

I sigh heavily. It has been three days since Ellis has left, and I don't know how to feel. While I'm happy he's finally putting his well-being first, a part of me dreads the thought of him forgetting about me and never returning. I must learn how to live without him all over again.

'By a thread,' I say. I pat my trouser pocket to ensure his letter is still there, his words something I prefer to keep with me at all times.

'It's never easy for the ones left behind,' my mother says quietly. After all, she would know first-hand, but unlike my bastard father, Ellis left for much more noble reasons. I purse my lips, feeling guilty.

'He may be different to your father, but you are still

allowed to grieve his absence,' she chides, seeming to sense the direction of my thoughts. 'You love him, and have done for many years now. It's hard to move on from someone so heavily engraved into all your hopes and dreams that you cannot fathom a future without him, even if you tried.'

I nod because that's exactly what this is. From the moment I met Ellis, something had sparked – curiosity, initially – but when he held my hand the first night he arrived at the prison camp, silently asking for me to stay, I had been a fool for the royal ever since. He had woven his way into my heart and stayed there forevermore.

'Violet,' murmurs my mother, watching me. 'True love is far from easy. It's not always manageable – it's painful, tricky, and a long and treacherous journey for most. But it's worth fighting for, and, in your case, repeatedly.'

Only now do I realise how much I've needed to hear that, to know she understands what I'm going through. My lips wobble at her words. My way of coping has been pretending nothing happened, plastering on a smile whenever anyone asks about Ellis, and acting like everything is fine when Hazel brings up baking school. Meanwhile, I know the strings my prince pulled to allow her a spot at the prestigious school, and the memory makes my heart tighten.

'So, will you wait for him?' she wonders, taking my silence in stride.

'Yes.' I nod once and wipe at my face as a tear escapes. I need no time to think of a response. 'I will.'

'That's my girl.' She smiles, pulling me in for a hug. 'Something as small as long distance will never threaten my daughter and her stubbornness.'

I squeeze her back hard, needing to be anchored by her firm grip. 'Thanks for that backhanded compliment.'

'My pleasure, darling. Now, help me crush these strawberries.' And with that, we ready the bakery for another busy opening.

49

THE PAST

They take the camp down, tent by tent. Us children are fed and covered in blankets with promises to be escorted home soon. While Alex directs the remaining survivors, I sit with a group of kids, searching for Violet.

Violet sits by herself, a worn brown blanket draped over her small shoulders. When I approach, her face lights up, and she wraps her arms around me before I can say a word. I pull her into a tight embrace and laugh at the feel of her.

'What's so funny?' she asks.

I shake my head, unable to answer. 'Nothing. I just can't believe this is finally happening. We're going home.'

Violet nods excitedly, and a strand of hair falls onto her face. I stare at it, transfixed. The lock is no longer gold, instead, it's light brown. Her piercing eyes look curious as she beholds her new look.

'I think it's pretty,' I say.

'I could be wearing a rag, and you'd say the same thing,' she retorts, and I shrug, a sudden heat flushing my cheeks.

'You're not wrong,' I confess. Violet watches me, absorbing my features as if trying to memorise every part of my face. 'Are you alright?' I ask, concern burrowing into my chest.

'I feel like I miss you already,' she says sadly. 'You'll be in the castle doing what royals do, and I'll be doing what bakers do.' I give her a puzzled look. 'Bake.'

I roll my eyes. 'Who would have thought?'

She laughs, and it's free without restraint – something I had a hard time believing I would hear again. I stiffen as shouts ring out around us. That's our cue. We're leaving. I find Alex in the crowd, and he meets my gaze, his forced smile making me feel a pang of guilt.

Violet's hand on my chest captures my attention once more. When I meet her eyes, I smile, realising how happy she seems, and how many times she's jump started my heart with a mere look in my direction. I gently touch her darker strand of hair and tuck it behind her ear, letting my touch linger.

'We are going to be best friends for the rest of our lives, remember?' I declare, resting my forehead against hers. Violet's eyes flutter closed. 'Even if we don't see each other every day, you'll always be my favourite person.'

'Do you mean that?' she rasps, seeming to enjoy our proximity. My heart lights up as if filled by lightning.

'Have I ever lied to you?'

She chuckles. 'No.'

'Well, there's your answer,' I retort as she moves away. I shiver at the sudden space between us. 'Best friends no matter what.'

She answers by giving me a kiss, light and playful on my lips. 'No matter what,' she echoes, pleased with my stunned reaction.

50

ELLIS

Dear Diary,

    I am to write everyday in hopes of documenting my thoughts and feelings. Apparently, it will help me when I reflect on this moment and see the improvements I have made. However, all I have accomplished this first week is making myself feel like a fool for writing to a <u>diary</u> of all things. So instead of that, I have decided to write letters.

    Wish me luck, I feel I am going to need it.

51

ELLIS

Dear Alex,

It has been three weeks since I have last seen you and I have my doubts. I came to Whitlocke in hopes of finding a new version of myself – a stronger, more open version that you would be proud of. But I fear he is nowhere in sight.

Amanda, the lady who owns this establishment, insists that healing takes time. But I am impatient and I already wish to come back. However, she is persistent and very persuasive. She says this feeling will always be present, but I must remember my reasoning for coming here in the first place.

So here I am, writing to you.

It's never been easy for me to share my thoughts and feelings, which you know first hand, but when I left, I was full of sorrow, guilt and anger. I have hurt people I did not wish to harm with dark magic I do not wish to own yet possess. I must remember that this magic is dangerous and must be controlled. I am to master it and do so with strength and courage. That is what you do with any obstacles in your way, and I shall follow in your footsteps.

I must go now, I have to endure the group sessions which are mandatory. Everyday, we sit in a circle and talk about our emotions. You can imagine how much excitement I get from such a set up.

Take care, and I hope I see you soon,
Ellis

52

ELLIS

Dear Aunt Melody & Uncle Hector,

I have been away from the castle for two months today.

Several weeks ago, I would have told you this place was a waste of time. Several weeks ago, I thought writing my thoughts and feelings in this diary was something they made us do to keep us occupied and out of trouble.

But now I have been here a significant while, I am beginning to find peace and something new blooms within me. I can see the small but significant difference in my way of thinking and in the way I carry myself. I must admit, the classes and the people here have grown on me — but only slightly.

I am far from the man I want to be, but I have hope, and hope is the best thing I can ask for right now. It is the goal I strive for everyday when I wake up.

Today, in our group session, we spoke about forgiveness, and I listened intently, finding relevance in this particular topic. It also left me wanting to write to you both as I think we have a lot of forgiving to do.

We have endured much grief in our lifetimes, and when the camp was torn down, it was the icing on a very sad, very darkly-decorated cake we call our family. No one should experience the horrors we have. It's simply unfair. But so is blaming you both for the trauma I hold.

Neither of you caused me pain – he did – and sometimes I forgot that. We have all made mistakes and said things we did not mean. I hope we can rebuild our relationship. I do not think my parents would want me to keep you outside of the walls I've built around myself. I think they would want us to listen to one another and forgive – to be the family we should have been over the last ten years. We all know how valuable time with loved ones is, and once they're gone, you can never gain that precious time back.

I would never have admitted this without learning what I have whilst being away, and I am forever grateful to you both. The best decision you made for me was sending me here.

I hope you are both well.

Your nephew,

Ellis

53

ELLIS

Dear Violet,

There is so much to say, but I'm unsure how to say it.

How do you write to the only woman you have ever loved that leaving was the right thing for you both? That being apart, as heart wrenching and torturous as it is, was the best decision I've ever made for the sake of both our well beings?

You don't. I know if you ever read this, which you won't, it will not be the same as if I told you in person. My words will twist in that beautiful mind of yours and this letter will make you think I left because of something you did, when in reality, it was because of something I could potentially have done to you.

I know how your brain works. I know how your emotions blaze like a fire – all passion and heart. I miss it so much. I also miss your frowns and your smiles. I miss the times we have spent together and the memories we could have made in the five months I've been gone.

But as I said before, I know now I've made the right decision.

When it comes to you, I'll make sure you are looked after. I will ensure you will never have to endure the pain I caused you ever again. Your face haunts my dreams. I have never seen such fear from you – not even in camp. And what's more devastating is knowing why. You felt safe with me, you gave me your unyielding trust, and I destroyed that within seconds and made you suffer.

I promise you, Violet, I will return a better man. I will be the master of my magic and I hope we can reunite again. I have nightmares that you have moved on, that someone like Luca has replaced me. Yet if that is something you have chosen, I will never come between that. But I know my heart will break piece by piece without you.

I selfishly hope you will be mine once more as I will forever be yours.

Sincerely,

Ellis

54

ELLIS

Six Months Later

My first few days were a blur – the same routine, the same pastel-coloured rooms, and the same faces surrounding me day in and day out. But I kept the faith. I knew if I worked hard, I would get to see my family and Violet again, sooner rather than later. That day is today. Amanda, the mastermind behind this operation, sits before me for our last session together.

'How do you feel?' she asks, her smile something I once thought as simply polite. But now I know its real meaning. Amanda's smile indicates I am improving, which means I am one step closer to being the person I want to be.

'Different,' I admit, and she nods in understanding. 'Like the old me who arrived here is a dream I conjured up.'

'You've worked hard, Ellis,' Amanda says. Encouragement has always been her preferred method of communication. 'Your aunt and uncle would be so very proud of you – Alexander, too.'

'I know.'

We sit in silence for a moment, and her words echo through the pale green room. The single window in her office has been left open, inviting in a faint breeze. I will be getting a portal back to Ivory Castle soon, where my family will be waiting for me. I swallow thickly.

'Are you nervous to see Violet again?'

My eyes lift to meet Amanda's. Violet has been a constant conversation topic for me – how we met, how we became friends, how we were rescued, and why we lost contact.

Now, though, I try not to think about it. Instead, I focus on how Alexander will receive me, and how my aunt and uncle will react to my return. Will they be happy to have me back, or will they think I need more time here?

Once, I would have deflected Amanda's question, deeming the answer too personal to share without revealing too much. My worries would be seen as weak or too vulnerable, but now I understand the importance of speaking your truth, and the benefits of voicing your feelings to others as a healthy means of communication. It allows those around you to have a deeper appreciation and perception of your personal limits.

'Yes, I am nervous. I'm worried she's moved on, and that she will still be angry at me,' I admit, taking a deep breath. I exhale, imagining all the negativity leaving my body. 'I wouldn't blame her for that, but I still have hope she hasn't.'

'That's a natural reaction to have,' says Amanda. 'But I

hope everything is as you wish when you arrive home.' She stands and offers her hand. 'It's been a pleasure working with you, Ellis. If you ever need anything, do not hesitate to contact me. I am always here.'

I rise to my feet and shake her hand. The stark difference between my first session with Amanda and last makes me feel a wave of fulfilment. I've come a long way, and I am proud of what I've accomplished these past few months.

I am going home, I think happily.

'Thank you, Amanda. I will.'

55

ELLIS

The first thing I notice is the castle seems brighter. It's as if the windows have been stretched to allow more light in. It's absurd, of course, but I remember home being smaller, more enclosed and caged in.

The second thing I notice are the three people waiting with neutral expressions but with eyes that glimmer with something I hope is excitement. My family stands side by side as the portal behind me closes, where Amanda stands and waves farewell.

None of us seem to know what to say or do as we stare at each other. It's been six months since I last saw them with no communication in the meantime – an obligation to ensure I had the best chance of recovery. I was a very different person then, and right now, they seem nervous.

'Ellis,' murmurs Aunt Melody with what I think is hope in her eyes.

Inhaling deeply, I step forward and wordlessly wrap my arms around her. Her small arms are firm as she reciprocates the gesture. All our past arguments – all the times we've never seen eye to eye – fizzle in that moment, as if they never mattered. I have found peace with our past, and I hope she has too. And if not, we will work together until we do.

I turn to my uncle next, whose steady support I've always taken for granted. He grunts as I grasp him, his body feeling smaller in my hold. He claps my shoulder when I release him. By his smile, I know he's happy to see me.

'Glad to see you in one piece, nephew.'

Finally, I face Alex. His pale blue eyes shimmer with relief yet he's an open book. I know everything he is feeling. I give him a timid but warm smile, and his gaze flickers with uncertainty. A bubble of regret forms in my gut, knowing my brother hasn't seen me smile so genuinely for years, and that any simple show of emotion from me is a novelty for him. I endeavour to change that.

'Alex,' I say finally, breaking the silence. 'Come here.'

We meet halfway, clinging to each other as if we fear being ripped apart again. He holds on tight, digging his nails into my back, and my throat constricts as I relish this moment and the closeness between us. I've forgotten what it feels like to hug my brother.

'I missed you,' he whispers, shaking in my hold.

'I missed you too, Alex.'

My brother pushes me at arm's length, flashing his infamous smile only for me. 'You did?'

I nod, keeping my hands on his arms. I'm not quite ready to release him yet. 'Of course. I've never been away from your side for as long as this. It was disorientating, to say the least.' A flicker of something changes in his gaze, and he's no doubt thinking of the months I was away from him, locked in Fral's prison camp. 'To say I missed you all is an understatement, actually.' I peer over to my guardians, finding Uncle Hector's arm around my aunt. Contentment shines through their expressions, and I can't help it as my lips tug up at the edges. 'It's good to be back.'

'Let's eat. I'm sure you have plenty to tell us,' says Aunt Melody, escaping my uncle's grasp and steering me away. Servants fuss over us as they prep the dining room, the cooks making delicious plates of all my favourite foods.

For the first time in a long while, we have our first family dinner where I talk the most – mostly about my group sessions, the people I've met and befriended, and the similar stories of other survivors. Everyone listens. I notice the way my family reacts to my candour and directness as I make myself present in every topic we cover throughout the meal.

It's like a weight has been lifted off their shoulders, and they're more relaxed in my presence than ever before. A flicker of hope shines through. My future is more vivid than I could have ever imagined.

* ☆ ° ₀ * ☾ * ☆ ° ₀ *

I glance down the street to Danes Bakery. A constant stream of customers enter and exit, satisfied with their purchases. Beside me, Hera watches, waiting for me to approach the shop. But I can't move.

'Whatever happens, you will be fine,' Hera says, meeting my eyes. 'She will not turn her back on you. I am sure of it.'

I swallow. 'I hope you're right.'

Taking a shaky breath, I head over and enter the bakery, greeted by the familiar smells of freshly baked bread and fruit tarts. People shuffle around each other as orders are called out, and I take in the establishment, remembering when this place used to be bare and fighting to stay open.

Hera waits outside, watching through the large windows. She offers a thumbs up in encouragement as I near the counter, where Maura and two other women handle the horde of consumers waiting patiently to order.

'Excuse me, is Violet around?' I ask the closest lady with burnish brown hair. Her dark blue eyes land on me, and she pauses momentarily, as if stunned by the sight of me. The line of customers sense the shift in her demeanour, too, and they all look my way.

'Your Highness,' greets an older man. He has a strange smile on his face as he studies me from head to toe – my lack of crown seems to confuse him. With the way he takes me in, you'd think I was away for years not months. 'You're back.'

I nod in greeting. 'Yes, I am.'

'Welcome home.' He tips his hat towards me.

'Thank you very much.' I smile, and he seems close to having a heart attack. Turning back to the bakery worker, I find her eyes still pinned on me. 'Is Violet here?'

She lifts a finger up for me to wait then heads over to Maura. The pair whisper to themselves, peering towards me. Maura pats the woman's arm leaving her to the line of customer's she was serving.

'Your Highness,' Violet's mother says cheerily. 'You look well. I hope your time away has been beneficial.'

'It has, thank you.'

'Wait outside. I'll let Violet know you're here.' Maura motions for me to leave the chaotic space that is her business, then heads into a doorway leading to the back kitchen. I slowly head for the exit, flashing Hera a nervous look as I stand in the street. My guard and I peer out into the crowds, who watch us curiously while we wait. My heart pounds with nerves, hoping with all my might I won't be let down from this visit.

Peering down, my fingers tingle and black coats the tips. However, I don't hide them away. I watch them. They don't spread any further as I apply every practice from the last six months into action.

You are worthy. You are a vessel of emotions. You are a power unto yourself. You are your own master.

'You're really here.'

I whip around at the sound of her voice, which strums something dark and deep within me. But I don't cower away from it like I would have. Instead, I embrace it, allowing those emotions to stir things inside of me to create something new and intoxicating.

Violet steps out from the bakery, as beautiful as the day I left.

VIOLET

Ellis' hair is no longer neatly clipped short. Over the six months he's been gone, his dark blonde hair has grown to where it now touches his shoulders. It suits him, as does his relaxed demeanour. I observe the prince from head to toe, and though he wears his usual royal garb of midnight blue – minus a crown — it seems tighter, like he's been exercising more. Further down, his fingers are stained black yet he does not curl them into fists or tuck them in his trouser pockets. Compared to me in my flour-covered apron, he's as hand-some as ever, and even more tanned from the Whitlocken sunshine.

We stare at each other, not revealing our emotions just yet.

'You copied my hairstyle,' I declare, realising my now short hair is the same length as his.

Ellis' cobalt eyes twinkle as he reaches self-consciously for his head. 'I thought we could match. I even asked to have black streaks through mine, but they sadly refused that request.' He shrugs.

I avert my gaze, fighting a smile. How can he make me feel so light and giddy with a simple jest, even after all this time? When I finally glance up, he's serious once more. My heart hammers.

'Walk with me.'

I lift a brow and tilt my head. 'Is that an order, Your Highness?'

'If you are about to refuse me, then yes, it is an order.'

We stare at each other again – a battle of wills – before I finally concede and look away. 'Alright.'

As we stroll along the bustling street, we watch and listen to the world around us. People don't notice the prince in their midst, too preoccupied with their own lives to give him a second glance.

I peer sidelong at Ellis, wondering what he's thinking as his cobalt eyes absorb every detail. He seems calm within the sea of people, unperturbed by the bodies surrounding us. There's no sign of tension and I find myself filling with pride at the sight of him.

'You're staring,' he states. I open my mouth to protest but he smiles down at me unexpectantly, and I can't help but give in.

'How are you?' I ask. The question seems too insignificant for everything we've been through – for all he has endured over the past few months.

His features smooth out into something I've not seen before. 'I'm great now, Violet.'

Violet.

The sound of my name on his lips makes my heart race.

'I learned a lot,' he continues, oblivious to my

thoughts. 'I met a lot of people with similar stories to me, and I never would have met them had I stayed here. Plus, I've missed my family much more than I was willing to admit.'

I nod, absorbing his words. He certainly looks happier in the way he carries and presents himself ... He's like a different person, untroubled and carefree.

'I was a little worried seeing you,' he admits. The vulnerability in his gaze takes me off guard.

I frown. 'You were?'

He stops and faces me, searching my eyes and stealing my breath. With just one look from Ellis, the world slips away, everything else fades from existence until there's only him and me.

'Yes. I thought you would pretend you didn't know me like before,' he jests, and the small tug of his lips makes me scoff. I'm unable to contain my smile as he scratches the back of his neck. 'And if that were the case, you have every right to do so.'

'No, I don't,' I answer, furrowing my brows.

'Why not? Not many people are worthy of second chances.'

I nibble on my bottom lip, delighted as his eyes lower with such intensity, watching my every move. He stiffens, and I'm back to wondering what's going through his head. He inhales deeply before releasing a breath.

'You're right. Not many people *are* deserving of second chances,' I say, and his eyes finally find mine. 'But *you* are.' Ellis clears his throat and averts his gaze. 'Was that the wrong thing to say?'

He shakes his head. 'No, of course not.'

'Did I make you uncomfortable?' Confusion and doubt creeps into my chest.

'You make me feel lots of things, sweetheart, but never uncomfortable.' The moment the nickname slips from his mouth, he appears to regret it. 'I'm sorry, it's a habit. If you don't like the name, I ...'

My hope dwindles. The uneasy looks, the regret.

He's here to let me go, once and for all.

'I came here today to apologise to you in person,' Ellis finally says, and my body prickles with nerves. 'I know I hurt you the day I left. It's unforgivable what I did, and I understand if it means everything has changed for us. But no matter what you choose for the future, or what you choose for us, I came to say I'm sorry.'

'You don't need to apologise.' I prepare myself, dreading to hear what he says next.

'I do,' urges Ellis, leaning forward to meet my gaze. 'I do, Violet. I know my leaving probably brought up old emotions you hoped never to feel again. I can never express to you how much you mean to me, hurting you is the last thing I ever wanted to do.'

I am quiet – contemplative – as thoughts rush through my mind.

'I was a wreck when you left,' I admit. He winces. 'But I understand why you left this time. You needed that time to find yourself – to heal.' I slowly reach back and take a piece of paper from my back pocket. As I carefully unfold it, his heartfelt words appear. The letter is crumpled and worn from the copious amount of times I've needed to read it – needed the comfort of his words. 'I had to remind myself you didn't leave *because* of me but rather *for* me.' I swallow, staring at the parchment as if it will aid the misery I fear he'll soon bestow upon me.

I must tell him how I feel. I must confess my feelings before I lose the courage to do so. He can't leave without knowing what I truly think of him.

'I've been afraid you would forget about me,' I say carefully. 'That perhaps you'll change your mind and think I am not worth coming back for.'

Ellis' hand gently grasps my chin, lifting it until my eyes meet his. I shiver at his touch, it's like returning home after a long time travelling.

'*Me* forget *you*? That's utter nonsense. Thoughts of you have been constant – wondering what you're doing, who you're with, whether you've met someone new ...' My heart soars. I offer a wobbly smile as my eyes water. His reaction is one of pure delight, and I know then my fear is for nothing. Six months apart and I haven't lost him. 'You are my everything, Violet. There's not a moment that's gone by where I haven't felt your hand in mine, imagined your breath on my skin, or your voice in my head. If anything, you helped me pull through on my bad days.'

I exhale. 'I was so worried about you.'

'And I was worried about *you*.' He wipes a fallen tear from my cheek. Warmth wraps around me as he steps closer, lowering his head so our eyes meet. Our lips are so close our breath mingles. 'But I'm here now to be by your side until you wish otherwise. I'm here to continue fighting for you, for me, and for our *real end*.'

I close my eyes and rest a hand upon his chest, where his hammering heart awaits my touch. The sensation brings back memories of him and I together – everything we have experienced – the good and the bad. He smiles faintly as if reading my mind and wraps his arms so tightly around me I know he'll never let me go.

'For our real end, Ellis,' I agree, brushing my mouth against his.

He exhales shakily and cups my face, trailing his thumb over my jaw. 'I've missed you, sweetheart. So very much.'

He presses his lips against mine, relieving every remnant of doubt that resided in my head for too long. I wrap my arms around his neck, and my shadows coil around him, too, like they have also missed him. I cling to Ellis, and his strong grip pulls me closer. The kiss is slow and deep, his tongue tantalising. He tastes as good as I remember.

Somehow, it's a conversation in itself, of everything we couldn't tell each other over the past six months – every feeling and every thing we've missed in our days apart.

He pulls away, and I narrow my eyes. This only seems to amuse him, his chuckle low – the sound something I'll never take for granted again.

'You have a bad habit of stopping when I wish for you to keep going,' I grumble.

He smirks, arrogantly licking away the stray tear on my cheek. 'I was going to profess my love for you.'

My half-hearted scowl softens as I reach to stroke his cheek. Ellis places his hand on mine, pinning it in place, and it's a feeling I wish will never end.

'Oh, well, if that's the case, don't let me stop you, Your Highness.' I grin, and Ellis' features morph into something earnest.

'I love you, Violet Danes. Now and forever. Don't ever

forget that.' He brings my hand to his lips and presses soft kisses to my knuckles. My heart swells.

It's been a long and winding journey to get to where we are today, but hearing those three little words from my childhood sweetheart somehow makes it all worth it.

'And I love you, Ellis Irvine. So very much.'

The End

AUTHOR NOTE

Hi there!
I hope you enjoyed reading
PRINCE OF NIGHTMARES.

Ellis was a character who wouldn't leave my head, his romance with Violet a passion project I wasn't planning on writing. But I'm glad I did, they deserve a happy ending and it was the most fun I've had writing a book.

Thank you so much for purchasing this book. Please consider leaving a review or recommending it to a friend.

Thanks again,
Hannah x

Look out for the next book here:

ACKNOWLEDGMENTS

Prince of Nightmares was written because I could not stop thinking about Ellis. If you don't already know, Ellis Irvine was first written in my book The Sapphire Crown (Book 2 in The Crimson Scar series). He was a minor character whose voice needed more space to grow and this book did just that.

A part of me needed to know he had a happy ending — as that's what most of us are here for. When Violet came to life inside my head with her fiery temper and easy banter I knew she was the right girl for him. Together they make such an entertaining couple and one I had so much fun writing.

But of course I couldn't have written Prince of Nightmares without these people...

To my family — in the years of writing you have always been my rock when I've needed support, opinions, or even just someone to talk out loud with to manage my chaotic thoughts. Thank you.

To my friends — for your shouts of encouragement, for your ability to keep me going when I want to give up because it's been hard or overwhelming. Thank you.

To Amy & Paul AKA the Joneses — a shout out to you two for the help in character names. Without you LUCA MOYE would never have been born and I would never have officially added a Kath and Kim reference into one of my books ... yeah, this will look good on my resume.

To my beta readers — Vee and Sacha. You girls were given a short amount of time to give me feedback and you said, 'Yeah I got this. No problem.' You helped make this story the best it could be. So thank you, I know I can always rely on you both.

To my readers — thank you for your continuous support and sharing my books. This is a little different to The Crimson Scar series. It is majority romance in a fantasy world. But it was nice to delve into the characters more, and explore the relationships with those around them at a deeper level. Hopefully you feel the same way and enjoy Ellis' book as it has been one of my favourites to write!

ABOUT THE AUTHOR

Hannah is a huge lover of tea, a passionate writer and an avid reader who claims buying books and reading books are two completely different hobbies. She is also the author of The Crimson Scar series.

As a Bachelor of Criminology and Law, Hannah has spent years reading and writing fantasy stories with morally grey characters, villainous crimes and lots of blood.

Want to know more?
Visit: www.hannahpenfoldauthor.com
Socials: hannahpenfoldauthor